DESERT OF THE HEART

■ **Jane Rule** was born in Plainfield, New Jersey, in 1931 and grew up in the Midwest and in California. In 1956 she moved to British Columbia where she now lives on Galiano Island. She has published numerous highly acclaimed novels, short stories and non-fiction. *Desert of the Heart* is the first of Jane Rule's novels to be published in paperback by a UK publisher. Pandora Press continues to publish Jane Rule's work in paperback editions for our UK readership.

PANDORA PRESS FICTION

ALSO BY JANE RULE

DESERT OF
THE HEART

Jane Rule

London

First published in the USA in 1964 by
The Naiad Press Inc.

First published in Great Britain 1986 by
Pandora Press
(Routledge & Kegan Paul Ltd)
11 New Fetter Lane, London EC4P 4EE

Set in Sabon 10½/12 pt.
by Columns of Reading
and printed in Great Britain
by Guernsey Press

British Library Cataloguing in Publication Data
Rule, Jane

Desert of the heart.

I. Title
813'.54[Fiction]   PS3568.U4

ISBN 0-86358-17-14

Conventions, like clichés, have a way of surviving their own usefulness. They are then excused or defended as the idioms of living. For everyone, foreign by birth or by nature, convention is a mark of fluency. That is why, for any woman, marriage is the idiom of life. And she does not give it up out of scorn or indifference but only when she is forced to admit that she has never been able to pronounce it properly and has committed continually its grossest grammatical errors. For such a woman marriage remains a foreign tongue, an alien landscape, and, since she cannot become naturalized, she finally chooses voluntary exile.

Evelyn Hall had been married for sixteen years before she admitted to herself that she was such a woman. But now, on a plane that was taking her from Oakland, California, to Reno, Nevada, she felt curiously unchanged. The anger, guilt, grief, and resignation that she experienced now were the same emotions that had always competed in her. And the same, small public securities she had left as a young wife were with her now. It was true that the Mrs, which had been an epithet, would soon be no more than a courtesy; and the ring she had never taken for granted would not, of course, be granted anymore. It was odd that she could not take it off. She had tried before she left the house, first casually at the kitchen sink, then frankly in the bathroom, but soap and water would not ease the ring over a joint thickened those sixteen years into obstacle. It would, she supposed, have to be cut off. It was impossible to have the Mrs cut off, too, but, just as she was not to be married, she was not to be single ever again either. She was to be divorced, a convention that might be as strange to her as the convention of marriage had been.

From the plane window Evelyn looked out at the new landscape, the mountains shelving down under her to the edge of the desert, to the town through which a river flowed and disappeared into miles of burning sand. If it looked familiar, it was not because she had ever been there before. She had seen the travel posters and the advertisements. She had reluctantly read westerns. And in dreams she had experienced what was now the actual descent, a lurching uncertainty toward earth.

In the airport waiting room, the calendar read July 27, 1958, and the hands of the wall clock hedged their specific way to four. Though the Chamber of Commerce had left its few stamped souvenirs, the syndicate its double row of slot machines, time seemed more local than place. The passengers waited in a slow humiliation of heat. The flies were terrible. They crawled across floor and counter. They settled with indifferent intimacy in the hair, on the face, refusing to be brushed away. But dirty and airless as the waiting room was, it provided shelter from the direct desert sun. Evelyn was reluctant to step out onto the pavement to claim her luggage. There the sudden brutality of heat made her sweat with a threatening nausea. She did not wait for the limousine. She signaled a taxi, the first of so many small, necessary luxuries.

The address of the guesthouse was in the lawyer's letter. He had suggested that it would be pleasanter and cheaper than a hotel. As Evelyn watched the cab meter, she wished she had asked Mrs Packer just how much she charged for room and board. It had seemed, at the time Evelyn was writing, indelicate to inquire.

2

Perhaps, after all, she was changing. She was full of new properties. She had bought two hats and made some effort to give up smoking. And she had caught herself twice in the last few days referring to George as Mr Hall. Guilt, not only at its source but in its expression, is reactionary. For years she had kept it in her house, as dull, vague, and persistent as the company of a cat; but now, more sharply focused, it struggled to become righteous indignation.

The billboards advertising restaurants, outrageously expensive motels, and gambling casinos only mildly offended her, but she was truly angered by the jewelers' exaggeration of their wares along the wide desert highway. Wedding rings were as big as hula hoops or moon gates, to play with, to walk through, to roll down a hill. And the all-night jeweler claimed to be just doors away from the famous neon chapel, which offered, in great block letters, twenty-four hours service, including a minister, flowers, a photographer, and witnesses. Perhaps they also supplied spare brides and grooms. As the billboards dwindled to the edge of town, they were replaced by the actual buildings, more substantial and garish than their copies. Evelyn was almost grateful for the occasional familiarity of a supermarket or used car lot.

The cab turned off the main street into an ill-defined neighbourhood of smaller public buildings, newly shadowing the few private houses, where homemade signs offered music lessons, alterations, and tea. There was a deserted school, a tall building with small windows, surrounded by a blank, baked-earth yard. Over the roofs of the next residential block there was the inverted exclamation mark of a church spire. It was Sunday.

As the cab pulled up to the curb, Evelyn looked out at a large, gray house set back from the street, silly with window boxes. She would not let her body falter as her mind did. She got out of the cab, paid the driver, picked

3

up her suitcase, and walked quickly toward the house.

Frances Packer opened the front door. She was a small, round woman in her fifties, mother-faced, proprietary. She greeted Evelyn by name and then called to her son, Walter. He came into the hall from the living room, a tall, square, bland-faced boy, blinking into the sunlight, the Sunday funnies still in his hand. He reminded Evelyn of so many anonymous youngsters who lounged somehow comfortably in the restrictive chairs at the back of her lecture room day after day, year after, repeating and spreading themselves like perennials.

'Will you take Mrs Hall up to her room, dear?' Then she turned to Evelyn, pleasantly. 'Dinner's at five.'

'That's fine. I'll just have time to wash.'

The upstairs hall smelled faintly of incense, but it was cool. The room Walter showed Evelyn into was large and leaf-dappled. The double bed had been modernized, the headboard, removed, the footboard now serving in its place so that the bed settled quietly and less importantly into the floor space, no longer a stage for a production, now a simple place of rest. It was the antique secretary in the corner that dominated the room. A social psychologist could not have designed a living space more appropriate.

'The bathroom's right next door. There ought to be clean towels just inside the closet there,' Walter said, as he put one suitcase on the luggage rack at the foot of the bed, the other across the arms of a chintz chair. 'Don't smoke in bed. There isn't any fire escape. Put toenails in the ash tray. And don't keep pets. Mealtimes and other house rules are in the printed folder in the Gideon Bible by your bed. Any questions?'

Evelyn grinned at him, grateful for his nonsense but unable to think of a suitable reply. Outside the classroom she had always been slow-witted with adolescents.

'Well, I have one,' he continued. 'We've been having an argument. I told Mother that she should call you Dr Hall. Isn't that your proper title?'

4

'It doesn't really matter at all,' Evelyn replied. She was one of the few women she knew who preferred Mrs to Dr, perhaps because her marriage had been more difficult than her PhD to achieve and maintain. Then, too, George had been sensitive about it. Walter was right, of course. Dr, now was her only 'proper' title, but it seemed too easy a solution, or too ironic.

'If you come down about quarter to – that gives you fifteen mintues – there'll be sherry in the living room.'

'Lovely. Thanks.'

As Walter closed the door behind him, Evelyn took off her hat and opened one suitcase to find her cosmetic bag. In the large, clean, old-fashioned bathroom she discovered the source of the incense. Airwick or a pine deodorant would have depressed her, but incense was her great aunt Ida, maiden and militant, who had lived alone in a house very like this; but she had mastered the master bedroom with nothing but her own royal virginity, which had deserved the stage, unaltered, on which she had been conceived. The bathroom, just like this, had fascinated Evelyn when she was a child, but she was never allowed to use the incense. Like snuff, like wine, like perfume, it was for adults only. Though now Evelyn had no intention of offending the air with more than the scent of her own soap, she could not resist the temptation to light a small stick of it and set it in the stand, candle of corporeal service, in memory of Ida; but the odor, confined in the room, caught in her throat. She had to put it out. 'Ah, Ida,' she said softly, 'it's true what you used to say: we are a weaker generation.' Evelyn looked at the tub, long, deep, claw-footed, and realized how much she wanted a bath, but there wasn't time now. After dinner she could be leisurely.

As she went down the stairs, cooler, cleaner, if not quite refreshed, the voices in the living room sounded cheerful. It might, after all, be quite a pleasant place to stay. The thought that she might actually enjoy herself had not occurred to her before, and, irreverent as she considered it, she did not rebuke herself.

'So there's a new arrival, is there?' It was a woman's voice, young and mock cheerful. 'Delivered, as every one of them is to this house, full grown and female out of our All Father's racked brain. And she looks like me.'

There were only two of them, Walter struggling up out of a deep armchair and the girl whose voice Evelyn had heard. She stood in a cage of sunlight by the bay window. Evelyn smiled, consciously amused and invulnerable because the girl was as young as a student; but as she turned, embarrassed and apologetic, to Evelyn, Evelyn was startled.

'Dr Hall, this is Ann Childs,' Walter said. 'How about some sherry? Would you like a cigarette?'

'Thanks,' Evelyn said. 'Hello, Ann.'

'Hello.' Ann stared at her.

'There's a line from Cummings,' Evelyn said. ' "Hello is what a mirror says" . . .'

'We do look alike,' Ann said. 'Frances was right. Don't we?'

'Yes, very much. It startled me.'

'Do you think we're related?' Ann asked.

'Maybe we are,' Evelyn answered, but she did not think so. There was no family resemblance, a turned eyetooth or a surprised left eyebrow that siblings share from a common grandparent. It was rather an impression which, when analyzed, seemed to have no firm basis. Ann's face was, for Evelyn, a memory, not a likeness. 'But probably not.'

'No,' Ann said, her own certainty fading. 'Walter says you teach at Cal.'

'That's right.'

'What department?'

'English.'

Walter handed Evelyn a glass of sherry. When she sat down, he did also, choosing a chair that would keep him at the edge of conversation. But Ann continued to stand. Perhaps it was the strain of looking up at her; perhaps it was the sherry: Evelyn felt a not altogether unpleasant lightheadedness. She found it difficult to follow and answer the questions Ann was asking her. And, as she watched rather than listened, she thought how extraordinary the girl's clothes were. On that hot evening, she wore black wool frontier pants, black boots, and a brilliant blue-green long-sleeved shirt. Evelyn had not been in the real West before, but she assumed that such a costume was reserved for rodeos.

'Do you think so?' Ann asked at the end of a question that had something to do with symbolism and Yeats.

'I'm sorry. I was admiring your shirt.'

Ann looked down at herself. 'It's a uniform. I work at Frank's Club, the night shift.'

'At *the* Frank's Club?'

'That's right.'

'What do you do?'

'I'm a change apron.' When Evelyn looked bewildered, Ann explained, 'I make change for the slot machine customers.'

'You do?' Evelyn could not help showing her surprise and amusement. 'How did you get the job?'

'I've been there for four years,' Ann answered. 'I live here.'

'She could be a dealer,' Walter said, 'but she doesn't want to, the idiot. That's where all the real money is for the women.'

Evelyn saw her own unconscious assumptions flower and fade in Ann's eyes like the blooms of transplanted bulbs. If Ann was not here for a divorce, if she lived in Reno, why was she in this house? Was she related to the Packers?

'Here's Virginia,' Walter said, rising from his chair. Dr Hall, this is Mrs Ritchie.'

Virginia Ritchie was a thin, pretty young woman. She

7

waited at the edge of the room even after the introduction, looking nervously from Evelyn to Ann and back again. It was obvious that she, too, saw a striking resemblance between them, but she could not comment on it. She clutched a hat and gloves, as if they steadied her uncertain balance, and waited for someone to explain.

'Have some sherry with us,' Ann suggested.

'Oh, thank you, but . . .'

'Come on,' Walter encouraged, almost brusque with awkwardness.

'Frances says dinner's ready.'

'Come along,' Frances called from the dining room. 'If we don't eat right away, Ann will be late to work and Virginia late to church.'

'Going to evensong?' Ann asked as they moved into the dining room.

'I thought I would,' Virginia answered. 'Dr Hall, perhaps you'd . . . ?'

'Thank you,' Evelyn answered quickly. 'I think not tonight. I haven't had a chance to unpack.'

'No, no, of course . . .'

'Mrs Hall, will you sit here?' Frances Packer indicated the place at Walter's right. Ann sat to his left, Virginia Ritchie beside her. 'You go right ahead and carve, dear. I'll just get the vegetables and gravy.'

Walter did not carve well. He was awkward and unconsciously brutal.

'Walter, dear, it's already dead,' Ann said wryly, as she watched him struggle. 'Relax.'

Walter sighed, stared for a moment at the leg of lamb, and then continued. In his real irritation, he apparently did not trust himself to answer. Evelyn smiled. She did like him, and she liked Ann with him. They were like brother and sister in a sentimental play, rude and obviously fond.

'How long will you be staying, Dr Hall?' Virginia Ritchie asked suddenly.

'Why . . .' Evelyn hesitated '. . . six weeks, I suppose.'

'Oh.' Virginia worked at her napkin furiously with both hands. In the silence Evelyn could hear Frances' spoon, dragging the gravy pan for foreign bodies. 'I'm so sorry.'

'For what?' Walter demanded with bursting irritation, but Virginia had begun to cry.

As Frances came in with the gravy, Virginia got up from the table and left the room to sob, step by step, up the stairs to her bedroom. Frances looked at Walter.

'It wasn't a deep cut,' he said defensively. 'She's hardly bleeding at all.'

'Walter, you're old enough to be kind,' Frances said. 'Fix me a plate. I'll take Virginia's dinner up to her.' She turned to Evelyn. 'She isn't usually like this. Sundays upset her.'

When Frances left the room, Walter began to serve.

'Did I upset her?' Evelyn asked. Surely she was not wrong about Virginia Ritchie, too.

'Everything upsets her,' Walter answered wearily. 'If I forget to pee down the side of the pot, she cries herself to sleep.'

'And Walter's obviously sensitive about being a boy; so you can see how tense and psychological the whole situation is,' Ann said.

'Two helpings of stringed beans for you, girl Childs, and no dessert.'

'Careful,' Ann warned. 'You have a date tonight.'

'Blackmailing capitalist! One of these days I won't need your car. If I weren't a poor, struggling young man, working my way through college . . .'

'You're breaking my heart,' Ann cried.

'I hoped I was.'

Their teasing was routine enough to be mindless, and they use it now with a tired nervous energy to cover the awkwardness of Virginia's departure. Evelyn watched and smiled and wished she could think of something to say.

She felt both curiously exposed and unknown.

'I hope you're not waiting for me,' Frances said, as she hurried back into the room. 'Have you had the gravy, Mrs Hall?'

'Thank you.'

The phone rang.

'I'll get it,' Walter said, as Frances started up from her chair. 'Sit down and eat your dinner.'

'I feel we shouldn't try to eat on Sundays at all,' Frances said. 'Walter says I'm a compulsive eater, but when I suggest . . .'

'It's a long distance for Virginia. Shall I call her?' Walter looked into the room from the hall.

'Well, yes, do. I suppose so. But don't yell. Go up. I must have that phone moved out of the hall. I wish I could think where.'

'How about the bathroom?' Ann suggested.

'I actually considered that, but it's something about the wires, being near water and all. Can I get you more meat, Mrs Hall? Ann? No, you won't. If everyone ate as little as Ann, we could go right ahead and feed China.'

'That's my theory,' Ann answered.

'Ann has a real Robin Hood complex,' Frances said brightly. 'It's much less complicated and much more subversive than communism. "Corrupt the rich to feed the poor." Isn't that it, Ann?'

'Frances doesn't like gambling,' Ann said.

'Neither do you,' Frances asserted.

This argument, like Ann's and Walter's teasing, was a familiar exercise without important malice, but Evelyn was made uncomfortable by it. There was a real tension between Ann and Frances.

Walter came back to the table and confronted the cold remains of his dinner glumly. Out in the hall, Virginia's tearstained voice was resonant and clear: 'Mummy loves you, darling. It's only three more weeks now. You be a good boy. Mummy loves you very much.'

10

'For God's sake, Mother, talk about something, will you?'

Frances did. She discussed fund raising for the Episcopal Church, legal adoption, the Reno flood. The connection between one subject and another was superficial but skillful. If Frances was extravagant in her subject matter, she was not undisciplined. Anne offered an occasional question or comment while Walter ate his cold potatoes. Evelyn sat silent, trapped between the competing voices, irritated and oddly ashamed. When Virginia finally said goodbye and rushed back upstairs, Frances also stopped talking and got up to clear the dishes to a tea cart, which she then wheeled to the kitchen.

'Thank you,' Walter said. He felt in his shirt pocket with his left hand and took out a pack of cigarettes. 'Smoke?'

'No thanks.' Evelyn's head ached. Her throat was sour with the food she had eaten. She longed to have the meal over.

'What time is it?' Ann asked.

'Six. You've got an easy twenty minutes. Relax.'

'Will you leave the car in the lot?'

'Oh, I'll probably come and pick you up.' Walter rose to take the last of the serving dishes away.

'What time do you get off?' Evelyn asked, forcing a question against the candid look of sympathy Ann gave her as soon as they were alone in the room.

'Three or three thirty. I'll be off at three tonight. Sunday's fairly slow.'

'You must have to sleep all day.'

'Oh, no. I'm always up by eleven. These hot days I get up earlier. There's no point in a night job if you sleep the day away.'

'I suppose not,' Evelyn said. She could not think of anything more to say that was not personal; and, because she herself disliked direct questions, she would not ask

11

any. 'I suppose not.'

'It really isn't usually as bad as this,' Ann said. 'I'm sorry about . . . all that nonsense I was talking.'

'Please . . .' Evelyn began but was troubled by the urgency in her own voice. What was the matter with her?

'Do you drive?' Ann asked quickly. 'Because I really don't use the car much during the day. Walt takes it to work. Any day you wanted to, you could drop him off and just have the car.'

'That's very generous of you, but I . . .'

'Don't refuse. You'll need things to do.'

'I have plenty of work to do,' Evelyn answered, her voice quite under control, her eyes consciously and silently reminding Ann of the fifteen years that separated them.

'I'm sorry again,' Ann said, her smile relieved and self-mocking. 'It's just playground tactics: if you won't be mad at me, I'll let you play with my car.'

'I shouldn't suppose anyone stays mad at you for very long,' Evelyn said, her voice still adult, but fond, as if to a child.

Frances came in with a berry pie. Walter followed with the coffee.

'Now you have plenty of time, Ann,' Frances said. 'You're to eat a piece of pie.'

'I didn't say I wouldn't.'

'She never wants dessert,' Frances said to Evelyn. 'She never did, not even when she was a little girl.'

Walter imitated an expression of maternal concern. Ann looked down, demure. Frances, unnoticing, cut the pie with haphazard generosity, and they ate.

After Walter and Ann had hurried off, Frances suggested a more peaceful cup of coffee in the living room. Evelyn raised the question of payment almost at once.

'I charge sixty-five dollars a week.'

'Fine,' Evelyn said, a little too quickly. She had not

really put her mind to any fixed amount, but her only experience with room and board had been the price set for students in Berkeley. She was, therefore, startled. 'Shall I pay you in advance?'

'A week at a time. If you make other plans, just give me a week's notice.'

'I'm sure I'll be quite comfortable here,' Evelyn said.

'I'm glad. But sometimes ... well ... people change their minds.'

'Do they?' Evelyn asked. 'Well, yes, I suppose they might.'

'Yes.'

The silence invited Evelyn to say nothing about herself, her own situation and intention.

'Let me get my checkbook,' she said abruptly.

'That's not necessary. Tomorrow's plenty of time.'

'I mustn't keep you then, Mrs Packer.' Evelyn got up.

'Do call me Frances. . . . Of course, you want to unpack. You run along. If there's anything you need, just let me know. I usually make tea around ten o'clock. You come down if you'd like to. Or before. I always like company; so don't ever feel you have to be alone.'

'*Have* to be alone,' Evelyn thought as she closed the bedroom door behind her. If she had known how much she would have to pay – it worked out to almost four hundred dollars for six weeks – she could have stayed in a hotel. Three meals a day of the sort she had just survived would drive her mad. The hysteria, the awkwardness, the prying, the solicitude were unbearable. As she looked at her not yet unpacked suitcases, she thought for a moment that she need not stay, that she could simply close them, call a cab, and be gone. But, at the fact of escape, her imagination balked.

'I can't run away from running away.'

Nothing was wrong, really. It was only Virginia Ritchie, a caricature of the wronged woman, who made the others behave as they did. She would be gone in three weeks' time, perhaps sooner. Evelyn wondered why it had never occurred to her that, once in Reno, a woman might change her mind. Regret, yes, even terror, but like the suicide falling, no way out. But that was ridiculous. Evelyn herself had waited until there was no choice, but perhaps other people acted on impulse. Virginia Ritchie was, after all, not much older than Ann Childs.

'All right. I admit it,' Evelyn said quietly in answer to a thought she was not allowing herself to have.

Ann was almost young enough to be her own child. But only a parent could be allowed to feel tenderness for his own likeness. In a childless woman such tenderness was at least narcissistic. And Evelyn had learned the even less flattering names applied to the love a childless woman might feel for anything: her dogs, her books, her students ... yes, even her husband. She was not afraid of the names themselves, but she was afraid of the truth that might be in them. This resemblance was, she knew, not a trick need had played on her; neither was it a miracle. Ann Childs was an accident; that was all. An accident, an illegitimate child, 'sprung fullgrown and female out of our All Father's racked brain.' Evelyn smiled.

'And I shall feel tender toward her if I like.'

As she crossed the room to open the drawers of the highboy, she noticed that, instead of the Gideon Bible Walter had promised, there was a small bowl of fresh fruit on the bedside table. Frances Packer was quite a nice woman really. She hadn't been trying to pry. She had only offered the opportunity for Evelyn to ask for sympathy. And, if many of her guests had been like Virginia Ritchie, Frances' friendliness was a calculated and saintly risk.

'I must tell her to call me Evelyn' she decided, as she folded nightgowns into the second drawer, trying to ignore the distaste she felt for such familiarity.

When Evelyn had settled her belongings, it was only seven thirty. She was not used to so early a dinner. All evenings would be long. It was just as well. She had

14

planned to do a lot of work during these six weeks. Already she missed her books. She had only had room for three or four in her luggage. If she had taken the car, she would have everything she needed with her. George would not use it, but she had refused to suggest anything that would threaten or anger him further. There were libraries. Perhaps she would go tomorrow after she had seen the lawyer. Or on Tuesday. That would give her something definite to do on Tuesday.

Sitting down at the secretary, Evelyn made a list of the notes she would write. Evelyn's correspondence, since her sister's death two years ago, had dwindled to nothing very much more than Christmas letters to half a dozen old friends. Of these, Carol was the only person she wanted to write to, but she must send some word to the others as well. It would hardly do to save the news of her divorce to include in Christmas greetings. Emily Post, or whoever did that sort of thing now, should produce a form letter or at least offer civilized suggestions for the announcement of a divorce. 'Mr and Mrs George Hall take pleasure in . . .' Or 'Mrs Evelyn Hall' – that was the right form now, wasn't it? – but not 'takes pleasure.' Did she regret it? 'Regrets the divorce of her only husband, George'? 'Is ashamed'? 'Unhappily admits'? For the contested divorce, the contesting partner could use 'Refuses to admit . . .' Evelyn put her hand up to her eyes, refusing to admit quite sudden tears.

She wanted a cigarette. She had none. Lovely. She would have to go out to buy some. It was only eight o'clock, still early enough to explore the immediate neighborhood.

Out on the street, because it was a pleasant evening and because the streets she had driven through were unpleasant, Evelyn turned east to walk further into what must be a residential area. At first she was able to walk slowly, naming trees and flowers, feeling against her face and arms the fine drifts of spray from lawn sprinklers, a

15

wavering pulse of sound everywhere, like evening crickets. She found a store before she wanted to, but, afraid on a Sunday evening that it might not stay open long, she went in. Waited on at once by a silent, tired woman, Evelyn bought several packs of cigarettes and a bottle of sherry. As she came out onto the street again, she was reluctant to turn back. Beyond the next intersection, the street she had been walking narrowed and steepened to block her view. Curious, she went on. At the top of the short hill, Evelyn stopped, oddly out of breath. The street fingered out from the main crossroad for just three short blocks of faded brick bungalows and no trees. At the end was the desert, sudden, flat, dull miles of it until it heaved itself upward and became the mountains. An irrational fear, as alien to Evelyn's nature as heat lightning seems to a summer sky, struck through her body. For a moment she could not move. Then she turned quietly, refusing in herself the desire to run, and walked back to the house.

Frances Packer was in the hall, but Evelyn refused the cup of tea she offered.

'Would you like to take the paper up with you?' Frances suggested. 'We've all finished with it.'

'Thank you, but . . .'

'Do,' Frances encouraged.

It was little enough to accept; so Evelyn carried the unwanted paper up the stairs to her room. She glanced at the travel clock by her bed, picked it up and listened to it. She had not forgotten to wind it. It clicked at her ear with precise regularity. How could she have been gone only twenty minutes? She put the clock down impatiently and began to undress.

Bathed and ready for bed, Evelyn stood by the window, looking out through the densely leaved tree to the sky, still transparent with the last, lasting light of evening. Safe now, the day like a door arbitrarily closed behind her, Evelyn could smile at herself. She could not remember a

16

night in recent years when she had been in bed before midnight. Now, at not quite nine o'clock, like a summer child she struggled to keep sleep off until the darkness arrived. Why? She had every right to be tired. It had been a long day, this last day of the long sixteen years that had brought her here. Surely now she could sleep. There was no harm in it.

– 2 –

Ann left Walter with the car and walked up the alley to the employees' entrance. Inside, the stale heat of the day smelled of brass ash trays and sweat and shoes. But the night shift employees, crowded around the board, lined up at the punch clock, sitting in the cracked leather chairs, were fresh from a day's sleep, newly shaved or powdered, in clean shirts, pressed trousers, and polished boots. Noisy with stories of the night before, because it had been Saturday, easy about the night to come, because it was Sunday, they relaxed together, the change aprons, the key men, the cashiers, the dealers, and the floor bosses.

'We're in the Corral again, darling,' Silver Kay called from across the room by the Coke machine.

'Out of the dollar machines, thank God,' Ann said, joining Silver and taking a sip of the Coke she offered.

'All very well for you. You're on the ramp again. I'm on the goddamned floor.'

'You like it,' Ann said.

'I like it. I like it. You've never been on the floor.'

'I'm not tall enough,' Ann said.

'You'll do. You're noticeable enough, love.'

'Thanks,' Ann said, looking up at Silver, who was over six feet tall in her heeled boots, hipless and brazen bosomed, her hair bleached almost white as the ten-gallon hat that rode on her shoulders like a rising moon, 'but I'm not in your class.'

19

'Why don't you enroll?' Silver suggested. 'It's reduced rates tonight.'

'Is it?'

'Umhum.'

'Joe out of town?'

'And I've got a bottle of your favorite Scotch,' Silver said, smiling.

'I might be tired,' Ann said, but she felt Silver's eyes trace a teasing and relieving suggestion from her throat to her thighs. 'I didn't sleep much last night.'

'Sleep with me.'

'You going down to the locker room?'

'I've been.'

'I'll see you later then,' Ann said.

In the basement Ann found Janet Hearle already there, the locker they shared open.

'I've just been up to supplies and got you a better apron,' Janet said. 'Here.'

'Thanks. How's everything?'

'We've got a date for the operation. A week from tomorrow.'

'That's good news,' Anne said. 'Have you got time off?'

'Do you think I ought to ask, Ann? They might just say I needn't come back.'

'But you have to be with the baby,' Ann protested. 'Ask Bill. He'll understand. He can work it for you.'

'I was late twice last week.'

'So you were late.'

'I can't lose this job, Ann. I've got to have the money. And Ken can get off. He's already checked with his boss. He can have ten days.'

'Ten days isn't enough, is it?'

'No, but by then we'll know. If he's going to live, he'll live.'

'He'll live,' Ann said.

'Your name's crooked.' Janet undid the plastic name-plate: FRANK'S CLUB INTRODUCES (a picture of a

20

covered wagon) ANN. She repinned it neatly over Ann's left shirt pocket. 'There.'

'You see Bill tonight. It won't hurt to ask.'

Janet nodded, uncertain. She closed the locker door. 'Well, here we go again.'

Ann would have spoken to Bill herself if Janet's uncertainty had been a simple matter of time off, but ten days away from work meant a loss of about a hundred dollars. She and Ken had not finished paying for last year's operation. They were buying their child's life on the installment plan without so much as a thirty-day guarantee. Well, Frances was right. Ann did not like gambling, but the sort people indulged in at Frank's Club, even when they lost more than they could afford to lose, was innocent enough. And at least, here, they knew the odds. Great signs in the lavatories announced, 'Remember, if you play long enough you'll lose.' And pamphlets handed out to customers carefully explained the varying disadvantages of each game. It was all a public relations stunt, of course, a way the Establishment denied that it was the House of Mammon in the City of Dis. But it was honest advertising. No university published the odds against learning, no hospital the odds against surviving, no church the odds against salvation. Here, anyway, people weren't being fooled. They were told that no one was intelligent enough or strong enough or blessed enough to be saved. Still, they played.

As Ann and Janet reached the top of the stairs, their way was blocked by a small crowd of employees, watching Silver give instructions to a new girl.

'Look, kid, out on the floor it's hell. Ask anybody. Isn't that right, anybody?' Several nodded, amused. 'For instance, it gets so crowded one woman passed out and had to ride two floors on the escalator before she had room to fall down. I'm not kidding. Am I kidding?' The others shook their heads. 'One Saturday night some cooperative customers helped us carry out ten drunks. We

21

didn't find out for an hour that those ten drunks were slot machines with coats and hats on. Tricky, eh? But what you've really got to watch out for is pickpockets. Now, do you know how to walk to keep off pickpockets?'

The youngster shook her head. Watching Silver, she tried to cover her fear with a mild scepticism.

'You hook your thumbs like this, see?' Silver demonstrated, her thumbs in her pockets, her hands cupped over her hip bones. 'And use your elbows to keep them clear.' She walked half a dozen steps. 'Now go ahead. Try it yourself.' The girl hesitated. 'Go ahead, I said. You have to learn.'

'She's right,' Ann said. 'You couldn't learn from anybody better. Silver was a pickpocket before she came here.'

'Only as a hobby,' Silver shouted above the laughter. 'Only as a hobby.'

'And she's proud of her amateur standing, because next year she goes to the winter Olympics.'

'Ann?'

Ann turned to find Bill standing behind her. 'Yes, Bill.'

'I want you to take the new girl tonight.'

'I like that!' Silver said. 'Here I am, volunteering my long experience . . . but you're in good hands, honey. Ann'll take care of you fine.'

'This is Joyce, Ann,' Bill said. 'She's got all her things. Her card's in. Ann will show you just what to do, Joyce. And I'll come by later and see how you are.

Joyce, rescued from Silver's towering burlesque, turned to Bill's protective, male height with gratefulness and relief. And, because she obviously did not want him to leave her, he walked across the alley with Ann and Joyce.

'You mustn't let Silver scare you to death,' he was saying. 'It won't be hard. Ann will show you . . .'

He did not consciously intend his speaking of Ann's name to be the repeated public announcement of his private feelings, but he could not help it. Ann moved away a little to be out of range of his tenderness. Because she could not accept it from him any longer, it touched her like a minor fear or pain. As they reached the door, he stopped and turned back to Ann.

'I've left my ledger,' he said. 'I'll see you later.'

'Is he married?' Joyce asked.

'No,' Ann said.

She put her weight against the door, pushing into the cold, conditioned air, the wrench and grind of the slot machines, the magnified voices of the dealers, the muted crowds. She took hold of Joyce's arm and guided her through the maze of machines and gaming tables to the escalator, where they rode, half a dozen people apart, to the second floor. It was not as crowded there, but the noise was still beyond measuring.

'Have you read any of those?' Ann asked, nodding to the mimeographed sheets and the book Joyce held in her hand. 'I don't mean *How To Win Friends and Influence People*. The only thing important about that book is that old Hiram O. Dicks thinks he looks like Dale Carnegie. So, if you ever run into him – he really looks like one of the janitors – tell him how much you enjoyed his book and how helpful it's been to you in your work. But that other stuff is important.'

'I haven't had time,' Joyce admitted. 'I just started this one.'

Ann looked down at the first paragraph:

   Hello! Welcome to FRANK'S CLUB. You may feel a little uneasy right now as you look around and realize that you are a member of this famous family of FRANK'S CLUB employees. Yes, you are a Green Horn in The Corral, and you aren't sure what is expected of you. Don't be nervous. Take it easy. All around you are other members of your family, ready to break you in. And every one of them was once a Green Horn himself. Remember, they also lived through their first day. . . .

'Well,' Ann said, 'when you get past the crap, there are

23

things in that one you should know. Look, you go up to
the next floor. Have a cup of coffee. Read some of this
stuff. Come down in half an hour. I'll be right over there.
Then I'll check you in.'

'Where?'

'Right over there by the wagons. If you get lost, just ask
anybody for the Corral.'

At the cashier's desk, Ann claimed the key for her floor
locker where she could put her purse away. The key
pinned to her shirt just below her name plaque, her
green change apron strapped high about her rib cage, the
change dispenser hooked in place, she went back to the
cashier's desk to check out her money. Janet was already
there.

'Five hundred tonight,' the cashier said, shoving a
setup, an IOU, and a free pack of cigarettes to each of
them. 'How's the kid?'

'He's going to the hospital in a week,' Janet said,
counting the money carefully before she loaded her
apron.

'San Francisco?'

'Yes.'

'Well, he's getting the best a kid could have. Hear you
had a fight with my ma last night, Ann.'

'That's right,' Ann said. 'I didn't think she'd tell on
herself.'

'She thought it was funny. She always says, "If I'm
tanked, I just stay near Ann. She's unlucky as hell, but she
keeps me out of trouble." '

Ann smiled. She had finished counting her money and
was signing her IOU. 'I'll be back in about half an hour
to check a new kid in. Okay?'

'Sure.'

Silver stepped up to the counter just as Ann and Janet
were ready to go on the floor.

'Well, you'll have an easy time of it tonight,' she said to
Ann.

24

'I don't need her. I wish Bill had given her to you.'

'But she needs you, darling. Just relax and enjoy her.'
Silver reached for the key the cashier was handing her.
'You give me the bottom locker and I'll . . .'

Ann moved Janet away from what was to be one of
Silver's graphic threats.

'Really,' Janet said. 'I don't wonder they took her off
the tables. She should be fired.'

'Oh, Silver's all right.'

'She's vulgar.'

'Sure.'

'Ann, why do you let her make all those remarks?'

'What remarks?'

'She's always at you . . . suggesting things.'

'This isn't a church sewing circle, Janet. It's a gambling
casino.'

'Well, there are a few decent people around. You, for
instance.'

'Because I have a limited anal vocabulary? Shit,' Ann
said softly and grinned. 'I like Silver.'

Janet smiled reluctantly and shook her head. 'All right.
I'm a prude. I know it. I don't like her. I don't like her at
all.'

Of course not. Janet was a faculty wife at a small,
isolated college across the border in California. Nowhere
was decency more honored and protected than at these
little cultural outposts built on the ruins of old mining
towns in the crude, uncultivated mountains. The only
way Janet could bear the degradation of her job was to
suffer not only the ninety mile drive over the empty
desert, the fifty pound weight she packed across her belly
for eight hours each night, the lack of sleep, but also to
suffer the world of the Club in all its corruption with
martyred indignation. Ann was her only friend, and even
with Ann she suffered, not allowing herself Ann's
company for so much as a glass of tomato juice at the
bar. Of course she hated Silver, who used to run a house

25

in Virginia City. 'I got sick of administration,' Silver would say. 'I'd lost touch with the people.' But Silver was as sensitive to Janet's disapproval as Janet was to Silver's vulgarity. Yet Silver admired Janet, perhaps even loved her in the gross sentimentality she had for suffering. Everything Silver thought or felt or did was gross, and she knew it. Her attitude toward herself was one of helpless indulgence. And Ann's attitude toward her was modeled on Silver's own.

Janet and Ann separated to take positions on their assigned ramps.

'How's it been?' Ann asked the girl she was relieving.

'Slow,' the girl said, stepping down onto the floor. 'I wouldn't want every day to be Saturday, but eight hours is a hell of a long time with nothing to do. I'd rather work downstairs.'

'How long's he been here?' Ann nodded to the single customer in the area, a young man who was playing three quarter machines at once.

'Him? Three hours maybe.'

'How much has he lost?'

'Oh, he's got lots of money. He's changed a couple of fifties since he's been here. But he doesn't tip. He doesn't talk either. Real friendly.'

Ann stepped up onto the ramp, careful of the weight and swing of her apron. 'Remember, they also lived through their first day . . .' No one had told Ann, on her first, that a quick turn, with the swinging weight of fifty pounds, could knock you down. Only a slot machine had saved her. And she had had nightmares for weeks after that: falling down the escalator in the brutal storm of six hundred dollars worth of change with a floor boss (Bill?) standing at the bottom waving her IOU. Was it a more significant anxiety dream than she had thought? Or prophetic?

Ann looked down at the young man, who had put his hand up but would not look up. With his free hand, he continued to play two of the three machines. Ann walked over to him, bent down to the machine to check the jackpot reading and the number. Then she returned to the center of the ramp, reached for the microphone, and called the jackpot in to the board. As she spoke, she could hear her own voice, separated from her, magnified over the noise. A key man came to pay. Ann witnessed.

'Will you play it off now, sir?'

The young man, still not looking at either of them, stuffed the bills into his pocket, put a quarter in the lucky machine, and returned to the full rhythm of his work.

'You think he was getting paid the way he works at it,' the key man said to Ann.

'Maybe he figures it that way.'

'Maybe.'

Alone, Ann leaned back against a slot machine to rest her back. She looked beyond the young man to the guns hung along the wall, the shelved violence of another time. In themselves they did not interest her, except as shapes, but through other people, who so often studied them, she had discovered nostalgia, possessiveness, fear, and she had sketched these attitudes into stances of the body in its alien clothes. Sometimes she overheard and remembered remarks of Freudian embarrassment exchanged between a tourist husband and wife. These had become the captions for at least two successful cartoons she's sold to *Saturday Evening Post*. But now, without people, the wall was a meaningless pattern. Her eyes shifted away only to catch themselves suddenly in a ceiling mirror. There was her own face separated from her, not magnified as her voice had been, instead made smaller. What a device of conscience that mirror was, for behind it, at any time, might be the unknown face of a security officer, watchful, judging; yet you could not see it. You could not get past your own minimized reflection. 'I do look like Evelyn Hall,' Ann thought, 'and what does that mean?'

'I'm ready.'

27

Ann started slightly, embarrassed. 'Right. I'll take you over.' She signaled to Janet to cover her ramp for a few minutes, then led Joyce to the cashier's desk. 'Did reading some of that help?'

'There's so much of it,' Joyce complained. 'I'll never remember it all.'

'I'll give her just three hundred tonight,' the cashier said. 'Now, you count it, kid. Don't ever sign an IOU without counting it first.'

'What happens if I lose any of it?' Joyce asked.

'Nothing,' Ann said. 'If it's over ten dollars, the floor boss has to sign you out, but you don't have to make it up.'

'That's Bill?'

'While you're working on this floor,' Ann answered.

'Won't I stay on this floor?'

'Maybe. Maybe not.'

'Count your money,' the cashier said.

Joyce resented the order but obeyed it. Ann felt sorry for her. She was the kind of girl who would not learn to give the cashiers the respect they demanded. In return, they would make her work impossible. She would always be given the bottom floor locker. She would have to wait for change. And she would always be the last to be checked in or out. Delayed in her work, she would be criticized by the other change aprons. The key man would hold up her jackpot payoffs. The customers would complain. Ann watched her counting out her money and gave her a month before she quit or was fired.

When they got back to the ramp, two or three other customers had joined the young man, who was as oblivious of them as he had been of Ann.

'How old do you think Bill is?' Joyce asked.

'That lady over there wants change.'

Joyce was clumsy and inattentive. Twice she gave the young man nickels instead of quarters. She could not remember machine numbers and so called the wrong jackpots in to the board. But she liked the microphone. It reminded her of this movie where this girl was announcing the trains and this guy hears her voice and couldn't get it out of his mind and just went back to the train station all the time to listen and try to image what she looked like. The fourth time Joyce called in a jackpot, one of the key men was sent down to complain.

'Look, kid, you're not running the late night show. You don't have to whisper. Speak up. And get the number right next time.'

'What's the matter with him?' Joyce asked.

The elderly gentleman who had hit the jackpot pinched Joyce on the thigh, winked, and handed her five dollars. She bared her teeth at him and slipped the bill into her pocket.

'Take it out,' Ann said gently.

'What?'

'The five. You have to turn it in to the cashier. She splits the tips at the end of the shift.'

'Well, but don't you think I earned that one?' Joyce asked, watching Ann. 'Why don't I just split it with you?'

'Look,' Ann said, 'do you see those mirrors? Behind any one of them, one of the security officers might be watching you. If you're ever seen putting money in your pocket, they don't give you time to explain. You're out, and that's that. And you won't get police clearance for any other job in town.'

'Pretty tough, aren't they?'

'Go turn the five in to the cashier,' Ann said.

'Anything you say.'

When the relief arrived for Ann's half-hour break, Ann longed for a few minutes to herself, but she took Joyce with her. Joyce had so much trouble getting her apron off and into the locker that they had time for only a quick Coke at the bar before they had to go back.

'Half an hour!' Joyce said. 'More like ten minutes.' She struggled against the weight and clumsiness of her apron while Ann strapped her own on. 'It looks so easy when you do it.'

'It takes practice. Here. Turn around and lean up against the locker. For one thing, you've got it too low.'

'Too low? Where am I supposed to wear it, around my neck?'

'It rides down,' Ann said. 'You can't carry fifty pounds on your kidneys.' She reached to lift it, her hands grazing the undercurves of Joyce's full breasts. She tightened the top strap around the small, fragile rib cage. Joyce was not built to carry the weight. 'Okay, now try the bottom one yourself.'

As Joyce turned around, Ann saw the dampness of the hair at her temples, the whiteness of her face.

'Sit down. Sit down right on the floor.' Joyce obeyed her at once. 'Put your head on your knees.' Ann looked down at her. After a moment, Joyce raised her head. 'Better?'

'Yeh. How did you know?'

'The first night's always rough,' but, if it was as rough as this, a girl was usually dismissed. Joyce did look better. Should Ann risk letting her back on the floor? How badly did she need the job? 'Come on. You'll be fine.'

Their section was more crowded now. The young man had to guard his machines from tourists who did not understand that, in the etiquette of gambling, to put hands on another man's machine was a greater offense than to put hands on his wife. Ann was grateful to be able to keep Joyce busy. While she had something to do, she would not have time to worry about herself. But, standing back to let her do the work, Ann had time to worry. The bravado and bitchery were gone. Joyce was as attentive to the shabby grandmothers as she had been to the affluent business men. Instead of talking, she listened to Ann's instructions with a desperate patience. Ann watched her with growing respect. Joyce was not simply afraid of being sick. She was determined not to make a fool of

30

herself. But she was very white. It was Ann who saw Bill come into the section and signal her off the ramp.

'Ann,' Joyce said, as she, too, caught sight of him, 'don't tell him, will you? I'm okay now, I really am.'

'I won't tell him,' Ann said. 'I'll be right back.'

'How's she doing?' Bill asked.

'Fine.'

'There've been some complaints up at the counter.'

'Not lately,' Ann answered. 'She'll be all right. She's quick.'

'How's her back?' Bill watched Joyce as he spoke.

'Killing her, I should think, but she hasn't complained.'

'She's pretty white,' Bill said. 'And she's not built for it. I was wondering about putting her on the elevators for a while.'

'Well, don't do it unless you can persuade her it's a better job.'

'All right. I'll leave her with you for a week,' Bill said. 'But she's had enough tonight. I'm going to check her out.'

'Okay.' Ann turned to go back to her station.

'Ann?' She turned back to him. 'How about a drink tonight?'

'Thanks but I told Silver I'd go home with her. Joe's away tonight.'

'I could drop you off there later.'

'She wants company, Bill.'

'Sure, of course she does,' he said quickly. 'Well, send Joyce down to me, will you?'

'Thanks anyway.'

'Some other time,' Bill said.

He was angry. It was the third time in two weeks that Ann had refused him, but she had no other choice. They had already tried going back to the old friendship, and it hadn't worked. Awkward politeness shifted to argument, argument to passion, and there they were again in that familiar bed, faced with another impossible morning. 'If a

31

wife is what you want,' she had said to him, 'go out wife hunting.' But Bill did not know fair game when he saw it. If the woods were not full of virgins, there were, at least, a number of recognizable amateurs. Bill went from whore to homosexual back to Ann again. He was incapable of understanding a woman who did not want to marry, who could not marry a man she loved. And Ann did love him. And now she would not see him. Of course he was angry.

'What did he say?' Joyce said.

'He says you've worked long enough for your first night.'

'You told him.'

'No, I promise I didn't,' Ann said. 'Nobody works a full shift the first couple of nights. He wants to see you now. Take off. I'll see you tomorrow night.'

Joyce hesitated, caught between pride and relief. Then Bill himself signaled to her and she went. As they stood together talking, Ann watched. In Bill's presence, Joyce's color returned, and with her color came her confidence. There were weights her back could bear. Bill looked up. Ann turned away, the palms of her hands aching.

At two o'clock, there were again very few people in Ann's section the young man, a middle-aged couple, and several college boys with fake identification. Half a dozen old men had begun to make their nightly rounds. Two of them had the guile to inspect the gun collection, but the others searched as frankly for dropped coins as barnyard fowl do for bits of corn. Half starved, trembling from lack of alcohol, they did not collect the dimes and nickels for food or drink. Each coin was to prime the pump which would, sooner or later, flood them with vaguely dreamed-of riches.

Ann saw Walt as he came through the doorway by the cashier's desk.

'Hi. Did you have a good time?'

'Wonderful,' he said. 'We went out to Pyramid Lake and went swimming. How's it with you?'

32

'It's been busy enough, just tapering off now.'

'You had your last break?'

'Yes. I've just come back. I don't think I will go home tonight, Walt. Joe's away. Silver's got a bottle of Scotch.'

'Just as you like,' Walter said, checking what might have been disappointment or disapproval. 'What shall I do with the car?'

'Take it home. Silver will drop me off tomorrow.'

Ann would like to have had him stay for a few minutes to help pass the time, but she did not suggest it. Now, he would not be in bed much before three, and he had to be up at seven thirty. Frances had given up scolding either of them for the way they so often neglected to sleep, but her silences or forced cheerfulness made Ann uncomfortable. She would rather not appear to be responsible for all of Walter's bad habits.

'Change!'

Ann took the young man's last five dollars and gave him a short roll of quarters. He had lost just three hundred dollars in eleven hours. He would not have had to work so hard at roulette. Ann leaned back against a slot machine and watched him in the last slow movement of his dance. In ten minutes, his hands and pockets were empty. He stood for a moment, resting. Then he looked up at the machines, at the college boys, at the guns, at Ann, his face pale and peaceful as if he had just awakened from a long sleep. He stretched, yawned, then turned away and was gone.

The college boys drifted to another section, and Ann was alone. Slowly she began to empty her change dispenser, to count and roll the coins. Walter was home by now, sitting alone in the kitchen. Ann half wished she had told him to wait. She was restless and depressed, reluctant to be with anyone, but her own room at the top of the house would be hot, too hot for sleeping, and she would not be in the mood for work tomorrow. It had been a month since she'd done a sketch that pleased her.

33

The girls of the graveyard shift had begun to arrive at the cashier's desk. The girl who relieved Janet was on the floor ten minutes early, and Janet had checked out before Ann and Silver arrived at the desk. Janet always went through first. She had a ninety-mile drive ahead of her, then only a couple of hours' sleep before the baby work and Ken got up to go to his summer job.

'Well,' Silver said, 'a real lively night tonight, eh? My biggest thrill was an old lady with weak kidneys. She wet her pants three times – not even for jackpots. For eighteen nickels she wet her pants. It's a good thing I've got catholic tastes. Other people I know might have been bored.'

Ann stood beside her, carefully stacking up her last bits of loose change. Just twenty cents out tonight. She wondered how Joyce had done.

'I'm a nickel ahead,' Silver announced. 'Now let's see. Who could it be who's wandering around town at three o'clock on the morning without money enough for the pay toilet?'

'You've got kidneys on the brain tonight,' the cashier said, tired and bored.

'You're wrong, love,' Silver said. 'It's pure substitution.' She reached over to claim her IOU. 'Ready?'

'Yes,' Ann said.

They went down through the Club together. Silver calling greetings to dealers, Ann nodding and smiling to other employees and customers. As they stepped out into the alley, the sudden heat and silence wrenched them away from the bright, timeless chaos of the Club. They were alone together.

'Well, love,' Silver said softly, 'will you come home with me tonight?'

'Yes,' Ann said. 'Yes, I think I will.'

They walked across the alley to leave their hats, their aprons, and change dispensers. They stood in line at the clock. Ann's card read 3:11.

34

'Not bad,' Ann said.

'Not bad at all. The car's this way.'

Ann had not been to Silver's house for several weeks. They came in through the back door to the kitchen, which Silver called, 'Secondhand Appliances and Son.' And it would have been impressive had there not always been at least one corner of it being torn up to install yet another of the latest kitchen conveniences. Silver turned in stoves and refrigerators, deep freezes and dishwashers as some men turn in cars. If she could not find an improved refrigerator, one that made juice as well as ice, she would decide to change her color scheme. Then all the blue-green equipment would have to go, replaced by yellow or pink or apricot. Counter tops and floors would be ripped up, towels and aprons thrown or given away. Consequently, there was rarely a time that the kitchen was fit to work in, but Silver liked to cook only occasionally and brilliantly. Most of the time she and Joe ate in restaurants or simply made themselves coffee and sandwiches at odd hours of the day or night. At the moment there were neither counter burners nor stove, but Silver had electric pots and pans, ovens and rotisseries. She could manage fairly well while she waited for the new installment.

'Hungry?'

'Not really,' Ann said.

'Well, I am. You fix us drinks while I cook myself something.'

'All right.'

Ann walked out of the kitchen into the heavy pile of the white carpeting that lay like six inches of snow all over the house. Silver admitted that it was a mistake. It was impossible for anyone to walk across a room without turning his ankle. But she would not have it taken out. The dining room was sedate with imtiation period furniture, the exact period not quite identifiable. The bar, which separated the dining from the living room, had been designed by Silver herself. From the dining room it looked ordinary enough, but from the living room, which was four steps up, it looked more like the communion rail in the Virginia City Catholic Church. The brass piping was barnacled with bits of ruby and sapphire glass, and, instead of bar stools, there were white leather TV cushions on the floor. Joe had hurt Silver's feelings when he dubbed it 'the holy hell saloon.' The living room was an obstacle course of overstuffed chairs, couches, and glass-topped tables, and everywhere giant, muscular rubber plants climbed poles and lamp standards to the ceiling.

Ann found the bottle of Johnny Walker and a bottle of Gordon's gin. Then she reached into the built-in refrigerator for tonic and ice. Among the bartender's tools, silver plated thighs and breasts, she found what she needed.

'I'm making baked eggs with chicken livers,' Silver called.

'All right. I'll have some.'

Ann carried the drinks back into the kitchen. Silver drank her gin and tonic like a glass of iced water, sighed, and set the glass down out of her way.

'Another?'

'Not now, love. Don't you want a bath? I'll bring this up when it's ready.'

'Sure.'

Silver did not like company when she cooked, and she could not settle to talk until she had settled to eat; so Ann took her drink across the house through Silver's bedroom into the bath, which was a large room, carpeted as the rest of the house was, the toilet three steps up, the tub a small sunken pool in the center of the room. Ann turned on the phallic fountains, put her drink down on one of the table ledges of the pool, and began to undress in the company of a dozen of her own reflections.

Just three months ago, she and Bill had stayed in this house while Silver and Joe went to the coast on a month's

36

holiday. Bill, who had never seen the bedroom and bath before, was selfconscious at first, but later, when they lay together in his own man-made bedroom, he would remember those weeks wistfully, then argue that you could with obvious basic changes, design a bathroom of this kind in good taste.

'No white rug for rolling dry,' Ann would say.

'Why not?'

'It's vulgar.'

'I don't think it's vulgar,' he'd protest with the earnest defensiveness he had for his own tastes.

'And certainly not a ceiling mirror. What would your mother say?'

'I'm not planning this bathroom for my mother.' He'd prop himself up on his elbow and look down at Ann. 'Remember that afternoon . . .'

Alone now, surrounded by her naked selves, Ann could not help remembering, but there was nothing erotic in her memory. That first afternoon, it had been Bill who was uncertain of playing the game of husband and wife. He had been perfectly content before with the two nights a week they spent together, the occasional weekend away. He was afraid of the trap of familiarity. But how quickly he had adjusted! If Ann cooked, he washed dishes. If she ironed his shirt, he polished her boots. He even wanted her to read the newspaper to him in the morning while he shaved. And his tenderness, which had been strictly scheduled before, grew so habitual that he could hardly keep his hands off her at the Club. Inspired by mirrors and fetishes, he was experimental. Passion became an engrossing hobby. He grew possessive, developed proud, little jealousies. Perhaps she should stop working. Perhaps they should buy a little house of their own. Ann had not been surprised. Perhaps, in one part of her mind, she had even hoped this change would come over Bill. What surprised her was her own reaction. At first she had felt only a little restless, but gradually her uneasiness grew to a kind of terror, and she longed for the days to pass, for the moment to come when she would be free again. He would let her go. He would have to let her go. She could not live, caught up in his love, tangled in his habits and needs until she could not maintain her own.

The afternoon she remembered was the last, a dozen Anns and Bills coupling in this nightmare of mirrors, not looking directly at each other, but at the images of each other they found most exciting. One of those faces of Bill had spoken to her out of a mirror, like a god commanding:

'Marry me.'

'I couldn't, Bill. I couldn't marry anyone.'

The pool had filled. Ann stepped into the warm water and turned off the fountains. Half floating, her head propped back against the edge of the pool, Ann felt the muscles of her back relax. She reached over for her glass and raised it to salute the single image of herself on the ceiling. 'Hello is what a mirror says,' she said softly, and then drank.

'Well, goldfish,' Silver said, as she came into the room carrying a tray of food, 'it's weeks since I've had anything as lovely as you to fish for.'

'The bait looks good,' Ann said, smiling.

'I'm going to play you a while before I land you. More Scotch?'

'Please.'

Silver set down a plate of eggs, chicken livers, and toast next to Ann's glass, which she refilled. She put the tray on a low stool and sat down beside it on the rug.

'Sil, have you ever met anyone who looked like you?'

'Like me? When God made me, love. . .'

'I know. . . . He broke the mold.'

'I broke it,' Silver corrected. 'Ripped my mother from her ass to her navel.' Ann smiled sceptically. 'Well, she died of me, poor soul. Somebody along the assembly line must have made a mistake.'

'Maybe you were her double,' Ann said. 'They say, when you meet your own double, you die. "The magus Zoroaster, my dead child, met his own image walking in the garden." '

'It's only a trick, love. We do it with mirrors.'

'I don't think so. I met a woman today who really does look like me.'

'I don't believe it.'

'It's true.'

'Well, if anyone's going to die of it, I will. Or she will. But you won't, love.'

'You think I'm a bitch, don't you?' Ann said gently.

'No, but Bill's beginning to think so. What in hell are you doing to him?'

'Nothing, which is terrible. If only he didn't want us to get married, Sil, if only we could just go on the way we were before, I could cope.'

'I thought you were in love with him.'

'Oh, I am. I am. In a way. Or at least I love him. But I can't live with him, not all the time.'

'He says whatever went wrong went wrong when you were staying here.'

'Does he?' Ann said, turning away from her food, resting her head back against the edge of the pool again. She focused her eyes beyond the mirror, trying to reach that unknown presence, that watchfulness beyond the glass, but all she could do was conjure up faces of doubt out of her own imagination. 'I don't know. I only know it is wrong. Don't you think that marriage just is wrong for some women?'

'I used to,' Silver admitted. 'For me, for instance. Men were my profession. I always had a woman until Joe.'

'But you haven't married Joe.'

'No, but I'm going to, love.'

'You are!' Ann sat up. 'But why?'

'Well. . . .' Silver paused, watching Ann. 'I suppose underneath I always kind of liked the idea.'

'One man. One woman. Forsaking all others?'

'It won't be quite like that,' Silver said, smiling. 'But then, it never is. I should know. And who am I, just a two-bit cheesecake, to think it's got to be Jesus-perfect for me or not at all? Don't you think Mr and Mrs would look good on our bath towels?'.

'Sure,' Ann said softly. 'Sure, why not?'

'Ann?' Ann turned to look at her friend. 'We'd like you and Bill to stand for us.'

'I'd love to, Silver. You know that. And I'm sure Bill would, too.'

'The only thing is, it would be nicer if you two were speaking to each other.'

'Give me a drink. Let's drink to you and Joe.'

'But on dry land, love.' Silver stood up and got a huge white bath towel out of the cupboard. She held it up. 'Come on.'

'What will this towel say?' Ann asked, as she stepped out of the pool into Silver's arms.

'Goldfish,' Silver said.

'But I won't come anymore after you and Joe are married.'

'No?' Silver asked amused.

'No.'

'You said the same thing when you started going with Bill.'

'And I didn't come.'

'Until you had a fight,' Silver said. 'Fierce, noble, little fish. You get caught, don't you? Then you get away, but you don't learn. The bait always tempts you. If you were an inch or so longer or if I wasn't scared of the game warden, I'd keep you.'

'I don't want to be kept,' Ann said, not quite sure she was telling the truth because standing there, independent and belligerent, she wanted Silver to take her up like a child, to comfort and love her with the familiar, huge crude tenderness of her body. But in the morning, which

40

was already in the gray in the sky outside this room, Ann would not be able to stay. She would struggle to get away, to be born again into that live uncertainty of her single flesh.

'I know,' Silver said, as she picked Ann up in her arms. 'I know all about that. I always catch you at night and let you go in the morning.'

'I love you.'

'You love all the world, little fish. You think God made even the desert for you to swim in. But you want to be free.'

– 3 –

Evelyn Hall woke early her first morning in Reno, refreshed. She lay for a while, watching the patterned shadows of leaves on the carpet, her mind still moving among the patterned shadows of dreams she could not quite recall. If she got up now while everyone else was still asleep, the morning and the house would be her own for an hour. She could begin in control of the day.

Dressed in the summer suit she had bought specifically for her first interview with the lawyer, her hat, gloves and purse ready on the bed, Evelyn sat down at the secretary to sort her papers and to write a brief note to George. She found it easy to begin the letter. She described the flight, the drive into town, the house, the people in it, her room, her walk out into the neighbourhood. As her thoughts returned to the crest of that short hill, she reached for words to explain, perhaps to explain away, what she had felt. It was fear, she wanted to say, but she did not know of what. Hybrid-faithed of Jungian and Protestant – children of jackass and mare, George had often bitterly called them both – Evelyn had nevertheless felt, at the sight of that Nevada desert, a Catholic desolation. 'It was as if I saw, in fact, what I do not believe,' she wrote. And having written it, she looked down at the letter and realized that she was not writing to George at all. It had been years since she had made any attempt to explain her own feelings to him. Puzzled, she set the pages of the letter aside and began again. She wrote one short paragraph and signed her name. It was already after eight o'clock. She would be late to breakfast.

Though her appointment with the lawyer was not until eleven o'clock, Evelyn walked into town quite soon after breakfast. On the way, she stopped at a gas station to ask for a city map. She was only several blocks south of the river. Walking toward it, she passed the Reno Public Library and was tempted to go in, but she remembered having set it aside for tomorrow. The heat, at nine o'clock in the morning, was already intense, but on a bridge that crossed the Truckee there was a breeze, and just the sound of the water made it seem colder. It was certainly not an impressive river. Evelyn could hardly imagine this stream, which seemed to struggle over the rocks of its own bed, in flood strength. The high concrete walls, which served as its banks, left a natural margin of shore where half a dozen old men loitered. Were they fishing? Two of them had poles, but the others were empty-handed. One looked up at Evelyn and shouted something she could not understand. Another laughed. Evelyn turned away quickly and crossed the bridge.

She found it impossible to stroll down the street. There were already too many people like herself, obviously killing time. They drifted and then were caught by a window display, a newspaper stand, or a private uncertainty, but none of these could hold their attention long. Walking or standing still, they watched each other with speculative, ironic eyes. Evelyn herself became uncertain, then self-conscious. She had somehow lost control of the day. She hurried along, as if she had somewhere to go, until she found herself in the crowds on the main street. Above their heads each angling for its own space, were the huge signs of the casinos, baroque with unlighted bulbs; and everywhere, in waves above the noise of the crowds and traffic, came the downbeat of the machines. Whatever Evelyn had expected when she imagined this Monte Carlo of Nevada, it was not this

44

false-fronted block of giant penny arcades, these rows of factories where shiftless consumers volunteered to operate money-eating machines for the Establishment. Here was no seductive, neon night where men of the world won and lost fortunes before women who drank scarlet cocktails to their victory or defeat. The men she saw could have been high school principals or druggists or house painters. One woman might have been her cleaning woman, another her mother. There they all were, these ordinary people, losing their groceries, their children's shoes, a week's rent, at nine thirty on this hot July morning. And they all looked as bored and at home as they would have been over the breakfast dishes or the morning's mail.

Evelyn walked on past one casino after another until she came to Frank's Club. It was no different from the others, neither more glamorous nor more frightening. Evelyn could have walked right in, right through the Club, no more conspicuous than she would have been in a market or department store. If she felt dislocated, no one would ever know. Tempted only because she knew Ann Childs worked here, Evelyn did not go in. It would have seemed to her as intrusively curious as her investigating Ann's room while she was out. And now, no longer able to imagine what a gambling casino might be like, Evelyn found the fact of Ann's working at Frank's Club a dragging weight on her already uncertain mood. She turned away to look for a place where she could get a cup of coffee, but she had to get off the main street before she found one.

Before eleven o'clock Evelyn had had several cups of coffee and had bought a cotton skirt and a bathing suit. She had not really enough money to buy anything, but she did not know how else to kill time. She had not been able to find a bookstore, and everywhere else, on the street and in shops and cafés, though she was inconspicuous, she felt vulnerable. Busy as she tried to keep herself, she arrived at the lawyer's office fifteen minutes early.

The secretary was middle-aged and solicitous. She offered to take Evelyn's parcels, moved an ash tray already within her reach, and, after Evelyn had begun to read a magazine forced on her, the secretary continued to chatter like a bird in a cage. Evelyn looked up, making her face a mask of polite interest, while she let an inner voice answer, 'If you don't keep still, I'll strangle you and put you in a pie.'

'Here's Mr Williams now,' the secretary cried enthusiastically, as a small, gray-haired man in a gray suit came into the room. 'Mrs Hall's been waiting for you for ten minutes.'

Evelyn had prepared herself emotionally for an Arthur Williams who would be rather like her dentist, tall, matter-of-fact, and gentle. She had always been fortunate in the men who officially surrounded her. Arthur Williams was quite obviously a new breed, and, if he had given Evelyn time to think, she would have judged him a catastrophe. But his apology rode in over his secretary's scolding with such a force of Southern oratory that Evelyn could only be amazed. He was a caricature of a Southern gentleman. The manners of his background had become in this climate almost hysterical mannerisms. He flung open his office door for Evelyn, rushed past her as soon as she had stepped inside so that he could be in the proper position to offer her a chair and to bow with a final flourish at the end of his welcoming speech.

But, once the stage was set and he had settled himself behind his desk, there was no trace of his recent, frantic activity. He smiled at Evelyn so pleasantly, so sanely, and spoke in so quiet a voice that her first impression of him took on for her the quality of an hallucination.

'When did you arrive?' he asked. 'Are you comfortably settled? Mrs Packer is a nice woman, isn't she?'

By the time he asked to see the papers, Evelyn's confidence in him was established. He made no apology for the silence that fell while he studied them, and, for the first time since Evelyn had arrived, she found herself able to relax in someone else's presence. She did not even feel that it was necessary to smoke. Instead she looked about the office, which was quietly and handsomely furnished. There were no family pictures on Arthur Williams' desk, but hanging on the wall behind him was the framed photograph of an elderly man in judge's robes. He looked so like the man quietly reading that Evelyn decided he must be Arthur Williams' father.

'Yes,' Arthur Williams said without looking up, then, 'Yes,' again. 'Any court would question this settlement without an explanation.'

Evelyn made no comment.

'This is the settlement you agreed to?' he asked.

'Yes.'

'You are at a disadvantage, of course, since you're the one who wants the divorce, but it's unusual for a woman not even to claim her share of the community property.'

'My only concern,' Evelyn answered, 'is to dissolve the marriage as quickly and quietly as possible.'

'And your husband agrees to an uncontested divorce only on these conditions?'

'He's not well,' Evelyn said, conscious of her need to defend George even now. 'He's in debt.'

Arthur Williams wrote something down. Then he looked up and smiled reassuringly.

'The papers are in good order. I've already made tentative arrangements with another lawyer to represent Mr Hall in court. I understand you will pay that fee?' Evelyn nodded. 'You'll need one witness who can testify to having seen you every day for the next six weeks. I'm sure Mrs Packer would be glad to do that for you. Now all we need to do is to establish the grounds for divorce.'

'Incompatibility,' Evelyn said at once. 'There are no other grounds.'

'Yes . . . that isn't actually a legal term used in Nevada.

47

Mental cruelty is the usual charge.'

'That's not quite the same thing, is it?' Evelyn asked.

'It really amounts to the same thing,' he said and waited.

A week ago, even a day ago, Evelyn had been certain that incompatibility was the only charge she would allow. Adultery, cruelty, even desertion were diseases a marriage suffered and could survive. The only incurable cancer was the inability of two people to live together. And, as a charge, incompatibility, if it laid blamed at all, required the guilt of both partners. But legally incompatibility did not exist. And divorce was not a private symbolic act. Like marriage, it was a social institution. Though she wanted to protest, Evelyn recognized the irrelevance of her morality.

'I see,' she said finally.

'Now,' Arthur Williams said, relaxing. 'I need only a few details, enough to establish the charge. Did your husband's behaviour ever cause you to suffer any nervous strain?' Evelyn looked doubtful. 'Have you ever had ulcers Mrs Hall?'

'No,' Evelyn answered. 'But my husband has.'

Arthur Williams smiled. 'How about insomnia?'

'No,' she answered and did not add that George never slept without pills.

'Have you ever been under a doctor's care for any kind of nervous ailment?'

'No.' She thought of George's psychiatrist.

'Has your husband's behavior ever embarrassed you in public?' Arthur Williams asked, a quiz master moving to a new category, determined to give the sponsor's money away.

Evelyn frowned. Her immediate response would have been negative, but she censored it, already feeling herself a willfully uncooperative child. But how could she answer? She and George had not been in public together for over five years.

48

'Has your husband's criticism of you ever undermined your self-confidence or your sense of security?'

Surely it was her criticism of him, never spoken, never even consciously indicated in a look or gesture, but so deep a silence in her it must have shouted at him every day of their lives together, that had undermined his confidence and security. Oh, he had been critical of her, but it was never anything more than a defensive attack when he was feeling critical of himself.

'Has your husband ever stopped speaking to you for any length of time?'

'Well. . . .' Evelyn was beginning to feel really desperate. 'Not actually stopped speaking.'

'Mrs Hall, these are only suggestions,' Arthur Williams said gently. 'Perhaps it would be easier if you told me just one or two things that have caused trouble between you.'

'Yes,' Evelyn said. 'I am sorry to seem so uncooperative. It's just that my husband and I never have fought. I suppose most people, getting a divorce, do.'

'Not always. Sometimes that's one of the troubles.'

'My husband and I. . . .' Evelyn began, sounding to herself like the Queen of England in her Christmas message, 'simply don't share any of the same interests.' She was immediately aware of how lame, legally and humanly, this statement was. And it wasn't really true. 'We don't share the same values.'

'Could you give me an example?'

How could she possibly say that she wanted to divorce George because he cheated book clubs, took advantage of the G.I. Bill and unemployment insurance, and had once sold a defective lawn mower to her mother? If there was some private validity in these complaints, publicly they were absurd. What was the fact, the event significant enough in itself to express the principle?

'I support my husband, Mr Williams. He won't – or can't – work, but he has to spend money, more money than I can make. The sound of the unpaid-for power saw

49

and stereophonic tape recorder do threaten my sense of security.'

'You said before, Mrs Hall, that your husband was not well. Does his poor health prevent him from working?'

'Well, yes and no.'

'What is wrong with him?'

'We don't really know,' Evelyn said.

'We?'

'My husband, the doctors . . . or perhaps names have been put to it, psychiatric names. He suffers from a sense of inadequacy, a sense of failure. But then the world for him is meaningless. It has no purpose. So there isn't any value, and we have no identity. All we have is a wish, or a need, that can't be answered.

'And that is what you mean when you say that you don't share the same values.'

'That's what I mean,' Evelyn agreed, but she felt uncertain. 'I could believe in despair if it weren't hungry, if it didn't feed on life with such an awful greediness. . . .'

'Let me see if I can't translate this into more pratical terms. I think what you're saying, Mrs Hall, is that your husband's emotional instability, his despair, has caused you deep distress, has, in fact, undermined your own living.' Evelyn nodded. 'Now, he refuses to support you and, furthermore, incurs debts you cannot meet. Are there other things he's done, intangible things? How does he behave toward you? Is he affectionate? Is he thoughtful?'

'No, I don't suppose so. I suppose he's indifferent, and yet he's dependent. He doesn't really want my company, but he doesn't like to be alone. He won't go out. He won't see people who come in. He sleeps a great deal – and reads and eats and buys machinery.'

'Has he always been like this, Mrs Hall?'

'No, no, it's been a gradual thing. You see, for a while after the war he was working on his PhD. Trying to. I already had mine; so I taught. But it didn't go very well, and we began to have debts. He took jobs then, part-time

50

jobs in stores and garages. Then he said he couldn't do both; so we tried to get along on my salary again. I don't know just when it was that we stopped pretending he was working on his thesis. It's years ago now, at least five.' Evelyn paused to think back. Still, she couldn't offer details, but she felt she was getting nearer the difficulty, nearer an acceptable way of saying it.

'I think that's all we need then,' Arthur Williams said cheerfully. 'We can go to court six weeks from today. That's September 8th.' He checked his calendar. 'So I should see you the Friday before. Then we can just go over the questions I'll ask you. It will be very simple. You'll just have to answer yes or no.'

'That's all you need?' Evelyn asked, bewildered.

'That's all,' and, as he rose from his desk, he began again his frantic, courtly ballet that was to accomplish Evelyn's exit.

Out on the street, Evelyn tried to recall exactly what questions she had been asked, what answers she had given. It did not seem possible that Arthur Williams had enough information to establish any charge. What could he say in court?

'Is it true that your husband sleeps a great deal, Mrs Hall?'

'Yes.'

'And you say that he is often indifferent to your company?'

'Yes.'

'He refuses to be entertaining to your guests?'

'Yes.'

'And he will not work.'

'No.'

Yes. No. Of course not. But it isn't his fault. Why shouldn't he sleep? Why should he be entertaining? How can he work? The man is suffering. The man is dying.

'Divorce granted.'

Was that, then, all that was necessary to cancel the

impossible vows she and George had taken and tried to live by for sixteen years? George had promised to keep her, but she had promised to keep him, too, and that was, anyway, the least of their promises. So little of their failure was willful. George could not comfort her. She could not honor him. What did she want of divorce procedings then; a systematic cancellation, vow by vow, of the marriage service? She did not know. But it should be something more or other than this.

As Evelyn walked along the street, Arthur Williams' actual voice came back to her, the accent, the almost lazy legality of the phrasing. 'Have you ever had . . . ?' 'No.' 'Have you ever been . . . ?' 'No.' 'Has your husband ever . . . ?' 'No.' She had not been able to answer one of the questions he put to her in such a way as to make the divorce seem necessary or even reasonable. But, if George had been asked, his answers would have persuaded any judge to set him free. George was the real victim of their marriage, so much the victim that he hadn't the courage left to want a divorce. 'Your honor, I charge this man with what I have done to him. I charge this man with being a victim to my circumstance. I charge this man with ulcers, insomnia, psychosis, insecurity, isolation, and despair. I charge him with my guilt which I cannot bear anymore.' Was there no legal term for this? Was there no social convention that could relieve the torturer's suffering? None. If this mock hearing did, in fact, set her free, she would still carry the mark of a strong, intelligent woman like the brand of Cain on her forehead.

Evelyn looked up to find herself approaching the house. She must have all but run those eight blocks back, absorbed first in bewilderment, then in fury. She walked into the house and up to her room, which she confronted with indignation and defiance. 'Well?' she wanted to demand. 'Well?' Well what? There was nothing here to confront but the indifferent furniture. She looked around her desperately to find some place to put her fury down.

Nothing here could receive it. Nothing but herself. 'I must do something.' There was nothing to do. At once, and for the first time, Evelyn realized precisely what that meant. She had done all there was to do. Arthur Williams did not want to see her again until the Friday before the hearing. 'But I must do something.' Evelyn sat down in the chair and stared. Gradually the rage died away, and she was quiet and a little sick.

There was work to do. She had one volume of Yeats with her. She would begin with that. Tomorrow she would go to the public library. Wednesday she would go to the University. With the books she needed, she would set up a schedule. Already she was conscious of measuring out the vital supply, rationing the hours that would keep her alive. Why did she feel so trapped? At any other time, six weeks would have seemed a gift. Now, because she had no choice, they were a sentence. 'Nonsense!' She got up to get her book and felt again the sudden dizziness. It was the heat, the altitude. How lovely it would be to lie down on the bed, to sleep awhile, but she mustn't do that. She had already discovered how long an evening could be. Sleep was too precious an escape to be squandered.

When Evelyn met Virginia Ritchie on the stairs going down for dinner, she felt much less critical of her than she had just twenty-four hours before. Younger, with children at home, with fewer of her own resources, she had already lived through three weeks of an isolation Evelyn found terrible in one day. She had no desire to make friends with Virginia, but she greeted her with some real gentleness and sympathy.

'Dr Hall, I do want to apologize. . . .'

'Please,' Evelyn said, 'call me Evelyn, and don't apologize for anything. There isn't any need.'

'I know I behave very badly,' Virginia said, 'but I find this waiting around with nothing to do just impossible. Everyone said it was best to go to Reno and get a quick divorce, but they don't know. They haven't any idea what it's like just to sit and wait. And this awful town. Even if I had to wait a year at home, at least I'd be busy. I'd be with the children. . . .' Her voice broke a little.

'But it's only three more weeks,' Evelyn said.

'Only three weeks,' Virginia cried softly, 'I've been here only three weeks. For only three weeks I've sat in tht room and thought. It's a lifetime.'

'Haven't you books to read?'

'Books? No, but I've read every magazine in the house. You know what they're like, all about young couples who. . . .' Again her voice failed her.

'You're reading the wrong stories,' Evelyn said, smiling.

'That's why I've stopped.'

Dinner that night was not as unfortunate as it had been the night before. Virginia was, as Frances Packer had promised, calmer and less self-consciously tragic. Walter did not have to carve and so divided his attention between his appetite and his role as host with some ease, while Frances tended the table and the gaps in the conversation. Only Ann was noticeably quiet and seemed grateful to have the meal done with, to be able to leave the house. Virginia, who had decided to go to an early movie, went with Ann and Walter, leaving Frances and Evelyn alone with their coffee.

'Another cup?' Frances asked.

'Thanks.'

'I am glad you're a coffee drinker. Walt and Ann never take the time. It is nice to have company. Now tell me, have you everything you need? Did you see the lawyer?'

'Yes, I did. Everything seems to be in order. Oh, he did say I'd need a witness. . . .'

'Don't worry about that,' Frances said. 'I can do that.'

'Frances,' Evelyn began tentatively, 'Frances, are all divorces here so simple?'

'Simple?'

'I mean, the lawyer asked me just a few questions. It didn't seem to me that I gave him enough information to make a case. And he says I don't have to see him again until the Friday before the hearing.'

'If it's uncontested, it doesn't take but a few minutes. I know. It doesn't seem right somehow when you first realize, but the wedding ceremony isn't all that much either, is it? Ann's father used to say to me, "Frances, don't prolong a thing just to make it seem important." He used to claim that nothing really important took longer than twenty minutes.'

'Twenty minutes?' Then Frances had known Ann's father.

'That's right. Conceiving, being born (we had our arguments about that), marrying, divorcing, dying.' Frances paused. 'It didn't take him even twenty minutes to die. . . .'

'But what a long time passes between events,' Evelyn said quietly.

'Ah . . . and that's what a woman knows, time. Nothing takes us really by surprise, does it?'

'No,' Evelyn said, 'I don't suppose so, really,' but she was out of her depth now.

Whenever there were generalizations about women, Evelyn weighed herself against them and found herself insubstantial. And talking in the kind of generality that threatened to expose her private living did not appeal to her. Though her curiosity had been aroused about Ann's father and the relationship that had existed between him and Frances Packer, Evelyn suppressed it. She chose, instead, to withdraw, reassured by Frances' friendliness and therefore confident that she could spend the evening alone with her work.

The desert island game Evelyn played with herself that night was only an amusement. The four books she had brought with her were not the ones she would have chosen, but she could make them last, like pans of rain water in a drought, perhaps two weeks. The game stayed an amusement because she could go to the public library in the morning.

Both her amusement and confidence were shaken a little when she walked into the library. The single room, furnished with only a few tables and perhaps ten bookshelves, was empty except for Evelyn and a single attendant, a middle-aged woman who sat at a desk reading the want ads in the newspaper. The collection of books reminded Evelyn of college dormitory libraries, which depended on private and haphazard donations from students and on books the main library could find no use for. There was virtually no criticism, and she found only a few of the standard works she needed. But books of any kind delighted Evelyn, and she would have been tempted to spend an hour investigating and discovering the occasional hilarious or real treasure any library can produce if she had not been uncomfortably aware of the attendant, who had begun to watch Evelyn with frank suspicion. But, when Evelyn walked over to the desk with the six books she wanted, the attendant was suddenly absorbed in the card catalogue.

'Excuse me,' Evelyn said. The woman ignored her. 'I'd like to take out these books.'

'Just a minute.' The attendant stopped to straighten some paperbacks on display and then walked around behind the desk. 'Have you got a card?'

'No, I haven't.'

'Are you a permanent resident?'

'No.'

'That will be a dollar for the card, then, and three dollars for each book you want to take out.'

'Excuse me?'

'A dollar for the card, three dollars for each book. You get the three dollars back when you bring the book back.'

Evelyn looked down at the six books she had chosen. In order to take them home, she would have to pay nineteen dollars. She did not have nineteen dollars.

'I don't quite understand,' she said.

'It's a policy with transients. We lost forty per cent of our books last year. We can't afford that.'

'No,' Evelyn said, 'no, I don't suppose you can.' She looked into her wallet. She had a five-dollar bill and some change. But she needed the books, and she could have the money back. 'I'll have to write a check.'

'We don't accept checks.'

'A traveler's check,' Evelyn said.

'We don't accept traveler's checks.'

Evelyn looked up from her wallet into the indifferent eyes of the woman before her. Evelyn closed her purse, turned, and walked out of the library.

She did not leave the house again that day, nor did she notice with any interest or regret that Ann was not at home for dinner. On Wednesday, the day Evelyn had planned to go to the University, she did not go. Instead, she slept until almost noon, and then stayed in her room, reading. The desert island was no longer a game. It was the new condition of her life. That other human beings were marooned with her made little difference. Seeing Ann at Wednesday dinner, Evelyn hardly spoke. And she did not stay with Frances and Virginia for coffee. In her room again, she did not allow herself to brood. She turned from Yeats to a journal.

At first the passage of time, marked clearly by each recorded date, gave her half-conscious pleasure, but time in a book can pass through many days in an hour and still drag at the spirit as heavily and specifically as its own confining skeleton There is no freedom in a journal. It is an accurate record of the prisoner. Even his greatest fantasies are only fantasies of a man trapped in time. A year had passed when Evelyn set down the book, but it was someone else's year. She had not turned on the lamp of her own evening.

She closed the book, got up, and lit a cigarette. At the

window, beyond the great tree, searchlights made pale crossings against the evening light. They signalled no plane. From somewhere near the center of town, a used car lot perhaps, they swung their aimless way through the empty sky. Evelyn grew conscious of a sound that had been going on for some time. Across the hall, Virginia Ritchie sat alone in her room, crying.

Nothing of real importance takes more than twenty minutes, nothing but the vast unimportance of life itself, which is just this . . . this terrible waiting. Before, it had always seemed a biding of time, her waiting to marry George, then waiting for the war to be over, then waiting for the child that did not come. Now she was no longer biding but killing time for the single ceremony, the little death of all her waiting. Evelyn turned toward the sound, dryly, almost viciously, whispering, 'Don't weep. Don't weep. It's already over.' But the weeping continued.

Evelyn could not go back to her reading, and she would not cross the hall to speak to Virginia. There was nothing she could say. Frantic, she left the room and went downstairs to read in the living room, but Frances was there.

'Cup of tea?'

'Frances, have you got any whiskey?'

'I do. Let's both have a drink.'

Frances went to the kitchen and returned with a tray. She put it down on a coffee table in front of Evelyn, a bottle of bourbon, an ice bucket, two glasses, and a bottle of soda.

'It wouldn't do you any harm to have several,' Frances said. 'It's the weather. I've never known it to be so muggy. Nobody can sleep. I could have offered you Scotch as well, but I got up at three thirty this morning and finished it off with Ann. She was in a terrible mood, but three drinks later we both went to bed and to sleep happy. It's just what you need.'

'You're a dear, Frances. I'll replenish the supply tomorrow.'

'And if you want to read, you just go ahead and read. I've got my own magazine.'

'I don't really want to. I've read myself out, I think.'

'You've been working too hard,' Frances said.

'Have I? I don't really know what else to do with myself.' Evelyn took a quick mouthful of almost straight whiskey.

'You're just like Ann. When she decides to work, she locks herself up in that terrible attic room of hers, and not even Walter can budge her until she's so exhausted she's made herself sick.'

'What does she work at?'

'She's a cartoonist, a very good one. You've probably seen some of her cartoons. She sells to all the magazines. You must ask her to show you some.'

'I'd like to see them.'

'I'm worried about Ann,' Frances said.

'Are you? Why?'

'I don't know what to do for her. The trouble is, I don't know what Ann wants out of life. She's not nineteen any longer. She's twenty-five. Most girls her age are married and having children. Ann's such an attractive girl, she could have had a half-a-dozen husbands by now, but she doesn't seem to want even one.'

'She must have seen a lot in Reno to discourage her.'

'Well, I don't know.' Frances took a long drink. 'I used to worry about that, too; but we all see a lot of dying, and it doesn't seem to keep us from living. Reno's no worse than anyplace else, really. If you want to find mistakes, you don't have to come here. Walter and Ann have heard a lot and seen a lot, but it doesn't have to hurt them, does it, to know something about the world?'

'I've always argued that way about books,' Evelyn said, 'but it never occurred to me to argue that way about life.'

'Somehow I don't worry so much about being wrong for Walter; he's my own, and anyway he's a steady sort of boy. If the world didn't shake him up a little now and then, he'd be dull. He's like me.' Evelyn smiled a protest, but Frances went on. 'Ann's not mine. I've taken care of her since she was ten, but I'm not her mother. I've never really tried to be.'

'Is her own mother living?'

'I suppose so, somewhere. But not for Ann. And her father's dead. When he was alive, I didn't have to worry about Ann. When he was alive, I didn't worry about anything. But she hasn't anyone but me now. And who am I? Frances, not really a mother, not really a friend, just a pair of hands and a familiar face.'

'Do you think Ann's unhappy?'

'I don't know. I really don't know.' Frances poured herself a drink and offered the bottle to Evelyn. 'I think she ought to be unhappy, but then I don't understand her. I'm not very bright, and she is.'

'You're a regular wise woman, Frances,' Evelyn said.

'No, no, I'm not. I'm a very narrow, silly woman really. Even things I used to know I begin to forget. It makes me wonder if I ever really knew them. Things Ann's father taught me. He used to say to me, "Frances, you collect conventions and clichés like old family china. Just pack them away now. Put them in the attic. If you leave them around here, they'll just get broken." And, you know, while I lived with him, I never missed them; but now, when the house feels lonely, empty of him, like a public place, I catch myself bringing them out again. Walter doesn't mind them so much, but Ann barks her shins on them every time. She's like her father. She can't live in a clutter. But I forget how I lived without it all those years. I did live, very happily but now I seem to need something in my house to keep me company: memories, the old notions of my grandmother, incense in the bathroom. I haven't any taste. I'm sentimental. Wall plaques, souvenirs. I'd like a great big plate with his picture in the middle of it. "Happiness," it would say at the top, and at the bottom, "Reno, 1943 to 1953." And I'd like widow's weeds and a wedding ring; While a man's alive, it doesn't really matter to have anything but him. When he's gone, that's the time you want all the little things. And I do forget about him. Do you know, I sit and plan a beautiful wedding for Ann, thinking I want it for him? He'd turn in his grave to see me.' Frances smiled and shook her head.

'Would he?' Evelyn asked. 'Why?'

'Because it's not real,' Frances said. 'One thing he taught me, one thing Reno taught me is that conventions can be a kind of trap. But you see, I forget. I want Ann to be happy, so I want her to have a beautiful, white wedding in a church. And why? The only aisle I ever walked down led me to the divorce courts. The happiness I've had is ten years of "living in sin," whatever that means. But I slip back a little more each year now into a kind of respectability. I can't help it. And it doesn't matter very much for me. I've had what I wanted. "I've had a love of my own." (That's a beautiful song.) I don't know. Thinking about a wedding is really just a way of thinking about love, isn't it? It's love I want for Ann. I don't think I really care very much how she gets it.'

'Why does she work at Frank's Club, Frances?'

'Ask her!' Frances said. 'I ask her and she just shrugs. She certainly doesn't need the money. I don't think it's the place for a girl like Ann – oh, for a lark for one summer. But Ann should be someplace where she meets people of her own kind. Ann's father was a lawyer. She belongs in a world like yours, Evelyn, among intelligent, creative people. Oh, she says, too, that she can get ideas there. There's no other place where she'd see so much of the world go by. And maybe she's right. But it's terrible work, taking money from people. Don't you think so?'

'I don't know much about it,' Evelyn said. 'But the idea certainly doesn't appeal to me. Did Ann go to college?'

'Yes, for a while. That was my fault. I talked her father into sending her down to Mills when she was sixteen.'

'Didn't she like it?'

'I think so really, but she was too much for them. She isn't ordinary. She never has been. Her father wasn't either, and he understood her.'

'What happened?'

'I never really knew much about it. They wanted her to go to a psychiatrist. Anyway, she just didn't go back. She went to the University of Nevada for a while, but she was restless. There was her sketching. She sold her first cartoons when she was nineteen. Oh she'll be all right. She's fine. I sometimes wonder why I worry at her so. And why do I tell you about it?'

'I like to hear about Ann,' Evelyn said.

'She looks enough like you to be your daughter.'

'I know. It's odd, isn't it?'

'You're the sort of mother she should have had.' Frances got up and poured herself a third drink. 'Come. Have another.'

'I think I've had plenty,' Evelyn said, covering her glass.

'One more will do just nicely.'

'I'll finish this first.'

'What did you come down here for?' Frances demanded. 'You came down to turn off your brain.'

'Did I? All right then. One more.' Evelyn helped herself. 'I really feel better.'

'So do I,' Frances said. 'It does me good to be able to talk like that now and then.'

Frances' speech had begun to blur a little, as much with tiredness as with drink. Her monologue had disintegrated, and, since Evelyn could not be primed, even by alcohol, to talk about herself, the conversation grew random and halting until it dwindled into a companionable silence.

'Well', Evelyn said, finally, 'you're right. I'm ready to sleep.'

'Yes, so am I. Sleep well,' Frances said, patting Evelyn's shoulder absentmindedly.

'Thank you, Frances.'

'Thank you, my dear.'

In bed, Evelyn felt the effect of drinking too much too rapidly. She could not close her eyes. One cigarette and a poem or two would be enough to settle the room. She reached for the Yeats and turned the pages slowly.

> And may her bridegroom bring her to a house
> Where all's accustomed, ceremonious;
> For arrogance and hatred are the wares
> Peddled in the thoroughfares.
> How but in custom and in ceremony
> Are innocence and beauty born?
> Ceremony's name for the rich horn,
> And custom for the spreading laurel tree.

Frances offered up such a prayer for Ann. This poor, guilty non-mother of a grown child burned incense in the bathroom, worshiped a great neon cross that hummed above the church door, and waited, idling among memories and wishes, to be redeemed by a dream out of *The Ladies' Home Journal*. Not quite fair. It was a prayer that had caught Evelyn, too. She had wanted to be 'rooted in some dear, perpetual place.' Why must sentimentality be culpable? It was Frances' ex-happiness, Mr Childs, who had prayed this world into existence for his child, where innocence was ignorance, where custom was the business of the throughfares. Iconoclast, petty devil, preaching anarchy and practicing law, he had uprooted the tree, preyed on his daughter, not for her. Evelyn closed her eyes and opened them again to restore her balance. She knew nothing about these people. Her rhetoric covered her own sense of guilt. All children suffered their parents' world. If she had had a child of her own, would she have done any better? Where would the child be now? She was guilty, too, not of the imagined child, but of the image of herself in Ann. They were all guilty, every man and woman who came, of the world they found. It was time she stopped pretending

63

to be a victim of it.

Evelyn dreamed lines of poetry, images, woke afraid and dreamed again. She was high above the city and could see far out across the desert the great stone images as they woke and began to move. Below her the old men on the river bank looked up and cried out, cursing and laughing at the desert birds that figured the sky in pairs. The water had turned to blood. The mist that rose was rank and warm as steam. Evelyn climbed down through it, hurrying. She came to a wood of petrified trees and ran. Far off she could hear the child calling, 'Evelyn! Evelyn!' She could not answer, but she ran on. 'Evelyn!' She made one terrible effort to whisper, 'Yes,' and woke.

'Evelyn?'

'Yes?' Evelyn sat up. 'Come in.'

She watched the doorknob turn slowly and carefully. Then Ann was in the room, smiling for Evelyn but at the cup of coffee and glass of orange juice she carried. Still half caught in her dream, Evelyn could not quite take in what she saw, the quiet, familiar room, the quiet, unfamiliar Ann. She wore a dress the color of old pewter, which was the gray of her eyes. Evelyn had not seen her in anything but trousers an a long-sleeved shirt. Her slim hips and long legs boyish, she had stalked the space of a room in boots. Now, delicate and unconfined, she seemed made in the image not of Evelyn's nightmare but of Frances' daydream.

'How very different you look,' Evelyn said.

'I suppose I do,' Ann said, 'dressed in my own clothes. I hope you don't mind waking up.'

'Not at all,' Evelyn said. 'What time is it?'

'After ten. It's cooler today. I have to go up to Virginia City and I wondered if you'd like to come along.'

'Virginia City?'

'It's not very far, an hour's drive.'

'An hour's drive,' Evelyn repeated, out on to the desert she had seen and dreamed. She could not lock herself

64

away from it. She looked up at Ann, waiting there. 'I'd like to go.'

'Good. Can you be ready in an hour?'

'Oh, twenty minutes,' Evelyn said.

She drank her juice and coffee as she dressed, feeling reluctant and yet relieved. The desert, a derelict gold-mining town, a day in the heat both bored and frightened her. Wide awake she could not be quite so resolute, but two days in the isolation of her work had made her value human company. She was through with silence and righteous indignation.

'Now you're to have some breakfast,' Frances said, as Evelyn came down the stairs. 'If you're going with Ann, you'll never get any lunch. She took me with her last week and didn't feed me a single thing until I absolutely demanded tea at four o'clock.'

'We'd had a four-course breakfast,' Ann protested.

'Coffee, juice, a piece of toast, and coffee. That's Ann's idea of a four-course breakfast. I'll just scramble you an egg,' Frances said, disappearing into the kitchen.

Evelyn watched her, wondering how much Frances had to do with Ann's invitation. If Frances had suggested it, was she thinking of Ann or of Evelyn? Probably both of them. Frances was, by nature, an organizer. She wanted to believe that happiness could be arranged. Well, perhaps it could.

'Are you going to be late for anything?' Evelyn asked, turning to Ann.

'Oh, no,' Ann said. 'It's just an errand.'

'Well, I wòn't need lunch if you don't have any.'

But they had lunch three hours later in the Bucket of Blood Saloon in Virginia City. While Ann sat at the bar, drinking draft beer and waiting for their hot dogs to be cooked, Evelyn moved away to look at the rock collections at the back of the building. They had gone first to the office of the *Territorial Enterprise*, where Ann had delivered some sketches. Then they had called on an alcoholic antique dealer who seemed to specialize in growing plants in ancient and ornate chamber pots. Ann had bought one for a friend named Silver. Up the hill from the main street was the old opera house. They had been let into the main auditorium by an attendant who had obviously run a speakeasy during prohibition. There among uncertain tourists, they walked across the sprung floor to the stage, where old posters and bits of scenery recalled the great performances of eighty years ago when Virginia City had been a city instead of a ghost town in thriving disrepair as it was now. Ann knew the facts and legends and talked with articulate energy to give Evelyn a real sense of the grand exploitation that had created and destroyed a way of life in fewer years than it took to forget the names of streets and barmaids. Without Ann, Evelyn would have been repelled by the shoddy self-consciousness of the second-rate relics, the pretentious commercial respect for so much colossal poor taste. But Ann's attitude, which both admitted and admired the crude extravagance, the ruthless energy, the sudden death, made Evelyn vulnerable to an interest in the place. Now, studying the samples of gold and silver ore and trying to imagine the honeycomb of mines that lay beneath the town, she felt a reckless pleasure at being in a saloon called the Bucket of Blood about to eat a hog dog with a change apron from Frank's Club. She was neither bored nor afraid. She was having a lovely time. Evelyn turned back to Ann and saw again the curious resemblance. It was as if Ann, sitting at the bar chatting with the bartender, were a much younger, freer Evelyn, an Evelyn who had never existed, at home in the world. She was a young woman no one need feel guilty of. Ann turned around and smiled.

'Your hot dog's ready.'

'I am hungry,' Evelyn admitted, taking a place beside Ann.

The bartender set out mustard and relish. 'I said to Ann

here, I thought she brought her mother in to see us. You two sure look alike.'

'Yes,' Evelyn said. 'I think we do.'

After lunch, they went to the Catholic Church, which was more like a religious dime store than a place of worship. Small gold crosses and rosaries were on sale at half price. While Evelyn looked at the priests' robes, woven of the local cloth of gold and silver, Ann told her a story of a fire in Virginia City. It had broken out in the mines first, fed by great drafts of air and the wooden timbers, until it burt through the earth and bloomed into a garden of flames. The men had to make a fire line across the city, blasting buildings to clear a path. The Catholic Church had been in the way. One of the mine owners had said to the priest, 'Let us blast the church and I'll build you another bigger and better than anything this town has ever seen.' 'Blast away,' the priest had said. And so they dynamited the House of God to save the city. But the miner was true to his word. He built a new church not only of wood but of gold and gems, and here it stood now, long after the city had disappeared, an empty monument to faith as the opera house was to culture.

'Is it ever used as a church?' Evelyn asked.

'In the summer. Now and then the grandchild of a gold miner is married here. But it has to depend on the guilty donations of the wealthy and this sort of cut-rate simony to survive. God can't be defeated.'

Ann took Evelyn then to the Protestant graveyard, a wasteland of dry grass and gray stone on a little hill overlooking the shallow valley. They wandered among the graves, reading the names and dates, the simple epitaphs.

'This one I've always loved,' Ann said, stopping.

Evelyn looked down and read aloud, 'Rest, Papa, Rest.'

'I would have put it on my father's tombstone if he hadn't insisted on a box in the crematorium. It's just like a general post office. He had no taste about death.'

67

'I'm not sure I blame him,' Evelyn said. 'Would you want to be buried in a place like this?' She looked about her at the barren mountains, at the weathered wooden skeleton of the town, at the desert valley and its aging heaps of yellow slag.

'Yes,' Ann said. 'I like it here.'

A wind had come up, and they stood in the shadow of a mountain, Evelyn shivered.

'Come on. It's time to go,' Ann said, and she took Evelyn's arm to guide her back to the main path. 'There's one other place I like to stop on the way down.'

They drove down the mountain to Geiger Point, where a few picnic tables and barbecue pits frailly furnished a landscape of outcroppings of rock and stunted trees. Here they stood together, looking down on the Washoe Valley and across to the higher mountains in the west. Evelyn tried to listen to Ann, to find each important landmark, but her imagination could not people this desert with wagon trains and Indians, which belonged to TV serials in one's own comfortable living room. It was empty, with an open emptiness that swung up at her, that dragged her down. She seemed to be falling with the drifts and falls of buzzards, toward, then away from the giant feathers of steam that rose from the hidden hot springs far below.

'Evelyn, are you all right?'

Ann's arm was around her shoulder. 'I'm a little dizzy.'

'Sit down here.'

Evelyn sat down on a rock step and covered her eyes, struggling against a need to cry or be sick or sleep. She felt Ann's hand on her shoulder move to the back of her neck, a strong careful hand against her skin. Gradually she lost her consciousness of the earth's spinning. It was still.

'Well,' Evelyn said, straightening up, 'how I welcome the convention of time and space.'

'Have you been dizzy before?'

'Umhum. It must be altitude.' Evelyn turned to Ann

68

and smiled an apology. 'I don't awfully like . . . heights.'
Or the adolescent depths of eyes, child, grown child. That
will do.

'You're the second one this week I've almost lost,' Ann
said, turning away. 'I'm going to have to carry smelling
salts.'

Ann closed herself so quickly that Evelyn could have
been uncertain of what she had seen, but she had taught
too many students not to recognize the unguarded look
and the silence. In her office, she would have known just
how to be behave. She would have assigned an extra
essay on Donne and turned the longing into scholarship.
Now, without a role to play, she was uncertain. She did
not want to turn Ann way.

'What did you major in at college, Ann?'

Ann glanced back at Evelyn, her eyes amused. 'I never
got around to deciding. When I was at Mills, I thought
about history or philosophy.'

'But you left Mills.'

'Yes, I made an indecent proposal to the special assistant
to the Dean and was expelled.'

The directness of the explanation shocked Evelyn into
laughter.

'It was funny,' Ann said, 'really terribly funny. You see,
I was only sixteen, and I didn't know anything at all
about your world. I was . . . is "naive" the word, I
wonder?'

'My world?'

'You know, the decent, respectable academic world, the
grove of grapefruit and lemon. The lady was apparently
interested in the state of my soul or the nature of my
problem, whatever the phrase is. She took me for a
moonlight ride, parked, and then sat, waiting. I was
terribly embarrassed. It didn't occur to me that she was
waiting for me to talk. I sat, too. Then finally I thought,
"Oh, what the hell" and kissed her. It shocks you, too,
doesn't it?'

'Why did you do it?' Evelyn asked.

'I thought that's what she was waiting for. You see, around here, if somebody takes you for a moonlight ride, it isn't to discuss the state of your soul.'

'Even if it's the assistant to the Dean?'

'Well, I'd never been to college before. I'd never known an assistant to the Dean. And, by the time I did go to the Universty of Nevada, I was a good deal more worldly. I haven't kissed an assistant to the Dean since.'

'I can't quite believe that.'

'That I haven't kissed . . . ?'

'Sorry, my pronoun reference is poor.'

'What don't you believe?'

'What kind of world did you grow up in Ann?'

'This one, and it doesn't teach you much about the customs of natives in other parts of the country. But I've learned. Here I am, discussing the nature of my problem. I am not disoriented or confused. It will never seem really natural, but . . .'

'In your mind,' Evelyn said slowly, hanging on to the conversation with growing uncertainty, 'cliffs are not places for discussion.'

'Why not?' Ann said, turning to Evelyn with an easy grin. 'I really loved your world. It taught me a lot. I'm just more at home here. Feeling better?'

'Yes,' Evelyn said, 'not exactly at home, but better.'

'Shall we go?'

Evelyn walked to the car, her mind retracing as precisely as her steps did the path that had led her to the conversation just completed. But she could not discover how she had got there by going back. She only recognized that she had been at the edge of a cliff and had retreated.

As they drove back to Reno, Ann began to tell Evelyn stories of Frank's Club, which made her laugh, and they arrived back at the house gay and relaxed from the day's outing. Walter was not at home for dinner. Virginia had asked to stay in her room. Only Frances sat down at the

70

table with them. Like a latecomer to a cocktail party, she tried to hide her sobriety, but Evelyn and Ann could not quite catch her up into their own mood. Funny stories were replaced by half serious discussion, which finally gave way to explanations.

'What's the news of Janet's baby?' Frances asked.

'Didn't I tell you? The last operation's on Monday.'

'Who's Janet?' Evelyn asked.

Ann explained Janet to Evelyn. 'So she drives ninety miles over the desert and ninety miles back every night.'

'When does she sleep?'

'When the baby does, I guess, and on her day off.'

'Well, she'll be going down to San Francisco then,' Frances said.

'I don't think so. Ken's going to take the baby.'

'Why?' Frances asked.

'She's afraid of losing her job. Anyway, she can't afford to take time off.'

'Well,' Frances said, 'it's hard, isn't it? But just think how lucky they are that surgery can do what it can. Just a few years ago there wouldn't have been any hope at all.'

'When I look at Janet,' Ann said, 'I wonder how lucky she is.'

'You don't know what it is to have a child and want it to live,' Frances said.

'No I suppose I don't.'

'I've left my cigarettes upstairs,' Evelyn said, excusing herself quickly.

Frances was wrong. Ann might not know what it was to have a child and want it to live, but she must know what it was to want a child. Any woman knew that. And there was a generalization about womanhood that even Evelyn could share. She had wanted a child just as this young Janet wanted her child to live. Like Janet, she had been willing to sacrifice anything in the world for it. And she had sacrificed, before she was through, a good deal of the world she had known. At first it had been only the

71

humiliation of doctors, for herself and for George. One appointment after another, one specialist after another, each result hopelessly successful: by clinical definition she and her husband were unquestionably female and male, fertile and potent. But there had been no child. After each alone had offered up his secret sex to the laboratories, had admitted to specialists his private, unscientific fears, together they submitted themselves to experiment, making love by the book, by the calendar, by the temperature chart. The cheapest and crudest pornography could not have been more destructive to the spirit of love, but the fact was accomplished. Evelyn conceived a child. When she lost it at three months, they did not try again. They talked once or twice of adopting children, but it was only talk. Neither any longer had confidence enough in himself or in the other to feel capable of children. And, as Evleyn realized what had happened to them, she felt a terrible guilt for the desire she had had. It was a sin to want so badly anything you could not have. That was an oversimplification, of course. And it wasn't just the one thing, the wanting children. It was much more complicated than that. But it would have been easier, so much easier, if they could have left themselves to an old-fashioned childless fate. There might have been, even after the hope was gone, some tenderness left. The final horror had not been the losing of the child, a simple clinical failure. 'It often happens that way,' the doctor had said. 'You'll see. There'll be nothing to the next one.' He'd had a new pill, she remembered, and ordered the prescription by phone for her. When it arrived, she paid for it, opened the bottle and flushed the pills down the toilet. The doctor was exactly right. There would be nothing to the next one. She would never again say to her husband, 'Now, tonight.'

Frances was wrong. The doctors were wrong. And that young Janet, driving across the desert alone at night, must know that her frail, crippled, living wish was wrong. Or could she know? While the child lived, could she be ungrateful. Could anyone really give up before it was over?

'Evelyn?' Ann was calling up the stairs.

'I'll be right there.' Evelyn picked up her cigarettes.

'Stay there. I'm bringing up your coffee.' They met in the hall. 'Frances is fixing a tray for Virginia. I thought we could have coffee in my room, and I'd show you some of my cartoons.'

'I'd love it,' Evelyn said.

'Are you all right?'

'I'm fine,' Evelyn said as she followed Ann up the stairs to her attic room. 'Virginia really shouldn't spend so much time alone.'

'She wants to go home,' Ann said, 'back to her husband, but she doesn't know how to admit it.'

'Do you think she won't get her divorce?'

'If she can think of a way not to. It's hard for someone like Virginia to admit she's wrong, even to herself.'

Ann opened the door and held it for Evelyn. It was a large room. On the far wall, under the window, was a long drawing table. Racks above it held tubes of paint, bottles of ink, brushes, pens, pencils. Shelves underneath stored paper. One sketchbook lay open before a high stool. Otherwise, it was a work area as orderly as an operating theater. But Evelyn's attention shifted almost at once from this focus of the room to the other walls. There were hundreds of books on bookshelves to the eaves.

'Look at the books! I've been living on four books for days with a library right above my head.'

'Come up and get anything you want any time,' Ann said.

She walked over to the drawing table and sat back against the high stool. Evelyn walked over to her.

'And this is where you work.'

'When I work.'

'Who are the children?' Evelyn asked, looking down at

73

five small photographs Scotch-taped to the wall.

'That's Kim from Korea, Ming from Hong Kong, Hung from Vietnam, Eftychia from Greece, and Carmela from Italy.'

'Isn't she a dear, little girl,' Evelyn said, looking at Eftychia.

'She's nine. She's in the fourth grade. She wants to be a teacher. Carmela isn't so practical. She's all for coming to America to be a movie star.'

'How did you find out about them?' Evelyn asked.

'Answered an ad. They only cost fifteen bucks a month apiece.'

'What a wonderful thing to do.'

'It's the easiest and cheapest way to have children I know,' Ann said. 'They're so little nuisance. A letter and a check a month is all they need.'

'So these are instead of children of your own?'

'I suppose so,' Ann said. 'With all the surplus children in the world – they're being dumped in India and China the way we dump wheat – I figure motherhood should become a specialized profession like medicine or law for people really suited to it.'

'How do you decide you're not one of those?' Evelyn asked.

'Ann! Ann!' It was Frances' voice, distant but urgent.

Ann was across the room before Evelyn had time to move. As Ann opened the door, her name came again, louder, almost a presence in the room.

'All right, Frances, I'm coming,' she called.

When Evelyn reached the hall, it was empty. Virginia's bedroom door was open. Virginia lay on her bed, Ann and Frances standing over her. Ann was shaking a pillow out of its case.

'Call the doctor, Frances, right now,' Ann said. 'And don't get into a flap. Virginia's all right.'

Frances came out of the room, crying.

'What is it?' Evelyn asked. 'What's the matter?'

74

'She's slashed her wrists. She's killed herself.'

'For Christ's sake, Frances,' Ann yelled. 'Don't stand there gossiping! Call the doctor!'

Frances hurried off down the stairs. Evelyn did not know whether to follow her or go into the room.

'Evelyn, get me another pillowcase off your bed,' Ann called.

Evelyn did what she was told. When she got back into Virginia's room, she saw the blood for the first time, great, purple-brown patches of it on the sheets, on the rug by the bed. Ann was finished a rough tourniquet on Virginia's left arm. She seemed unconscious.

'Thanks,' Ann said. 'Now take the top sheet and tear me strips of it.'

Evelyn hesitated, reluctant to uncover Virginia.

'Quickly!' Ann said. 'Then get a blanket to cover her. Grab one off the closet shelf there.'

By the time the doctor arrived, Ann had stopped the bleeding and was sitting quietly by the bed, adjusting the tourniquets. Evelyn stood just inside the door, ready to do anything she was told. Frances stayed in the hall, talking unhappily to herself.

'Well, this is a pretty amateur job,' the doctor said, after he had uncovered both wrists. 'If a job's worth doing, it's worth doing well. You don't want to be a simple butcher. All the same,' he said, turning to Ann, 'it's a good thing you found her. She done a fair amount of bleeding.'

Virginia stirred and moaned.

'You go right ahead and moan, young lady, and be grateful you still can.'

'Dave . . . Davie,' Virginia whispered.

'He'll be here shortly,' Ann said. 'Well, I'm going to wash. Is there anything you need, doctor?'

'No. Here's the ambulance now.'

'Could I borrow your towel?' Ann asked Evelyn. 'Mine are all upstairs.'

'I'll get it.'

When Evelyn brought the towel to Anne, she was soaking her hands in a basin full of water.

'You certainly knew what you were doing,' Evelyn said, 'Is she really going to be all right?'

'Oh, sure,' Ann said. She reached over to take the towel. 'She wasn't even trying, or she's ignorant. You don't slash a wrist like that. You cut it like this.'

Ann demonstrated with her finger across her own wrist. Evelyn, looking down, noticed for the first time the fine diagonal scar across Ann's wrist.

'An old attempt,' Ann said, 'but not my own. It was an idea my father had before Frances came along.'

Evelyn stared at Ann, too shocked to reply.

'Well, now it seems to me we should give Dave-Davie a ring and tell him it's time to come to take Virginia home. Pride has only drastic ways out, doesn't it?'

'You're angry.'

'Yes, I'm angry. I love life. Despair always makes me angry. It's the one sin I believe in.'

Evelyn turned to watch the stretcher-bearers carry Virginia out of her room and down the stairs, but it was not Virginia he saw; it was George. 'I don't quite,' she said quietly. 'I mean I don't quite believe in despair, whether it's a sin or not.'

'I'd better go to the hospital with her and phone from there.'

From her own bedroom window, Evelyn watched Ann talking with the doctor and then getting into the ambulance. Why must she go? Why was Virginia Ritchie Ann's responsibility? Because Frances had not taken it. Because Walter was not home. Because Evelyn herself had been no more than a reluctant sightseer – all day. Frances had said, 'She's not ordinary.' Ann herself had wondered, ironically, if 'naïve' was the word to describe her own incredible innocence, her absurd sense of duty. Evelyn was seeing again, in fact, what she did not believe. Ann, marked on both wrists by her father's death wish, wandered among ruins and graves, looked out across the desolation of desert as her inheritance, and loved life. How? With a confusion of humor, tenderness, and rage, with aggression, reluctance, and generosity. Any special assistant to the Dean would certainly recommend a psychiatrist. Evelyn herself, from behind her desk, would have no other choice. As the ambulance door shut, Evelyn wanted to call out, 'Ann, wait. I'll go.' But it was too late. Evelyn turned from the window, ashamed. There was something she could do. She could face the simple, physical unpleasantness of Virginia's room. It must be cleaned up. And there was Frances. She could comfort Frances. Ann would not be long.

− 4 −

Ann did not go back to the house. Instead, she asked Dr Riesman to drop her off at the center of town.

'It's late, Ann.'

'Not for me.'

'Where's Bill tonight?'

'I don't know,' Ann said. 'I don't see him much anymore.'

'Oh?'

'No sympathy required.'

'For you, you mean?'

Ann did not answer.

'Ann, when are you going to leave that house?'

'I don't know. Is there any reason why I should leave?'

'Things like tonight seem to me reason enough.'

'You think changing an address can change the world?'

'In a way. At least you could choose the kind of trouble you get into.'

'Oh, come,' Ann said. 'I have a choice now, as far as anyone does.'

'Four years ago I told you . . .'

'I know. And I am free.'

'You're not. You're as tied to your father's memory as you were to him.'

'That's not true.'

'It is. Why aren't you seeing Bill?'

'Because I am free. Because I want to stay free.'

'Because you don't want to let any other man have the

right to your life that your father had.'

'Something like that,' Ann said.

'All men aren't your father.'

'No? Well, it's kind of you to take such a fatherly interest.'

Dr Riesman glanced over at Ann and smiled. 'Let me take you home.'

'No.'

Ann opened the door before the car had come to a full stop. She no more than nodded good night to the doctor. A blunt, good man with an oversimplfied sense of psychological history, he had always irritated her. Of course she missed her father. She missed him because he had borne down on her like a weight of gravity, and given her substance, had caged her in the knowledge of her own flesh. While he lived, her world was the prison of his need. She missed him now with a relief that used to seem almost a kind of madness. It was not simple, missing with joy the weight of earth. It was not simple, love freewheeling over fear of earth. She was not tied to his memory. If she had been apprenticed to her father's need, she was now at least a journeyman and could choose the need she served. It was her own.

There was no one she knew in the employees' lounge. Idly she read notices on the bulletin board, most of them orders from the Management to the Employees, always a dyspeptic paraphrase of the Golden Rule set out in large type among the bits of gambling jargon. 'The Admonishments' Ann called them. She turned away from the board and saw two children standing quietly by the matron of the movies, an ample, tired grandmother of a woman whose job it was to accept, send to the free movies, and return children to their parents. The last movie ended at eleven. It was now after twelve. Because the employees' lounge was always crowded, the children were not allowed to sit down to wait for their truant parents. They had to stand, as these two did, until they claimed.

The boy was younger, perhaps seven. He had been crying. The girl was nine. She might have comforted her brother if her own humiliation had not closed her off from his fear. She stared straight ahead of her at the door. Ann walked over to the matron.

'Every night. Every single night it happens. I should have been home an hour ago.'

'You'll get your overtime,' Ann said.

'What about my sleep?'

The boy looked at Ann. The girl refused to listen.

'Are you hungry? Would you like something to eat?' Ann asked, squatting down beside the boy.

'No, thank you,' the girl answered, still not looking at Ann. 'My mother will be here in a minute.'

'How about a Coke?'

'No, thank you.'

Ann looked at the boy. 'How about you?'

'He doesn't want any either.'

'If she doesn't turn up in fifteen minutes,' the matron said, 'I'm calling the police.'

The little boy bgan to cry again. The little girl stared at the door.

'It's all right,' Ann said, putting an arm around the boy. 'It's all right. She's just tired and grumpy.'

But in fifteen minutes the matron would call the police if they hadn't already come of their own accord. Rarely a night passed that a child or two weren't taken to the hospital to sleep. Before the free movies was instituted, the police found children locked in cars. In the summer it wasn't so bad. In the winter the children were a real trial to the law.

'Say, why don't we do something while we wait?' Ann said. 'Do you like to draw?' The little boy shook his head. The little girl did not respond. 'I do. Shall I draw you a picture? What kind of a picture shall I draw?' Ann helped herself to the matron's pencil and looked around for a piece of paper. 'What's your favorite animal?' Ann looked down at the children. 'Horse? Dog? Cat?'

'Dog,' the little boy said softly.

'Do you have a dog?' The little boy nodded. 'What's his name?'

The little boy turned away from Ann as a tall, well-dressed young woman came into the room. He cried out and ran to her. The little girl did not move. She stood, staring in front of her, forcing her mother to walk the full length of the suddenly silent, hostile room.

'Now stop making a fuss, Tommy. Stop it!' the mother said in a loud, cheerful voice. 'Come along, darling,' she said to her daughter. 'Don't keep mother waiting.'

Ann could not watch the child. She turned away, rage rising in her throat like nausea. Why save Virginia Ritchie's life? I should have slashed deeper, made a decent job of it, let life out of that house of petty horrors, the female body. 'Mummy loves you.' Of course she does. Having opened her thighs to that faltering hero, your father, having swelled and ripened to your appalling birth, she has to love you. If she has eaten off your arm or your leg, if she has consumed you altogether, you must understand that she is nothing more than a young animal herself, ignorant, clumsy, hungry. She has needs of her own. Of course, she loves you; you're one of them, I should have cut deeper. Stop it! Don't rage. She really is no more than a young animal herself. As I am. As I am.

Ann walked out into the alley to the Club entrance. She opened the door and let the noise beat against her nerves like a thousand fists. The abscess of fury broke. Ann stepped up to the bar and ordered a double Scotch.

'I'll buy that for you.'

Ann looked up at the not very drunk young man who stood beside her.

'Thanks, but I'm waiting for a friend.'

'You don't have to wait for me.'

'Thanks anyway.'

Ann put her money on the counter and took her drink

away from the bar. She stood at the edge of a roulette game, letting the alcohol mute the dying fanfare of indignation in her head. At last, at the center of the noise, she was still, but anger had kept her a kind of company. As she forced it away, grief could too easily sound the silence of her heart unless she could find human company. Bill would not be here. A year ago they had arranged the same night off. He might be at home. But to go to him in need was to incur a debt she could not repay. Silver? It was two hours before the end of the shift. And, anyway, Joe was home. Home. Frances might have gone to bed. Evelyn might still be awake. At one o'clock? Evelyn welcomed the conventions of time and space, fifteen years and the Sierras. One does not play games with ladies from California. No? No. What were you doing today then? I was . . . being kind. That little maneuver on Geiger Point as well? All right, that was a mistake. Which you won't make again? No. How will you stop? I won't go home. I won't see her.

'Here you are. A double Scotch.'

It was the same young man. Are you human company, random antidote to grief? Must I take you? A habit of will forced Ann to response.

'Thanks.'

She stood beside him, watching the roulette wheel spin. If it lands in black, I'll say no. If it lands in black, I'll go home. The wheel slowed. The ball swung slowly, round and round, dropped, bounced, dropped again into red.

'Have any money on it?'

'No *money*,' Ann said, 'no.'

Had she really tied the night to chance and lost? Of course not. Red or black, it didn't matter. She would not see Evelyn. And if you look in a mirror? I'll see myself. Will you? It doesn't matter who I see. She's in another time, on another earth.

'Where are you from?' Ann asked.

'Frisco.'

The City. Even here in Reno they called it the City, a promised land across the mountains, a promised sea, her earth. But that was years ago on a beach of cypress, sea sand, kelp. She's a wish I've outgrown. An image. My mother. Myself. The wheel spun again. He put money on red. The ball swung round and round. A need I haven't got. A need I mustn't have. Evelyn is . . . herself. The ball swung slowly, dropped into black.

'Damn!'

'Everybody loses,' Ann said.

'Red again.'

He stacked chips on numbers too, watched, waited, won.

'That will buy the drinks,' he said. 'Shall we try for more?'

'More?'

'Yes, more,' he said. 'Let's go all the way.'

All his simple way could not be far. Ann looked up, willing.

But in the morning, when she woke and looked at the naked dog-tagged man asleep beside her, her will broke as a dream might. She had been here before in this stale, hot motel room, the sun an orange insistence against the heavy drapes, the rattle of the cleaning wagon outside the window. She reached out to the metal circle on his chest and read his name. He slept on, secure in his identity. Ann got up quietly, dressed, and walked out into the parking area. At a public phone booth she called Silver.

'Little fish, do you know what time it is?'

'Haven't a clue.'

'Eight o'clock in the morning!'

'Oh.'

'Where are you?'

'The Rancho Something-or-Other Motel.'

'Where's the nearest café?'

'Next door.'

84

'Go have a cup of coffee. I'll pick you up in fifteen minutes.'

'Thanks.'

Silver, huge and haggard, arrived with a prepared list of insulting questions. Ann had been called in on Silver's own excursions often enough not to feel guilty, but she did apologize.

'I scared hell out of the paper boy, and his dog howled. Say you're sorry to him.'

Ann laughed.

'Now, what's the matter?' Silver asked, pouring an unmeasured quantity of sugar into her coffee.

'I didn't have my car. I needed a ride home.

'I heard a rumor the other day that there's a cab company in Reno.'

'Really? Did you hear anything about the drivers?'

'It's not the hour,' Silver said. 'You're just not funny.'

'Are you really irritated?'

'No.'

'Sil, did you ever want to kill yourself?'

'But I might get irritated.'

'I'm serous.'

'I somehow picked that up. I'm a sensitive sort.'

'Well, did you?'

'Christ, Ann, everybody wants to kill himself sooner or later. It isn't exactly what you'd call an unusual experience.'

'Isn't it? I've never wanted to, never ever.'

'What have you been doing in the last twenty-four hours?'

'I went up to Virginia City yesterday.'

'Alone?'

'No, I took Evelyn Hall.'

'That's the mother figure of the moment, isn't it?'

'What do you mean, "of the moment"?'

'Haven't you ever noticed that you have a thing about women?'

'What kind of a thing?'

'Oh, go to hell. I'll charge you twenty-five bucks an hour when I decide to tell you who you are.'

'It's a funny thing,' Ann said. 'Dr Riesman . . .'

'That bastard!'

'. . . has me all figured out as well. Only his theory is that I have a thing about men.'

'Clever! I wonder if he's ever met a woman who didn't.'

'There's something about figuring people out and summing them up that I don't like. You find out who somebody is in order to cure him. I haven't the least desire to be cured.'

'So you're sick, so sick you want to live.' Silver finished her coffee. 'Then what did you do?'

'Well, we went home for dinner, and then I took Evelyn up to my room to see some cartoons.'

'Now we're getting to it.'

'But Virginia Ritchie chose that moment to slash her wrists.'

'Jealous?'

'Cut it out,' Ann said.

'I'm just trying to get the picture.'

'So I went to the hospital with her, and then, after Riesman and I had a little chat about my complexes, I stopped at the Club.'

'I didn't see you.'

'I didn't go upstairs. There was this guy . . .'

'Just tell me one thing: why didn't you go home to mother?'

'I don't know. She's – you know – different.'

'Sure,' Silver said. 'Different.'

'Don't you think some people are?'

'This Evelyn Hall's really rocked your boat, hasn't she?'

'Everybody rocks my boat,' Ann said, grinning suddenly. 'There's a cartoon that will sell.'

Drawings never came singly. The first of these was the

simple, comic sickness, passive, sexless. Then there was a man with an oar, beating off mermaids. In another, a woman wore a cockeyed red cross and was helping a wounded whale into her rowboat. They were good sketches, but, as Ann turned away from her drawing table to undress and to sleep, she was aware the she hadn't caught herself. She did not often have the courage to. Instead she chose near misses to catch the breath but not to touch the heart. Aim at the apple on Master Tell's head, not at the apple that tempted Eve. *Eve's Apple* was her private sketchbook. In it were drawings she would not sell. They were drawings she often wished she had not made.

Ann did not want to accept the view of the world she sometimes revealed to herself. Because she had named her needs and was determined to satisfy them, moral insight was a kind of despair. It involved judgment. To judge was to condemn. In *Eve's Apple* were the portraits of the condemned, cruel, comic, tender, indifferent. Her mirrored insights, Ann was not sure whether they were reflections of conscience or vanity.

Ann lay down and stared at the ceiling. From the hall below, she heard Evelyn calling to Frances. Ann closed her eyes, guilty not of erotic visions but of the ridiculous, beautiful inhibitions of desire, an infant's lust for nurse or nun, for virgin mother. Ann sat up abruptly. What would you say, doctor, if you knew that my secret sin was dressing the world in virtue? Infantilism. She lay down again, and self-mocking, curled herself into sleep.

Frances woke her several hours later with the news of David Ritchie's arrival.

'Where is he now?'

'Downstairs.'

'Has he been to the hospital?'

'No,' Frances said. 'I think he hoped you'll go with him.'

'Oh, grand.'

'I hated to wake you up, but I didn't now what else to do.'

'Oh well,' Ann said, swinging out of bed, 'sleep is only on way of passing the time of day. How is he?'

'Very upset, I should think.'

'And contrite?'

'I hope so,' Frances said firmly.

'You have an attitude for every occasion, Frances.'

'Don't be ugly.'

'It's four o'clock now. Get me coffee and juice. I'll have dinner downtown.'

'Ann, where were you last night?'

'Shacked up with a drunk from Frisco in the Rancho Something-or-Other Motel.'

'Oh, Ann!'

'Now, be a dear, Frances, and get me some coffee.'

David Ritchie was dressed in his wedding suit. Ann did not know why she was sure of it, except that he looked such a used groom, a service button in place of his white carnation, guilt instead of fear trapped in his doubtful eyes. He was still a new husband five years after the fact.

'I wanted to talk to you,' he said, holding the car door open for Ann.

'Sure,' Ann said. As she watched him walk around the car, she wished she had offered to let him drive. 'Do you want to go somewhere for a drink?'

'Coffee?'

'Sure.'

'Could you tell me exactly what happened?'

As Ann reported the details she knew, careful to keep her own interpretation of the events to herself, she wondered how useful exactly-what-had-happened could be to anyone. She remembered her own repeated questioning of Frances. What had her father said the night before? Where did he say he was going? Now, again, when the man phoned, exactly what did he say? Had he seen the accident himself? When did the doctor arrive? Ann had asked the same questions over and over again, had taken the answers away with her and worked over them, trying to reconstruct the death until it was as accurate and vivid as if she had been there herself. Even if she had been there, would seeing it have made her understand any better than she did now?

'How much blood do you think she lost?'

'I don't know. As I told you, they gave her a transfusion at the hospital.'

'Could you guess?'

'I really couldn't.'

'A pint?'

'Look,' Ann said, 'can you estimate pints from a wet diaper?'

'I'm sorry.'

'The thing is . . .' Ann went on more patiently, 'that she's right there to ask about it. Here's a coffee shop. Do you still want to stop?'

'If you wouldn't mind.'

Ann waited behind the wheel as he hurried around the car to open the door for her. His careful manners must have been taught him by his mother and not his father. He was subservient rather than protective. Every gesture was an apology for his manhood.

'Do you want to hear my theories?' Ann asked, after they had ordered coffee. He nodded. 'I don't think Virginia had the slightest intention of killing herself. I think she had come to the conclusion that she didn't want a divorce and didn't know how to admit it.'

'She wants me back?'

'That would be my guess.'

'Did she tell you about . . . us?'

'Not a thing.'

'She said she couldn't ever . . . well . . . be my wife again. She wouldn't even see me. And she said the kids mustn't see me.' He stared at his coffee. 'I don't really blame her.'

89

'Because you got drunk and went to bed with one of the girls in the office?'

'Then she did tell you . . .'

'Oh, Dave, come on. You're not really that contrite.'

'What if she'd died?' he demanded.

'She had no intention of dying.'

'How do you know?'

Ann paused. 'I don't really.' She was tired and vaguely ashamed of herself. If she was going to play God, the least she could do was to be good at it. And she was very bad at it with people like David Ritchie, with all the tourists. Just as she was certain of melodrama, she caught the faint, peppery odor of something quite other. Conscience? She didn't know.

'Will she see me?'

'She asked for you,' Ann said.

'Do you think she'll give me another chance?'

'Try her.'

David Ritchie looked straight at Ann and swallowed, obviously moved. 'I will,' he said.

Ann would not have been surprised if, at that moment, the room had been filled with organ music. She imagined that David walked out of the restaurant in time to his own private wedding march. They drove to the hospital in silence.

'I want to thank you, Ann . . . for everything.'

Her father used to say, thanked for the sugar or a fur coat or a kindness, his voice an exaggerated haughtiness, '*I'll* never mention it again.' Ann said, 'Good luck, Dave.'

She watched him walk up the hospital steps, not Everyman so much as Anyman, carrying his little guilt like an offering to the shrine of his wife's righteous indignation. It was after six. Ann would have no time for a meal before work. She'd get a sandwich in her long break.

'So all stories have a happy ending,' she told Silver as they stood together at the cashier's counter, signing their

90

IOU's.

'You need to get some sleep,' Silver said.

'You don't have to block my view. It doesn't bother me.'

Silver shrugged and turned away to her station, leaving Ann to watch Joyce and Bill, who leaned together at the other end of the counter, silently looking into each other's eyes.

'You want any change tonight, or has the boss got other plans for you?' the cashier asked.

Bill stared away from Joyce, embarrassed. Joyce turned to the cashier, bared her teeth, and then winked at Ann. Ann smiled before she turned away.

'Ann?'

'Yes,' Bill.'

'Has Silver spoken to you?'

Ann looked up at him, questioning.

'About the wedding?' he continued.

'Yes.'

'They want us to witness together.'

'I know.'

'Are you going to?' he asked.

'Sure.'

'It's a little awkward. I . . .' he hesitated.

'There's nothing in the rule book about the *witnesses* having to be one flesh, is there?' His jaw tightened. 'Bill, give up on it. It's all right. And we don't have to change the world over it. We can still go to the same weddings.'

'Don't you ever . . . ? No, I don't suppose you would.'

Miss you, Bill? she wanted to ask. Yes, I miss you. Find it hard, Bill? Yes, I find it hard sometimes, but not as hard as it might have been if we'd gone on with it.

'Tell Joe you'll witness, for *him*.'

'I'll think about it,' Bill said.

'You must have had a rough night last night,' Joyce said, swinging up onto the ramp with almost professional assurance.

91

'Don't bite the hand that feeds you, love.'

'What are you feeding me?'

Ann grinned and turned to a customer to make change. Two ramps away, under the wheels of an old stage coach suspended from the ceiling, Ann saw Janet, tired at the beginning of this Friday evening, the beginning of their week. Tomorrow Ken would take the baby down to the City. Then, of course, Janet would have time to sleep, if she could sleep. The days were so very hot. Ann's own tiredness was insignificant really. The energy she had spent was only the extra change she had found in a coat pocket, at the bottom of an old purse. Janet was drawing, day by day, on her life's savings.

'You stay on with the first relief,' Ann said to Joyce, 'and take your break when I get back.'

'You trust me?' Joyce asked.

'I told you the place is full of mirrors.'

'It's not tips I want to pocket.'

'I don't own him. You're welcome to him,' Ann said, stepping off the ramp before Joyce had a chance to reply.

'*You're* in a hurry,' the relief said as they passed on the floor.

'I haven't had any dinner,' Ann said. She took off her apron quickly, put it in her locker, then stopped at Janet's ramp on the way out. 'I was wondering if you wanted to stay in town this week. We may have an empty room at my place by tomorrow. Anyway, I could put an extra bed in my room.'

'Oh, thanks, Ann. I don't know. There are so many things to do at home. Could I think about it? I'll talk to Ken.'

'Sure.'

'I could let you know tomorrow.'

Janet could not stay in town. With Ken and the baby away, she needed the house. It had become her Pandora's box, the last place on earth where hope was trapped. While she waited, hope was the only company she could

92

keep. Ann nodded to her refusal as they checked in on Saturday night.

'You look awfully tired, Ann,' Janet said.

'It's the heat, that's all. Every summer I think I'll buy an air conditioning unit for my room. Then I never get around to it. Anyway, when I can't sleep, I sometimes get some work done.'

'What's the latest on Lady Suicide and Anyman?' Silver asked as she joined them.

'They're flying off together into the sunset tonight,' Ann said.

'It's the B movies that always make me cry,' Silver said. 'And speaking of B movies, Bill told Joe he'd stand. Have you heard I'm going to be a bride, Janet?'

'I had heard, yes. Congratgulations.'

'According to the best books, you should congratulate Joe.'

'Brides are always hypersensitive,' Ann said.

'It's losing their maidenheads and all,' Silver explained to the back Janet had turned to her. 'Now what have I done?'

'Nothing, ' Ann said. 'Ken took the baby down to the City today. She's edgy. That's all.'

'Jesus, I'm tactful.'

'You didn't do anything, Sil.' Ann looked up at the great grotesque of a woman, stricken with unimportant, misplaced guilt, and wanted to laugh at and comfort her in the same moment. 'Come on. We'll be late.'

As they pushed open the doors of the casino, the cold air cracked and pounded and shrieked and moaned with the Saturday night that was going on inside. All hands had been called, the brightly-shirted, white-hatted crew, riding herd on the shifting crowds, their hands on the silver. Across the floor, the down escalator, like a slow motion waterfall, fed the already flooding sea, the drain of doors clogged, backing up.

Separated at once from Silver, Ann made her way

through the crowd slowly, her eyes choosing paths that closed before she could follow them. Often she stood still, waiting for a way to move, then touched an elbow or shoulder or waist, carefully, gently moving the bodies of strangers out of her way. Before she reached the escalator, she had settled to the infinite patience, to the isolated peace she almost always felt in this crowd. Reality was so powerfully and presently restricted that nothing outside it had meaning. The plane that was taking off at that moment for San Francisco was no more than the conventional end of a magazine novella. Evelyn and Frances, sitting together over coffee, were passengers on a train Ann had not taken. Even Janet somewhere ahead of her and Silver somewhere behind her were lost in an archaic image of time and space.

'Christ!' Joyce said, as they met on the ramp, 'Silver wasn't kidding about Saturday night. It's hell.'

Ann had time only to nod. Hands reached up on all sides, for change, for jackpot payoffs. In less than an hour she was at the cashier's desk, buying more silver, and it seemed to her that she had sold most of it again before she was able to reach her ramp. Raised above the floor, it was like a small island of safety, but the currents of the crowd pulled her away from it again and again. She could hardly hear the shouting of a customer against the pounding, erratically belching machines, the spilling silver, and the magnified, disembodied voices of her friends, competing for the attention of the board.

'I was beginning to think you'd never make it,' Joyce said.

'So was I', Ann answered, as they crossed at the center of the ramp, back to back so that their aprons would not foul.

'Where in hell's the key man? I've got eight jackpot payoffs waiting, two machines out of order.'

'Here he is now,' Ann said. 'I'll witness this end.'

'Mexican coins in the quarter machines downstairs.

Keep an eye out,' the key man said.

'Which eye?' Joyce growled good-naturedly. 'Is he kidding?'

'More or less,' Ann said, checking the coin escalators in the quarter machines while she made change. 'Anyway, we're all right now.'

'Will you look at that?' Joyce said, nodding to the end of the ramp.

A girl, dressed in white and burdened with orchids, chewed gum to the rhythm of her dime machine. Three machines away her button-holed groom idly spent his spare change. Ann went down to the five-dollar bill he waved.

'Buddy, you've got the wrong idea,' the man next to him shouted.

Another dug him in the ribs and made an obscene gesture. People nearby made faces of laughter, stared, nudged, pointed, began to press closer. The young groom continued to play his machine.

'Why doesn't somebody tell him?' the man next to him yelled.

Shouts burst free of the already terrible noise, single catcalls, high notes of laughter. The young groom began to eye the crowd, watching for a way to get out. Someone thumped him on the back. A drunken grandmother rumpled his hair. When he shruggd her off, she grabbed at his carnation. He turned suddenly into the crowd, trying to shove through but no one made way. His bride, separated from him now by a dozen people, chewed her gum and played her machine.

Ann leaned over and shouted into her face, 'Get him out of here before they tear him to pieces.'

The bride in the white dress looked behind her, then back at Ann, and shrugged. The groom was moving away now with a mob escort of crude advisers and well-wishers. He smiled, got angry, smiled again. Only once he looked anxiously over his shoulder, but he could no longer see his bride.

'What a wedding night, eh?' Joyce shouted. 'The bride's got a jackpot.'

Ann· reached for the microphone and read off the number of the lucky machine, her quiet voice sounding accurate and colossal across the room.

Sunday morning, battered out of bed by the brutal sun and church bells, Ann sat at her drawing table, making exhausted sketches of the Detached Man and the Self-Contained Woman. Evelyn knocked and came in with juice and coffee.

'It's awfully hot up here, Ann.'

'I don't notice it much.'

'You go ahead and work. I just want a book or two.'

Ann nodded and turned back to her table.

'Oh, before you settle again, Frances and Walter were talking about having an early picnic supper.'

'Could you tell Frances I have to be out for supper tonight?'

'All right.'

Evelyn took the books she wanted and quickly left the room. Ann turned with the closing door, about to speak. Instead she put her head down on her arms, but it was too hot for even private melodrama. She could not cry. She could only sweat. Suffering was a winter luxury. Now all she did was balance her tiredness between work and work, the silent satire of her room and the crashing sentimentality of the casino. It was too hot, she was too tired for love.

Willfully cut off not only from Evelyn but from everyone in the house, Ann tried to take rest also in her less voluntary isolation from her friends at the Club. Bill, giving more time to Joyce, gave less attention to his angry sorrow. And, as Ann felt relieved of his need, she was also relieved of her own desire for Bill. Silver's growing preoccupation with plans of the wedding left Ann a little more wistful, but she was grateful, too, to be less often the direct object of Silver's strong, crude verbs. On both Monday and Tuesday evenings, no one interrupted Ann's rhythm of work. The hands that signaled, touched her sleeve, asked for nothing more than the change in her apron. Provider for and witness to the world, she stood on her ramp, surrounded by guns, reflected in mirrors, alone. Even Janet, working nearby under the weightless bulk of the hanging stage coach, was too preoccupied with worry to share it. When on Tuesday night Janet's relief was late, Ann only signaled from a distance to let Janet know she could go home. Ann would wait.

When the relief did arrive, it was quarter to four. All Ann's friends had gone. The few change aprons and key men on the graveyard shift were strangers to her. So were the tactful janitors who cleaned around late customers, a gay, drunken party of locals, scattered traveling salesmen, and a couple of old women, spending their pensions. Just as Ann stepped up to the cashier's desk to check out her apron, a great trolley arrived, already loaded with sacks of change. The two cashiers turned away from Ann to the more important business of the night's cash clearance. Ann stood, patiently counting out the stray coins from her change dispenser. Thirteen dimes . . . no, fourteen . . . no, twelve. She counted again and tried to stack the coins. They toppled over. Ann's hand shook as she restacked. The nickels fell over. She stopped to rest, her elbows against the high counter, her head down. She tried again. Her hand shook violently, her eyes focused through tears. She did not know how long she had been standing there, how long she had been crying. Odd to be crying.

'All right. Come on. Let's have it,' the cashier said impatiently.

Ann kept her head bowed while the cashier took the count.

'You're out fifty dollars.'

'I can't be,' Ann said, trying to focus on the rolls of

change, trying to count.

'Well, you are. Where's your paper?'

'Paper?' Ann repeated, fumbling at the pocket in her apron, which was behind the change dispenser. 'That's it. Here we are.' She handed the cashier fifty dollars in paper money. 'Sorry.'

'Are you going to make it home, kid?'

'Sure.'

'Don't forget your locker key.'

'No.'

Ann found herself outside. The heat had fallen down over her like a sack. She struggled to breathe, to see, and found her way to the employees' entrance as if it were at the other end of a maze. Her card, when she punched it, read four forty-five. She was still crying as she climbed the stairs to her attic room, as she took off her clothes and lay down to sleep. Tired. She was just tired. But for a long time she did not close her eyes. In the ruthless desert dawn, she still stared at the slanting ceiling and waited for the inevitable intensity of the full morning sun. Then, resigned, she slept.

Ann did not get up until late afternoon on Wednesday. She went over to the table and looked at her drawings of the Detached Man and Self-Contained Woman. Wryly she scribbled down names of new characters: Share Bath and Basement Suite, All Found and Unfurnished. Among these couples of forlorn comics, she could find a few for sale. But she hadn't time or energy to begin sketches now. She herself was only semidetached and felt personal about everything. Even her body was so vulnerable that it was compromised by the heavy frontier pants she had to pull on. In her stiff, announcing boots, in her tight-sleeved, tight-necked, loud shirt, she threatened herself in the long mirror. But it was Wednesday. Tomorrow was her night off. Then she could rest, dressed in her own clothes.

'Ann, you look dreadful.'

'Thank you, Frances.'

98

'I'm serious. Do you feel all right?'

'Yes, I feel fine.'

'Well, I'm glad you're home tonight for dinner. All this running around, not taking time to eat . . .' Frances was interrupted by Walter and Evelyn, who came into the dining room, carrying their glasses of sherry.

'So I said "Sold!" ' Walter turned to Ann, put an arm around her waist, and almost lifted her from the floor. 'Girl Childs, today I am a man.'

'What's all this?'

'I've bought a car.'

'Hold dinner, Frances. We'll go out and smear him with oil.'

'Isn't it a shame I've already been circumcised?'

'Walter!'

'Sorry, Mom. Anyway, I've got wine for dinner.'

Walter followed Frances into the kitchen. The tones of his voice were loud and deep with pleasure, and Frances' protesting laughter was almost girlish.

'He is excited,' Evelyn said, smiling. 'You know, he almost makes me wish I'd had a son.' Ann looked up sharply. 'He's very generous with his pleasure.'

'He said he wasn't going to buy a car until next summer.'

'But he got an awfully good buy.'

Ann shook her head. She wanted to disapprove, but she knew she was simply disappointed. She had liked loaning her car to Walt. She wasn't really possessive of him, was she? Obviously, she must be. And now a little jealous, too? Her guilt made her angry. How long did Evelyn Hall think she had a right to stay, threatening Ann with her self-possession, her candid gentleness, her intelligence, her decency, until Ann could not eat a meal in peace, until she was driven out of her own house? Why couldn't Evelyn leave her alone? Why did Evelyn leave her alone? Ann grinned. Fatigue and irritation had not quite canceled her sense of the ridiculous.

'All right, Walt,' she said, as he came back into the room, 'I want the full story.'

'You'll have it. What's more, you're going to have a demonstration. I'm going to pick it up on your way to work. Will you come with us, Evelyn?'

'I'd love to.'

Frances declined the same invitation. She would wait for a ride until Walt and Evelyn got home. Ann struggled against tiredness and reluctance into an almost acceptable mood. For her own sake, as well as for Walter's, she did not want to be left out. She let herself be rushed through dinner, worked hard at a kind of wry gaiety, until, when the three of them got into Ann's car, she felt almost identified with the role she played. After all, she and Walter were almost brother and sister; and Evelyn, amused, serene, indulgent, was almost old enough to be their mother. They were all, at that moment, more willingly related than blood would ever have allowed them to be. But, after Ann had exclaimed, teased, taken a ride around the block, she had to leave Walter and Evelyn. Without their need for her gaiety, it died. The almost real world was not real enough. Like saccharine, its aftertaste was slightly bitter.

Bill was waiting for her in the employees' lounge. 'Ann, I need you on relief tonight. Would you mind?'

'No, that's fine.'

'With Joyce on the ramp, you're the easiest one to move.'

'Sure. I don't mind.'

It was a foul job, moving from one station to another all night long, twenty minutes here, forty minutes there. Each station had its own peculiarities. At one, the change apron did her own jackpot payoffs and had to keep a record. At another, she had to report directly to the cashier. And, because each station had different numbers and kinds of machines, a relief had to carry her full allotment of change, cups of silver dollars, an extra twenty rolls of nickels. If one girl was late coming back from her break, the relief had to make up the time by sacrificing her own time off. A few of the change aprons actually liked the job during the week because it broke the monotony of a slow evening. But Ann, like most of the others, preferred the set routine that freed her mind from the details of work, and tonight not only her mind but her body was reluctant.

She strapped her apron very high, carrying it like a fetus in its seventh month, careful to lift and turn the weight as if it were her own flesh, for she had to walk some distance with it, and maneuver on and off escalators, her back burning, the veins in her legs aching with the drag of sixty pounds of dead weight: the ironic emancipation of woman, martyred to nothing but her own belligerence, surely. Why did she do it? At the center of this desert industry, symbol of it, she wanted to take her place, for there was no nature. The apes could not have survived. Only man could have invented a living independent of earth, related to no physical need, yet satisfying them all. Out of his own nonanimal nature, he had found a weakness, a faith, by which he could survive. Ann was novice to her world's only passionate belief. She moved from station to station, to serve and to witness.

At the third, she began to lose time. Her first break, which was supposed to be forty miunutes, was only twenty-five. When she took her apron off, the sudden loss of weight seemed to disturb the law of gravity. She felt she could step into air, up and up over the crowd like a child's balloon, not quite in control of herself. She drifted instead uncertainly into the ladies' room where she asked the attendant to order her an illegal drink. Then she locked herself in one of the cubicles and sat down with her whiskey. The door next to her banged shut, and Ann stared at the pigeon-toed feet of a woman, who began vomiting noisily. Ann was due at her next station in five minutes. She took the escalator to the second floor, took an elevator from there to the fourth floor, which was the night club, where the band had always just stopped playing, where the floor show was always just about to begin. Ann nodded to the girl she was to relieve and took her place close to the crap table.

'The wife wanted a silver tea set sort of thing. So, when I was in the City, I thought, "Why the hell not?" Do you know how much the goddammed things cost?' The speaker paused to watch his chips swept off the table. He placed new bets. 'Fifteen hundred bucks! I was wild! I told the salesgirl, "Shit, it's cheaper to buy a new wife." '

'Watch your language, sir,' the dealer said quietly.

'Watch your own,' the man answered, but good-naturedly. 'What do you think you're running, a Sunday school?'

'Yes sir, and taking up a collection,' the dealer said, sweeping the board clean again.

Ann did not like the fourth floor. She was glad, at the end of half an hour, to step back into the waiting elevator. A sign at the back: 'Thank you. You may have helped put a student through the University of Nevada. Frank's Club Scholarship Fund.' Ann looked over at the elevator girl who stared at the closed door not six inches from her face. She had an aging, well-powdered black eye. Two young men stepped into the elevator when it stopped at the third floor.

'I told you to watch it,' the first said. 'All these places are run by a bunch of crooks.'

'Jesus, fifty bucks,' the other said.

'Two?'

'Main floor,' Ann said.

As she reached her assigned ramp and signalled the girl on duty, she felt a hand on her arm. It was Jerry, the main floor boss.

'Ann, take a look over there, will you?'

Ann looked towards the roulette table he had indicated, saw the crowd, and recognized the standard symptoms of

102

luck. Someone at the table must be betting heavily, winning enough to collect riders.

'Is that guy Janet Hearle's husband? The drunk in the white shirt?'

Ann, who had met Ken Hearle only a couple of times, could not be sure at that distance. She remembered him a tall, crude-boned man, sweating quietly in a suit, a conservative academic farmer.

'I'm not sure, Jerry. I hardly think so.'

'Will you take a good look?'

'Sure.'

He had obviously lost a jacket and tie somewhere, and one patch of hair was still glued in place by the lacquer and comb of another, forgotten, mood. His face and neck were blotched with color, as if he had been slapped several times by a vicious but inaccurate hand. Ann stood near him, still uncertain.

'Ken?'

'Here's a sweetheart,' he cried as he saw and obviously recognized her. 'You're just who I need.' He reached out and put an arm around her shoulder. 'Will you tell this phony cowboy he can't close me out of the game? Tell him I'm a relative. Tell him I'm a dependent. Tell him I'm a next of kin.'

The dealer's eyes questioned Ann while the crowd encouraged her to defend the gambler.

'I'm not closing you out of the game, sir,' the dealer said cooly. 'You're welcome to bet as long as you observe the limits.'

'What the hell do you care? You're making money off me.'

'I'm sorry. It's a rule of the house.'

'Okay. Okay. Just don't spin that little wheel yet. Hang on to your ball.' With his free hand, he sprinkled chips across the board. He reached back to the stack before him and picked up twenty dollar chips, which he dropped on number six. 'That's the lucky number, sweetheart.

Watch.' He leaned heavily on Ann, as the wheel spun, as the ball spun, slowly, more slowly, then dropped into number six. 'There you are!' he cried. 'Seven hundred smackeroos! And that bastard wanted to keep me out of the game!'

'Now, why don't you take it off and cash it in?' Ann asked.

'Are you kidding? I'm just even. I'm here to *make* money.' Another customer handed him a drink. 'Thanks, friend. Gotta send spies. They cut me off at the bar. Just as soon as I break the bank, I'm complaining to the management.'

'Ken, listen . . .'

'You listen. You watch. Didn't you see that last one? Old number six? It'll pay again. It'll pay until midnight.' The luck riders listened and patterned their next bets after his. 'It's my lucky day.' He drained his glass and set it aside.

'I'll go and get Janet,' Ann said.

'No, you won't, not yet. You see,' he said, dropping his voice to a loud whisper, 'she doesn't like this place. She doesn't like it at all; so I'm going to surprise her. I'm going to win a lot of money. Then I'm going to take it up to the big man himself, and I'm going to say. "Here you are, you bastard. Now gimme back my wife." ' He smiled happily at Ann and did not notice his bets being swept off the board. 'But it's a surprise.'

Ann caught sight of Jerry, standing at the edge of the crowd. She mouthed, 'Go get Janet,' at him, and he turned away quickly.

'Oops. The cowboy's after my money again, but it can't last, ladies and gentlemen. Just have a little faith and follow me. This is my lucky day.' He no longer placed his chips. They fell from his hand. In three turns of the wheel, he had only twenty dollar chips left in front of him. 'Now comes the payoff. With this stack of chips, ladies and gentlemen, I intend to quit fooling around.' He put all his chips on number six. 'Black six of August has to win.'

'Ken!'

He raised his head from where it rested against Ann's hair and focused dimly on his wife. Bill and Jerry stood right behind her.

'Shh . . . honey . . . shh.'

'Ken!' Janet took hold of his arm.

'Oh, Christ!' he said, as the ball dropped into number seven. 'It's past midnight after all. That's the only trouble, ladies and gentlemen. Like the sign says, if you play long enough, you'll lose.'

'Ken.'

He seemed to see Janet now for the first time. He looked down at her, bewildered.

'What about Kenny, darling?'

'He's all right, honey,' he said softly. 'He's dead.'

Ann turned to Bill and Jerry. 'Help her get him out of here.'

– 5 –

Evelyn fell awake as the front door closed. She checked the time by the luminous dial of her travel clock. It was four thirty. Ann came uncertainly up the stairs. The bathroom door closed quietly. The rush of water from the tap muted the sound of violent wretching. Evelyn sat up in bed, turned on the light, and lit a cigarette. It could not be a simple miscalculation of the number of drinks. Ann hadn't had time to make such a mistake. In just a little over an hour, she would have had to be willful to get so drunk. The toilet flushed. The water was turned off, then on again. Ann was brushing her teeth. Evelyn got up, put on a robe, and combed her hair. She had accepted Ann's awkward, unhappy evasiveness for a week, waiting for her to recover from rage at Virginia's suicide attempt or from embarrassment about their conversation at Geiger Point or from a mood of defensiveness vaguer and more general than Evelyn could identify and understand. But Ann was not recovering. She was getting worse. Evelyn could stand it no longer. She did not know what she would do, but she had to make some kind of obvious gesture. When she heard the bathroom door open, she opened her own.

'Do you need a towel?'

Ann laughed softly. 'How thoughtful. Thank you. How are you this morning?' She came into the room carefully, squinting against the light. She had washed off her makeup and had splashed water over her hair and down the front of her shirt. Her face was white and blurred with fatigue. She took the towel Evelyn handed her and then sat down heavily in the armchair by the window. 'Nice of you to be awake.'

'You probably ought to go right up to bed,' Evelyn said.

'Nonsense. I'm much too drunk to go to bed.'

'How did you get drunk so quickly?'

'Not so quickly. I started on the sly early in the day. It's my day off. I can celebrate.'

'Because tomorrow's Thursday?'

'Today's Thursday. At midnight, when all the stages turned into pumpkins, when the horses turned into rats, when not only little natural Gasella but all the people at the party turned into paupers, the place was lousy with glass slippers. Then the real miracle occurred: Wednesday turned into Thursday. Every midnight is a fairy tale, the end of one.'

'So you celebrate every night.'

'No. This is special. Today I'm celebrating the death of Kenneth Hearle, junior, aged two and a half, on Wednesay, August sixth, survived by his parents, grandparents, and great-grandparents, and God knows how many other relatives and wellwishers.'

'Janet's baby?'

'Janet's ex-baby. Please do not send flowers. Donations to a fund to pay the surgeon's fee for a successful heart operation may be addressed to . . .'

'Thank God,' Evelyn said quietly. It was over then.

'Oh, I intend to. I intend to. Mind you, I think He's a bit late. Two and a half years and several thousand dollars ago, it might have been more useful. But I'm a practical sort. I'd like to send a donation to the anti-heart fund for research on how to stop it quickly and cheaply. And we must write a poem. Have you got a newspaper? They have poems ready-made, just like TV dinners. A three-course grief with rhymed gravy. I bet Frances has a bottle downstairs.'

'I have one right here,' Evelyn said.

'Are you a secret drinker? I wouldn't have thought so, but then I'm easily deceived. I can even deceive myself.'

'Do you want a drink?'

'No, I don't want a drink.'

'Coffee?'

'No! Sober me up and I can't be sad.'

'Why not?'

'At the Club we have a name for people who bet with a man who's winning. We call them luck riders. I'm a grief rider. I have all this capacity for grief and nothing of my own to grieve about.'

'You don't grieve. You rage.'

'Do I? Well, I shouldn't. There's nothing wrong with the world.'

'Are you serious?'

'Quite. If drunk. I'll tell you a secret. I don't believe in the signs, not really. But then I don't gamble either. I have a sign of my own: "If you don't play, you can't lose." It's not a mass philosophy, you understand.'

'I don't think I do understand.'

'Oh yes you do,' Ann said, getting up out of the chair slowly. 'And, what's more, you approve. Never mind. Why don't we go to Pyramid Lake tomorrow afternoon?'

'Ask me again when you wake up.'

'No,' Ann said firmly. 'I don't want the chance to change my mind.'

'Do you think you'll want to?'

Ann gave Evelyn a long, significant, not quite focused look, intended to make her laugh. 'My tragedy is comedy,' she said. 'I'm in love with the whole damned world. The only problem is maintaining aesthetic distance. You're elegant at it.'

'Am I? Yes, I suppose I am.' Evelyn held the door open. 'Get some sleep.'

Ann went off, singing softly:

109

'The other night our baby died
It neither cried nor hollered.
It lived but twenty hours.
It cost us forty dollars.
It was a lousy baby anyhow.
We didn't like it anyhow.
It died but for to spite us,
Of spinal meningitis.'

Evelyn closed the door, cautious and regretful. Simple comfort was something you could not offer without risk to anyone but a small child. Yet adults needed it, too. Where were they to get it? From lovers. From children. If you had neither? Did you learn to live without it? She had learned. By now she was 'elegant' at maintaining aesthetic distance from suffering and from delight that were not her own. 'If you don't play, you can't lose.' She did understand. She did approve, didn't she? Ann was making melodrama of a death that did not belong to her. She was right to make fun of herself. But there was passion in the sparring, grieving, angry comic that had to find an acceptable disguise somewhere between sentimentality and brutality so that the world could decorously and sympathetically respond. She was just too truthful to make a success of it.

'Must I be careful?'

Evelyn snapped out the light and walked away from the question to the window, where she lifted the shade. The tree-defined patch of dawn was sea-gray, oddly oppressive, the tentative predication of a storm. Ann might be forced to change her mind about Pyramid Lake. Evelyn felt a quick, protesting disappointment. She very much wanted a fair day.

The morning suffered only a fitful overcast. Above the city, the sky was occasionally quite blue, and by early afternoon the sun had consumed any alien possibility of rain. Evelyn worked, for the first time really grateful for

110

the heat. The weather could break some other day.

Ann knocked at her door at three o'clock. She was dressed in pedal pushers. Her hair was freshly washed. Her eyes had a young clarity of recent heavy sleep.

'Well, you look quite recovered.'

'I am,' Ann said. 'Did I ask you to go to Pyramid Lake today?'

'You did.'

'And did you accept?'

'I told you to ask me again when you woke up.'

'I see,' Ann said and then paused with mock thoughtfulness. 'Well, I'm awake. Will you come?'

'Yes.'

'Frances is packing a picnic supper for us. You'll have to change. Have you got slacks and a suit?'

'Yes.'

'And some sort of jacket. There's sometimes a wind in the evening.'

Ann's energy quickened the ordinary preparations into importance and pleasure. She teased extra pieces of chicken from Frances, chose towels to match bathing suits, and sent Evelyn to the attic for a book of particular poems, Eliot if she liked or Auden, but not Thomas, not Frost. Their landscapes suffered in this particular out-of-doors. Her gaiety had only a slight brittleness about it, as if she remembered but refused to include her tiredness and her angry, uncertain grief of the night before.

Evelyn took her mood from Ann. As they drove through the outskirts of the town and arrived at the desert's edge, she did not allow herself the reluctance and vague dread that threatened her. Instead, she was determinedly curious, observant, gay. Ann listened, answered, and turned sometimes to Evelyn, her eyes easily forsaking the straight, empty road before them.

'They say, wherever the sage grows in abundance, the soil is very rich. If there were water, this whole valley would be valuable farmland. Around Salt Lake City, the

111

Mormons did irrigate, of course; but they had the rivers.'

'And the vision?' Evelyn suggested.

'Perhaps. But Mormons settled in this part of the country, too. In some of the little towns, like Genoa, Mormon houses are the historic sites. I'll take you there some time. The Mormons started duplex building in the west, a different front door for each wife. But they couldn't manage here. It's no place for the God-fearing visionary. The men who stayed either knew they were damned or didn't believe in damnation. It's still so.'

'What category are you in?'

'I?' Ann turned to Evelyn. 'I don't know. One of the damned, I suppose. It's hard not to believe in an Old Testament sort of world. Fire and brimstone have weathered some four hundred towns into dust already. Every place is a Sodom or Gomorrah: it's only a matter of time, and very little time at that. The faithful say the plain was well watered, even as the Garden of the Lord, before He destroyed the cities. I don't believe it. There was never water here, not fresh water.'

'But you love the whole damned world,' Evelyn said, 'or so you claimed last night.'

Ann smiled. 'Yes, I do. The desert seems to me the simple truth about the world.'

'What simple truth?'

'The earth's given out. Men can't get a living from it. They have to get it from each other. We can't have what we need, but we can take what we want. It's true everywhere. Here it's easy to see.'

'I don't agree,' Evelyn said. 'Everywhere is not a desert.'

'But the desert's beautiful,' Ann said. 'Look.'

Reluctant, Evelyn watched the place of Ann's vision, a wind-shaped land of dry, muted grays, tans, and greens. But, as Evelyn looked, she forced herself to see, too, a bolder ochre, a deep orange, an almost clear blue-green. The wind took up the tumbleweed which rode the stubble

112

of sage like the shadows of clouds. The sky was clear, and the scent of sage, sharp in the heat, gave even the dust a kind of clarity. The road cut straight across the uneven floor of the plain, its line never broken because it continually merged with its own horizons, but in the unexpected pockets were sudden views. The car rushed up a rise of land to the crest of a subtle hill, and there at the center of the endless desert was a vast body of water.

'Ann!' Evelyn cried. 'Stop!'

Ann pulled the car off the road. Below them, a mile away, the southern shore of the lake was a long, straight line, bone-white against a blue so deep it seemed the night of the day sky. Five miles away, the land rose again in severe steps of rock, not so much shaped by as ascending, escaping from the water. To the left and north, the far shore disappeared. The water met and closed with the sky.

'How big is it?' Evelyn asked.

'I don't know. Bigger than Tahoe. Around thirty miles long, I should think.'

'But there's nothing here.'

'No, nothing but an Indian reservation to the east (we're actually on reservation ground now) and a couple of gas stations and grocery stores on the road going north. People talk about developing the Lake. I suppose some day they will.'

'But there aren't any trees.'

'No. Not even sage. Nothing can grow. The water's alkaline. Lovely for swimming.'

Evelyn wanted to refuse. She wanted Ann to turn the car around and drive back to Reno, which, alien and hostile as it might be, was at least human. There was no way Evelyn could comprehend this unnatural, dead body of water, still, killing, blue. Yet she could not ask to leave. She lacked both the courage and the cruelty to refuse. As Ann drove the car down toward the edge of the Lake, Evelyn sat, silent with apprehension. They traveled along

113

the paved road to the east for a while, then turned off on to rutted sand which took them to within two hundred yards of the water.

'Can you take the towels and blanket?' Ann asked, her voice thrown past Evelyn by the wind. 'I'll take the food.'

They labored across the barren, burning dunes to a small sandcliff edge, where Ann told Evelyn to wait. As Anne disappeared over the side, Evelyn stepped closer to the edge to keep her in sight. There only twelve feet below was a narrow curve of beach, flat, hard and white with a kind of crude sand. Ann left the picnic basket and ran back up the shifting sand to help Evelyn down. The beach itself was sheltered by the cliff from the wind and from the sun and from the view of the unending shore line. In that great openness of water, desert, and sky, it was curiously private; but the security kit provided was, for Evelyn, a frail illusion. She was, nevertheless, grateful for it. She set the blanket and towels down almost against the cliff itself, twenty feet from the water, and sat down to watch Ann who had kicked off her shoes and was wading out from the shore to plant a bottle of wine.

'The water's marvelous,' Ann said, as she came back. 'It's a curiously gentle lake.'

Evelyn reached out nervously for a handful of rough sand. As she looked down as it slipped through her fingers, she caught at it suddenly.

'This isn't sand at all.'

'No,' Ann said, kneeling beside her. 'They're tiny shells.'

White snail shells, no bigger than the head of a pin, caught along the lines of Evelyn's palm. She studied them with uncertain wonder, then looked up at the beach itself, white with billions of dwarf deaths, free fossil washed, yes, gently, into petrified rhythms along the shore.

'Isn't it beautiful?' Ann asked.

'I suppose it is,' Evelyn said. 'Don't other people come here?'

'Occasionally, but not right here. I don't know why people don't come. Everybody goes to Tahoe, I guess. I'm glad. I like miles to myself.'

Evelyn watched Ann almost enviously. Was she really innocent enough that she could leave the world behind? 'You could almost imagine there were no other people,' Evelyn said.

'Yes,' Ann said. 'Almost.' She stood up and began to unbutton her shirt. 'If we're going to swim, we should. In another couple of hours, it will be too cold.'

Evelyn did not want to move. She could not imagine walking into the water of her own free will. Why was she so frightened? Irritated with herself, she stood up and reached for her suit. Ann, more quickly changed, waited for her at the edge of the water. Evelyn walked out of the shade of the cliff into the sun. She would not refuse.

'Ready?'

Evelyn smiled. Something of Ann's young animal eagerness touched her own memory. Evelyn had been a good swimmer, and even now, though her body had adopted the mannerisms appropriate to settled middle age, it was strong and capable. The water, as she looked right down at it, was clear and shallow, innocent somehow of its own great size. When she stepped into it, the quick shock of its coldness startled her into pleasure. She wanted to swim.

They did not swim together. Ann chose a solitude far out from shore. Evelyn swam near the edge, beyond the curve of cliff to another beach, longer and more open to the view. She grew braver, more curious, and her body, released from a long stillness of work, relaxed in the rhythm of pure, physical energy. When she finally turned and swam back to the small, private beach, Ann was already on the shore.

'You're a beautiful swimmer,' Ann said.

'I used to be. It's been years since I've done anything more than play in the surf.' She took the towel Ann

115

handed her. 'I wonder why.'

Ann spread the blanket out nearer the water in the sun. 'It's not too hot now. Are you thirsty? There's wine, coffee, or water.'

'Water? What an odd, good idea!'

Evelyn stretched out on the blanket on her back. The muscles in her arms and legs were tired, but the sun warmed and quickened her blood.

'I feel simply marvelous,' she said, as Ann lay down beside her.

'It's nice here.'

'I'm glad I came. An hour ago I wasn't sure.'

'Why not?'

'The desert frightens me, I think. It looks too much like the seventh circle of hell. I'm afraid of damnation.'

'Why?'

'Why?' Evelyn repeated, peering at Ann from behind her hand. She lay back again and closed her eyes. 'I don't know. I've always supposed everyone is.'

'Well, they're not. I, for instance, am a hell of a lot more frightened of being saved.'

Evelyn chuckled.

'I'm serious,' Ann protested. 'Virtue smells to me of rotting vegetation. Here you burn or freeze. Either way it's clean.'

'Sterile,' Evelyn said and felt the word a laceration of her own flesh.

'I wonder. It's fertility that's a dirty word for me.'

'Is it?'

'Yes, I'm terrified of giving in, of justifying my own existence by means of simple reproduction. So many people do or try to. And there are the children, so unfulfilling after all. And they grow up to do nothing but reproduce children who will reproduce, everyone so busy reproducing that there's no time to produce anything. But it's such a temptation. It seems so natural – another dirty word for me. What's the point?'

'You'd have the human race die out?'

'No. We'll multiply in spite of ourselves always. We'll populate the desert. One day there will be little houses and docks all along this shore, signs of our salvation.'

'What would you have us do instead?' Evleyn asked.

'Accept damnation,' Ann said. 'It has its power and its charm. And it's real.'

'So we should all get jobs in gambling casinos.'

'We all do,' Ann said, her voice amused. 'What do you think the University of California is? It's just a minor branch of the Establishment. The only difference is that it has to be subsidized.'

'Are you talking nonsense on purpose?'

'No, I'm serious.'

'You think nothing has any value?'

'No, I think everything has value, absolute value, a child, a house, a day's work, the sky. But nothing will save us. We were never meant to be saved.'

'What were we meant for then?'

'To love the whole damned world,' Ann said, delighted. ' "In the destructive element immerse." Perhaps there's some truth in it. I might learn. I don't know. I'm old to learn. And I'm not sure I'd like a world without guilt or goodness. It might seem very empty.'

'Like the desert?'

'Yes,' Evelyn said.

She lay quiet then, the sun a dark heat against her closed eyes. She felt Ann turn and sit up. Guarding her face from the glare with her hand, Evelyn opened her eyes. Ann was looking down at her.

'Have you ever been special assistant to the Dean?'

'No,' Evelyn said.

As Ann bent down toward her, Evelyn took hold of the soft damp hair at the back of Ann's neck and held her away. But, as Evelyn looked at the face held back from her own, the rain-grey eyes, the fine bones, the mouth, she felt the weight and length of Ann's body measuring her

117

own. Her hand relaxed its hold, all her flesh welcoming the long embrace. But simple physical desire could not silence her recovering brain. Slowly, carefully, almost painfully, she turned Ann's weight in her arms until she could withdraw.

'I live in the desert of the heart,' Evelyn said quietly. 'I can't love the whole damned world.'

'Love me, Evelyn.'

'I do.'

'But you don't want me?'

Evelyn looked at Ann, the child she had always wanted, the friend she had once had, the lover she had never considered. Of course she wanted Ann. Pride, morality, and inexperience had kept her from admitting it frankly to herself from the first moment she had seen Ann. Guilt and goodness must now keep her from admitting it to Ann.

'No relationship is without erotic feeling,' Evelyn said. She had heard it somewhere at a cocktail party, an academic cocktail party. Someone else had added, as she added now, 'But that doesn't necessarily mean it has to be acted upon.' Ann looked away. 'I'm sorry, Ann.'

Evelyn wanted to say something else, to explain, to justify. 'I'm married, Ann,' she wanted to say. 'I mustn't. I can't.' But George could hardly save her now. He was not even a conventional excuse. 'I don't know anything about this sort of thing,' she wanted to say, but it was not true. If she had never actually made love to another woman, she was intellectually emancipated in all perversions of flesh, mind, and spirit. Her academic training had seen to that. 'Forgive me, Ann,' she might say; but Evelyn did not really want to be forgiven.

She sat up and stared across the lake to the naked rock of the northern shore, to the sky which only a few moments ago had ben a clear, empty blue.

'Is that a storm blowing up?'

'Maybe. Maybe not. It's pretty far away.' A fresh damp

gust of wind came in off the water. 'We probably ought to eat. Are you hungry?'

'Yes, I think I am,' Evelyn said.

She watched Ann wade out for the bottle of wine, that young, beautiful body she had so carefully admired an hour ago to take her mind off the terrors of the landscape. Its sudden erotic power bewildered and offended her, whose taste and decorum usually governed her private thoughts as firmly as they governed her public living. Evelyn blushed with impatience and embarrassment. Physical response was no more significant than a hiccup, a sneeze, a twinge of gas, functional disorders which caused discomfort but not alarm. If she were to mistrust her own psychic health and morality every time she crossed her legs during the ballet or the reading of a French novel, she would keep a psychiatrist and a minister as busy as a hypochondriac keeps a doctor. It was not important. To exaggerate a single kiss into significant guilt was a real loss of aesthetic distance. And Ann was not a child. It was no traumatic experience for her. Ann had found the bottle and was wading ashore. She did not force her steps. She moved with a slow, unconscious grace. Evelyn turned away and looked for a cigarette.

'Are you getting cold?' Ann asked. 'Shall we change?'

'I'll just throw a jacket over my shoulders.'

Their conversation, during the meal, was desultory and inconsequential. Ann was being entertaining. Evelyn, reluctant to ask Ann to control the situation, was nevertheless grateful to be moved in time and mood farther and farther away from the moment. Suddenly, near lightning startled them both, and, as the first large drops of rain fell on the beach, they hurriedly gathered their belongings and started toward the car, leaving their unimportant intimacy like a scrap of paper on the empty beach.

'May I drive?' Evelyn asked, as they reached the car.

119

'Sure, if you like,' Ann said, handing her the keys.

The wheel, firm and restricting in Evelyn's hands, gave her back a simple feeling of authority and independence. She was in control, and she had an excuse to keep her eyes away from the vast expanse of desert, away from Ann, carefully on the long, straight road back to Reno. Evelyn wanted to keep the storm behind them. Her foot hard on the accelerator, she drove toward the sunlight to the south, toward the open blue of the sky, but it was a losing race. The storm bellied over them, beyond them. Rain and wind struck the car at the same moment, knocking it almost off the road. Evelyn held the wheel firm in her memory of where the road had been. She could not see. Ann reached for the windshield wipers.

'A real cloud burst.'

Evelyn nodded, driving more slowly, leaning forward to see, playing the car against blasts of wind that seemed to come from every direction. She was not at all frightened now. The storm was a simple force that could be met and challenged, a welcome violation of the desert. Even the skidding gravel and the sudden disappearance of the road could not shake her confidence. Then, as they dropped over the crest of a hill, the rain stopped, and before them was a valley of brilliant, burning sunlight, arched with rainbows, edged with lightning. Its beauty broke into Evelyn's vision like an explosion.

'This is the desert of the heart,' Ann said quietly.

'No!' Evelyn said, refusing to shout because she refused to lose control of herself.

She held the car steady through the awful sunlight and back into the storm. As they reached the outskirts of Reno in the full night of the storm, the culverts that had been dry three hours before roared with water. Low places in the road were flooded. Evelyn drove slowly, watching the red brake lights of the car ahead, which wavered through the watery darkness like giant fireflies.

'This is the most incredible place,' she said quietly,

naïve most incredible world.'

'Is it?'

'I've never seen a storm like this.'

'You've been driving it like a veteran.'

'Well, I did get us here, didn't I?'

'With determination,' Ann said, laughing.

'I want a good, stiff drink when we get home.'

'You shall have one.'

A drink muted the desperation of Evelyn's confidence. Sitting in the living room with both Frances and Ann, she began to relax into the decorous kindness and self-possession that was her habit, but, when Walter came in, she used his arrival to achieve her own departure. She went to her room, which was so familiar as well as impersonal, cell and sanctuary, a comfort as ambiguous as her work which she turned to at once. She read until she was ready to sleep.

Evelyn's dreams that night were literally pedestrian. Childhood playmates, half-forgotten acquaintances, college friends, several quite unlikely colleagues, walked casually and continuously through the peculiar, storm-shadowed sunlight on great crosses of pavement, cruci-fixes like airstrips flattened against the desert. They said nothing. They did nothing but walk up and down the hours of the night, limited by patterns of concrete. Evelyn was not in her dreams. She witnessed them as if her vision encompassed the world, and she was aware that she had created it; yet she could not, or would not, feel responsible for it. As she recognized one after another among the girl children, the young women, the aging female relatives, each seemed to merge with an image of Ann. Then Ann had the face of Carol. All the figures were Carol, and words which were neither seen nor heard thought themselves into the landscape, creating it again: 'This is the desert of the heart.' Evelyn, distant, omniscient sleeper, stirred in disbelief, woke in protest.

At once she had a perfect knowledge of the dreams'

121

significance, followed by a perfect contempt for the lies they told. With love she had condemned no one but George to a wasteland. These dozens of females, Carol-faced and Ann-bodied, were aberrations of an overactive and naïve conscience, a ridiculous melodrama of the psyche.

But Evelyn's mind, informed, logical, and ruthless, could not quite destroy the image of the dreams. All day she struggled through desolation toward an oasis of work, and she did not arrive. It was her mind that betrayed her with fragments of other visions, world of words juxtaposed. Out of them she involuntarily composed a hollow woman prayer of her own, rhetorical, mocking, terrible, from the *Twenty-Third Psalm*, *The Inferno*, and *The Second Coming*.

'It's your Sunday school morality that drives me up the wall,' George said. 'You're so God-damned sure of yourself you don't even have to believe in God.'

She kept her back to him and went on kneading the bread dough.

'You have the I.Q. to go mad but not the emotional courage.'

She went out the back door to get the clothes off the line.

'All intelligent women are latent homosexuals. I like you in trousers.'

She was on her knees, weeding the garden.

'They say husbands often have their wives' nervous breakdowns. I wonder if I'm going through yours.'

She was ironing his shirts.

'You're so kind to me, so forgiving. If only you could be generous enough to have sins of your own, I could forgive you.'

Surely guilt and goodness will follow me all the days of my life unless I can dwell in the desert forever. For Thine is the ... City of Dis, the River of Blood, the Wood, the Burning Sand. There is no beast to wake. There is only yesterday's empty cradle relieving no one of the future. They are innocent, these suicides, profligates, blasphemers, sodomites, and usurers, against whom God, Nature, and Art have been violent. Only the good can be guilty. And surely guilt and goodness will follow me all the days of my life unless I can dwell in the desert forever, a voluntary exile, a permanent resident.

'But I can't,' Evelyn said aloud. 'And it isn't necessary. At the end, I can go. At the end, I'm free.'

She would not cluster fragments of memory into fixed shapes of fear and failure. If she had been wrong before, the error was in her nature, not in her will. She had never excused herself. She had never indulged her weaknesses as if they were needs. Surely she could not be judged for a nature her will had never consented to. She had been good.

'I have been good.'

But wrong, over and over again, wearing one ill-fitting uniform after another of the world's conventions. The only dress that ever suited her was her academic gown, but it was hardly appropriate for the daily occasions of her living. She could not be a wife with a wardrobe for parades.

'I should never have gone back to the university at all.'

But what else could she have done? Clumsy, terrified of machinery, she had spent one month, overalled and goggled in a shipyard, making an incredible amount of money that she did not need. A signed letter of protest to the *San Francsico Chronicle* about the treatment of the American Japanese lost her a more reasonable job with the government. She had finally settled on volunteer work at Oak Knoll Naval Hospital where she spent her days writing angry, apologetic loveletters for armless and eyeless sailors. The evenings she spent sitting at the desk in her one-room apartment, writing love letters of her own to George, her old friend and new husband, somewhere in the Pacific. Or she visited next door with

Carol and the baby. She often wrote to George about the baby. She knew it was silly, but, after she had talked about the books she had been reading, there was not very much else to say. They had both overwritten the past until speaking of it was like rehearsing a play after the production is over. And each of them was reluctant and superstitious about speaking of the future. They had to write of a suspended present, of which most of the details were either censorable or not interesting enough to record. The only person with whom Evelyn could share the unimportance of her day was Carol, who like Evelyn, only waited for the war to be over. If Carol had gone on waiting, perhaps Evelyn would have, too.

'What else could I have done?'

Carol, standing there, saying in so flat a voice, 'It's happened.'

'What?'

'Sam's dead.'

Evelyn had gone back to Carol's apartment with her. They had sat together, waiting for grief. It had taken time, but they were patient, and when it came, Carol did not really weep. She began to rock herself gently and then to wail, high in her throat, like a distant singing. Evelyn sat beside her, an arm around her shoulder, letting her rock, letting her croon her song of disaster into the early hours of the mild California morning until the factory whistles screamed in the day.

'You must sleep now,' Evelyn said.

She undressed Carol and put her to bed. She could not stop rocking. She would not stop wailing. Finally Evelyn changed into one of Carol's nightgowns and lay down beside her.

'Sleep now.'

Carol turned into Evelyn's arms, her face pressing against Evelyn's breast. As she began to suck, the rocking and wailing stopped. Evelyn looked down at the infant grief she held in her arms. She rested a hand on Carol's

124

temple and watched over her long after she had fallen asleep, Evelyn's own grieving sympathy turning slowly into rage.

For this curled need in her arms could be the end of waiting, months and years wasted in longing until, at last, the desire for comfort and nourishment could be nothing more than a perversion of the flesh, a blind sucking. Carol would wake, and in decorous forgetfulness they would cancel out this night. The baby would also wake, his need reason enough for the day. But, if George were to die, what day could Evelyn wake to? What day did she wake to even now, the meaning of her life dependent on a man she had not seen and would not see for months, might never see again? There was no role to play. There was no marriage. Not now at this moment. And this moment was all there might be for her or for George or for anyone. If George were teaching, if George were writing a book, his coffee, his shirts, his card catalogues would be purpose enough for Evelyn. But he was not teaching and writing. He was on an island somewhere, waiting to kill or to be killed. He could not help it. She could not help him. Even his underwear was the business of the United States Government.

'Then I'll teach. I'll write. I'll make a world for you.'

She had been wrong. It was not a world for George. It was a world for herself, but she had not meant it so.

That first week after Sam's death a letter had arrived from George. Evelyn did not know what to do with it. She went to her own apartment almost guiltily, not so much to find privacy to read the letter as to hide it from Carol, but Carol followed her into the room.

'Letter from George?' she asked. 'It's all right. I had one from Sam, too. Even dying takes a while by mail. I wonder how many more will come.'

'George isn't dead,' Evelyn said angrily.

'I'm sorry,' Carol said. 'Evelyn, I'm sorry.'

They had forgiven each other, but their absent

husbands, who had once made up a part of their friendship, became an awkwardness between them, Sam forming the large letters of his canceled future, George minutely and conservatively reporting the present. Carol, for Evelyn's sake, did not speak of Sam, and Evelyn, for Carol's sake, did not speak of George. The silence gave the two women a reserve that perhaps protected them from an intimacy they did not quite forget and did not really wish to remember; and it may also have helped Carol to give up her memory of Sam. It forced Evelyn to move George from the center of her concern into the few quiet corners of the day that she could save. At first, she had found it difficult, but gradually, after she had returned to the university and was busy with teaching and preparing for her PhD examinations, George's minor role in her life seemed quite natural. She had, after all, lived with him only several months before he had gone overseas. Before that she had been a student. A student again, working in a world she understood and valued, Evelyn was really very happy.

With the baby, Carol could not work, but she needed money. Evelyn needed time; so she paid the grocery bill, and Carol did the cooking. It was pleasant to come home to a meal already prepared, to see the baby, to tell the day, and then to settle to work. Sometimes Carol went out. Evelyn enjoyed that, too, for often, when she was alone with the baby, she allowed herself to imagine her own children.

There was nothing unusual in the relationship between Evelyn and Carol. It grew out of affection and circumstance. There must have been relationships like it all over the country, young women separated from their families and friends, separated from their husbands, living at the quiet edge of oceans, waiting together. When the men began to come home, first from the Atlantic, then from the Pacific, there was enough joy and relief and inexperience to cover regret. Carol married again just a

126

month before George came home and moved east with her new husband. Evelyn might have been lonely if her own future had not been immediate.

Nothing unusual. Nothing at all. Except, perhaps, that single night. And surely grief excused the blind, passionate needs of the flesh. For the rest, the moment of unacknowledged tenderness and vague desire, the unconsenting will must surely ransome nature. And, if Evelyn sometimes looked back on that year with Carol, remembering ease and delight, it was no betrayal of George. Evelyn simply accepted the new knowledge that friendship is a happier, less significant relationship than marriage. And one she would prefer? It was not a thought she allowed herself. George had said, after he had been out of work for six months, 'What you need is a wife, not a husband. That's what I should try to be.' Perhaps it was true. At the time, Evelyn could not have admitted it. She not only worked but insisted on doing all the jobs around the house. She cooked like a farmer's wife, baking her own bread, canning. She would not send even the sheets to the laundry, and, though she loathed sewing, she made her own clothes. If she could not bear a child, there were a hundred other conventions through which she could prove she was a woman. And George would never have played wife. They were very alike really, she and George. He had frenzies of building cupboards, mending the roof, chopping wood. They lived in the middle of Berkeley as if they were homesteading a thousand miles from civilization. Yet nothing they did could cancel the central failure each felt in himself and in the other.

'So we've given up. We've admitted it. I've admitted it. What difference can anything make now?'

As some people cannot smoke, as others are poisoned by alcohol, Evelyn could no more than entertain despair as a habit of mind. Even as she scorned the old image of herself, she could not give it up until she could find another to replace it. And, though her mind admitted a number of possibilities, her imagination continually faltered. Sitting across the dinner table from Ann, Evelyn studied her with the intensity and distance she might have given a painting. What she saw was no longer an imperfect reflection of herself but an alien otherness she was drawn to and could not understand.

Evelyn did not know any longer who she was. Perhaps she had never known. Perhaps her identity had always been made up of bits and pieces of other people, her thumbs, her collarbone, her ears, her left-handedness, even the tones of her voice dictated by the random and absolute coupling of genes. Her tastes and her moods had been handed down to her from a great uncle, a second cousin, a father. Not exactly handed down. Everyone was the common property of inheritance. The self was, surely, the will that shaped the arbitrary and meaningless fragments into identity. The will chose. Or was it, too, dictated to by an inherited morality?

'But my particular bones refuse my will.'

Mistaken then. Badly mistaken. The will? Or the nature?

'I don't know.'

The will bakes bread the nature chokes on. The nature turns the wheel the will breaks on.

'I don't know.'

If there is no face in the mirror, marry. If there is no shadow on the ground, have a child. These are the conventions the will consents to. But there is a face. There is a shadow. They are simply unsuitable.

'I'm a case of mistaken identity.'

So is George? So are we all? When we are children, emulating the giants, being little men and little women; when we are grown emulating the dwarfs, being little people. But we are not petty, George with his unpaid-for machinery, I with my cookbooks and clothespins. There is no house big enough to contain our failure. We should be granted tragic space.

128

'The desert,' Evelyn said quietly. 'But I'm afraid. I'm afraid of damnation.'

It was a fear duller than the first involuntary vision of the empty desert. Her dreams had since populated it with so many people she knew, and Ann was, in fact, so at home in it that Evelyn felt her reaction shifting from her glands to her mind where fear, in a negative morality, could be called cowardice and then should be overcome.

In a week, fragments of poems, desire and tiredness, worked against fear and guilt until Evelyn had established a new, tentative and precarious balance between what she called nature and will. It was the same distance she restored between experience and understanding, but the way between was different. The moral landscape had altered. Melodrama turned into quiet satire so that she could gently mock rather than furiously accuse and justify herself. Her habit of reserve remained.

Ann did not challenge it. She was busy during the day, working in her room. In the evening she was taken up with her job and her friends at the Club. And, though a tiredness still sometimes stained her face, she was not tense and restless as she had been. Her conversation at the dinner table was amiable and affectionate. She was kind to Frances, gentle with Walter, casual and careful with Evelyn.

'I'm going Christmas shopping tomorrow afternoon,' Ann said to Evelyn on Wednesday night. 'Would you like to come?'

'Christmas shopping at this time of year?'

'I have to get packages off to Vietnam and Korea and Hong Kong right away. The deadline for Greece and Italy is only a month away. I thought I'd do it all at once.'

'For the children, I see. What kind of things do you get?'

'Clothes, mostly, and a few canned foods. I always put in a toy or two and school supplies as well.'

'I'd love to go,' Evelyn said.

The excursion, unlike those of the previous two Thursdays, presented no problems.

They set out right after lunch. Ann had a list for each child, which included measurements and sizes, fifty dollars in cash, and a plan for shopping. In the boys' department at Penney's, they stood together, Evelyn measuring the waists of khaki shorts, the legs of blue jeans, the shoulders of T-shirts, Ann feeling materials, examining stitching, matching colors.

'No loud patterns,' Evelyn said to the clerk. 'Plain white or khaki or dark blue.' She had rehearsed the names and sizes so that she could say, 'It's too big for Kim, but it might do for Ming Kin,' and she had asked Ann about different climates so that she could say, 'That's too heavy a material for Hung, in long trousers anyway.'

Never so much interested in boy children, Evelyn was surprised at the delight of choosing among such ordinary clothes exactly the right size, color, and material. Each child, who had been only a name and a face in a photograph, became a person with special tastes and needs. Evelyn pronounced their names possessively, proudly, and asserted their individuality against the random suggestions of clerks. When the boys' clothes had been bought, they went to the girls' department. Here Evelyn had a more difficult time being practical. Carmela, dreaming of being a Hollywood movie star, would so love a bottle-green velvet, which was just her size, and there was a beautiful white sweater for Eftychia. While Ann looked for durable materials and dark colors, Evelyn lingered with extravagance. Once, when she looked up, she found Ann watching her.

'I'm being silly,' Evelyn said.

'It would be fun.'

'No, not when they need things so badly. But it's fun to think about.'

School supplies were even more of a temptation than clothes. Evelyn had never outgrown her childhood love of

130

erasers, paper clips, chalk, pencil boxes, and small pads of paper.

'Now remember,' Ann said, laughing at the handfuls of small treasures Evelyn was collecting, 'the parcels can't cost over ten dollars.'

'Oh, I know,' Evelyn said, 'but look at these stickers of birds. They're just ten cents.'

'Put them in then.'

They chose carefully among toys for the useful and educational. There were pocketknives and flashlights and scissors, map puzzles and picture books.

'We're running over our budget,' Ann said. 'We won't be able to put in any food, but it doesn't matter. I can send extra money. That's better anyway. They can get a lot more things they probably like better.'

'It's sad to be finished,' Evelyn said. 'I like feeling mother of all the world.'

'We're not finished. After dinner, we have to wrap everything up in Christmas paper. I like that even better than shopping.'

They sat on the floor in Ann's room, sorting their purchases. On Ann's worktable were five, sturdy cardboard boxes, stacks of newspaper, a box of Christmas wrapping paper.

'Oh, and I mustn't forget the photographs,' Ann said, getting up and opening a drawer.

'What are they?'

'A picture of me for each of them. They like pictures.'

'Let me see.' Evelyn held out her hand for the five small snapshots. 'When were these taken?'

'Three or four months ago.'

'Who's the man?'

'Bill, a friend of mine at the Club.'

'I like his face.'

Ann turned away to get the box of wrapping paper. 'Now, which ones do you want?'

'Carmela and Eftychia, may I?'

'Sure.'

'Or should I take one of the boys and one of the girls? That's what I'll do! Give me Hung, and you take Eftychia.'

Ann smiled. 'But the lovely thing about these children is that you can have favorites. You can even like girls better than boys (my preference in the adult world only), and no one will grow up with bad bathroom habits or unattractive aggressions. If anyone does, it isn't your fault. Childbirth without pain, Motherhood without guilt, Mother without child.' Ann paused. 'I wonder if I could get that: "Mother Without Child." If I got it, I couldn't sell it.'

'You know, I still haven't seen any of your cartoons.'

'Another night. We have work to do.'

Their wrappings were very different, Evelyn's careful and traditional, Ann's bold and handsomely shabby. She worked more quickly than Evelyn because she didn't stop to count, to admire, to compare, to play with. When she had finished two stacks of presents, she went downstairs for glasses and whiskey. They stopped for a drink.

'Where's Frances?' Evelyn asked.

'In bed with a book.'

'I should think she'd like to be in on this.'

'No. Didn't you notice at dinner? All the things she wasn't saying?'

'Like what?'

' "Charity begins at home." Or "People busy doing good have no time to be good." Or "Woman's place is in the home," her own, that is. She doesn't really believe any of it, but I just generally make her nervous.'

'She's devoted to you.'

'I love Frances, in an irritable sort of way.' Ann got up. 'I'll leave these last two piles for you, okay? I'll start packing the boxes.'

It was midnight when they stacked the five parcels, complete with customs declarations, on Ann's worktable.

Ann poured them another drink, and they sat down on the bed together and surveyed the untidy gaiety of scraps of tissue paper, scattered stickers, bits of ribbon. Evelyn reached down to pick things up.

'Don't bother. I'll do that in the morning. I like the mess.'

'What an extraordinary, ordinary day,' Evelyn said, leaning back against the wall, 'like bringing water to a picnic.'

'Tired?'

'Not exactly. Are you?'

"No,' Ann said.

'You look terribly uncomfortable.'

'I am. I like standing up or lying down.'

'Lie down then. Here, I'll move.'

Ann turned her head, awkwardly propped against the wall, and looked at Evelyn.

'I sometimes think I can forecast the weather in your eyes,' Evelyn said.

'What's your prediction?'

'Hot and clear.'

'I want you,' Ann said.

'I want you.'

And, if you can't have what you need, you take what you want. Accept damnation. It has its power and its charm. You love the whole damned world in the alien, not quite accurate image of yourself.

'Take off your clothes.'

'Turn off the light.'

Then, among the unseen scraps of Christmas paper, in the close heat of an attic room, with blind, gentle precision you take for its own sake the grotesque miracle of love.

Evelyn lay back, Ann asleep against her right shoulder. She stared at the dark shapes of parcels on the drawing table. Christmas Eve for the Mother without Child. She must have the emotional courage to go mad. It had taken

133

only three weeks. Virginia Ritchie in three weeks had slashed her wrists, a transient despair to save her life. Evelyn could not despair. Then she could not be saved. She looked down at Ann's young, sleeping body.

'Damn the will then,' she said softly. 'I don't want to be saved. I want you.'

– 6 –

Ann woke alone, saw the parcels on the drawing table, saw the Christmas wrappings on the floor, then turned into the space where Evelyn had lain and closed her eyes again. She did not sleep. She breathed a new fragrance, which was not so much sexual as personal, a faint perfume on her own arms, in her own hair. She felt the strangeness of the carefully arranged sheet that covered her. She listened to the morning silence of the room. Ann was the one to get up quietly and go, away from Bill, away from Silver, away from occasional strangers. She had never made love in her own room before. She had never been left before. She lay for minutes, unthinking, peacefully bereft. Then quite suddenly her drifting consciousness caught on a sharp memory of the night before and hung there, unable to set itself free.

She sat up and shook her head fiercely, trying to dislodge an ambiguous wonder.

'It's nothing,' she said to herself. 'It's nothing important.'

But it had not been just another casual night. She had thought about it, planned it, and worked toward it for over a week. It was an accomplishment, the result of a calculated campaign. For what? *For* nothing. It was waged *against* humor, decency, and aesthetic distance to free Ann from the weight of sentiment she would not carry around with her. Smash Evelyn, that image of Evelyn that had tempted Ann to a memory of innocence, of virtue, of salvation. Then view the shattered mother with slight distaste or distant curiosity, a little disappointed, vastly relieved.

'I think you're lying to yourself.'

How could she be? Didn't she fit neatly into her own image: Ann Childs, free-lance lover, proud craftsman of passion, cartooning cavalier against the mystic rose and all colors of blue? She was her own understood self. Denied the imagined romances and sweet sufferings of adolescence by actual experience which had sharpened her wit and dulled her appetite, she could indulge in the skills of lust for purposes of friendship or amusement or protection, but she could certainly not indulge in the clumsiness of love. Not love that woke her reaching for some lost joy as if it belonged to her permanently like an idea or a rib, making her safe singleness only partial, a poverty. No. She made love, as she made sketches, to keep her free. She made love to break love.

'Love.' An idea. A sound. A name. A calling. 'Love.'

She had smashed no image. She had not even tried. And she felt no distaste, no disappointment, no relief. She felt, instead, a ridiculous tenderness that no self-mockery could defeat. It was foolish. It was dangerous. It did not make any kind of sense.

'I don't want to make sense.'

Why did she have to? Even great men, the wise and the clever, abandon taste and fear sometimes, indulge themselves; '*Dulce est despire*.' Was that it? 'It is sweet to be silly at times.' Father's Latin. Father's Horace. But need it be silly? 'This meeting and melting into one another, this becoming one instead of two ... the desire and the pursuit of the whole is called love.' Didn't that make a kind of sense? And think of the real poets, even now in a world shrewd from love. The hundreds of indefensible sweetnesses '(for love are in we am in I are in you)' are child-tongued, crude, and innocent. Why not?

Easier to know why. The sciences of love tell the truth,

explaining away in -exes and -ologies and -alities and -isms all myth and private reality. In womb thou art, to womb returneth, oh, but clinging to small flowers and double nakedness and shells and spindrift clouds to decorate the tomb. Scarred on the walls are the tender and reckless imaginings of a world outside, a simple mystery of sun.

'Get up and decorate the tomb then,' Ann said, angry and hopeful, not knowing whether she would scrawl 'Evelyn' across the wall like a dirty word or print it with the careful inaccuracy and pride of a small child for his own name.

She put on a cotton smock, a gift from Frances, her cliché and concession to Ann's craft, and sat down on the high stool to try her first sketches of 'Mother Without Child.' Frances brought breakfast to her room. Ann heard her grumbling at the far edge of consciousness. She was absorbed in work, hiding there, until it was time to dress for dinner and for the Club.

Evelyn came out of her room just as Ann reached the hall.

'A good day's work?' Evelyn asked, smiling.

'I don't know. I never know right away. You?'

'A good day.'

'I didn't get out to mail the packages.'

'I should have thought to do it for you.'

'It doesn't matter.'

Ann stood, awkward and defenseless. If Evelyn had been either indiscreet or distant, she would have known what to do. But decorum was a climate in which Evelyn lived. Within it she could move with a kind of candor Ann could neither imitate nor reject. And she had no attitude of her own. She did not know what to feel.

'Will you have a drink with me tonight when you come home?'

'You'll be asleep.'

'Wake me then,' Evelyn said, unsuggestive, direct.

137

Ann nodded and turned away to the stairs. They walked together into the dining room where Frances and Walter were already waiting for them.

'You look absolutely sweet today,' Walter said to Ann. 'Are you in love?'

'She's had a decent night's sleep,' Frances said.

'And a good breakfast. That was good coffee, Frances.'

'You see? There is something wrong with her,' Walter said, turning to Evelyn to find an ally.

'You're projecting,' Ann said.

'I am not. I'm in a miserable mood, not a bit sweet.'

'What's the matter?' Evelyn asked.

'I've been jilted – again, the second time in one summer. Last time I could blame it on Ann's car. This time, I haven't even that excuse. And everybody here's been ignoring me as well. Tonight Mother won't even go to the movies with me. When a man can't get his own mother to go to the movies with him . . .'

'I don't like sad movies,' Frances said. 'If you'd go to something cheerful . . .'

'When I'm suffering? Evelyn, will you go to the movies with me?'

'I ought to work. Sure, I'll go to the movies with you.'

Ann smiled quickly to conceal an unreasonable envy. After all, if she had wanted to spend time with Evelyn, there had been the whole day. And, if she chose, she could spend what was left of the night. If she chose . . . why was it that Walter could always find needs simple enough to be answered if not by one person, then by another? He took what there was, a car, an absentminded affection, a piece of pie. Ann took only reluctantly what was offered or asked for something else. And, when she got what she wanted, she almost always managed to be suspicious of her need or the gift itself, in this case both. Ann looked over at Evelyn. The wry celebration of images had left her head. Only the questions remained. Evelyn looked back at Ann and smiled. Then she turned her

138

attention to Walter again, willing to explore with him his cheerfully broken heart. Ann left them over coffee, engrossed in amiability.

Silver was waiting for Ann by the board, 'Have you heard? It worked. Janet's been fired.'

'Bill can work miracles when he puts his mind to them,' Ann said, grinning. 'When did it happen?'

'Yesterday. They sent her a telegram. Bill doesn't know exactly what it said, but they gave her enough to cover all Ken lost that night as well as medical expenses.'

'Did Bill say anything about how he worked it?'

'All the floor bosses went in together. They weren't in there more than five minutes. The old man just said, "How much?" And that was that.'

'Glory be to Hiram O. Dicks.'

'Joyce is moving into your locker with you. For a straight bitch, she's not a bad kid, you know?'

'She's fine,' Ann said. 'I like her. I'd better go down.'

'I'll go with you,' Silver said. 'You free this weekend?'

'Well, yes and no. What's on your mind?'

'You. Joe's gone down to the City for the weekend to buy his Adler Elevators for the wedding. I thought maybe I ought to do some shopping, too, buy something wifely and useless like a dress. How do you think I'd look in a dress?'

'Just a plain, old, ordinary dress?'

'That's it. Both breasts covered and a zip up the side.'

'I can't imagine.'

'But I'm counting on you to help.'

'I suppose I have to. I'm your maid of honor.'

'What a title for the little fish!' Silver said, shaking her head. 'So we'll go shopping tomorrow afternoon, and, as a reward, I'll take you home with me tonight.'

'Why not make it tomorrow night? I'd have to pick up some clothes to go shopping.'

'We can stop by your place in the morning, and, if you're very good, you can stay tomorrow night, too.'

139

'I don't know about both nights, Sil.'

'It's the last weekend we'll have, love. Remember your principles.'

'Oh yes, my principles, my honor.' Ann frowned.

'I'll get my hat and meet you at the locker.'

Joyce was already at the locker, remaking up her eyes and smoking a cigarette at the same time.

'Silver tell you about our hero?' she asked as Ann reached in for her hat and apron.

'It's good, isn't it?'

'Good for Janet.'

Ann looked at Joyce sharply. 'What's the matter with you?'

'I lost every sou I made last week; so I'm doing the landlady's laundry and cleaning this week to pay the rent, and I borrowed for the groceries.'

'You're a fool,' Ann said.

'I like sympathy.'

'If you get hooked, you might as well quit.'

'Well, if the old boy would like to fire *me* for five or six thousand, I might just consider it. Too bad I don't have a kid with heart trouble.' Ann's anger rose slowly enough so that she did not have time to reply before Joyce added, 'Mine's a healthy little bastard.'

'How old?'

'More or less just out,' Joyce said, grinning. 'He'll be six weeks on Monday.'

'No wonder you had a rough first night!'

'I meant to thank you for that, you know?' Joyce said. 'I could have lost the job.'

'Let's go, girls,' Silver said, standing at the end of their row of lockers. 'We don't want to get there after all the money's gone.'

They were all in the Corral for another week, but Ann worked her ramp alone. Joyce had taken Janet's place under the covered wagon. Ann looked over, missing Janet who

140

always doled out change as if she were giving the neighbourhood kids money for the Good Humor man, her natural
generosity threatened by a frugal frown, which had been her
perpetual expression. She worried about people. Ann
wondered how she had taken old Hiram O.'s generosity.
She had probably wanted to refuse it, but her pride and
principles would not have been as strong as her concern for
Ken. That was the saving grace of morality, even the
strongest sort. It always gave way to need or love. Ann
heard Evelyn's voice, asking, 'Are you talking nonsense on
purpose?' Janet might have asked the same question. Hers,
like Evelyn's, was a Purgatory logic, seeded in a pious
mother by the gentle guilt of a father, born into a small
town, brought to crippled fruit. . . . Ann's silent rhetoric
hurt her guts. Neither of them would ask that question now.
Conversion, in one form or another, was inevitable. Perversion in one form or another? 'Take. Eat,' said the serpent, a
communion with good and evil. She and Walter had looked
up 'evil' in the dictionary one night and had found, among
other things: 'That which hinders prosperity and diminishes
welfare.' Whose prosperity? Whose welfare? Ann looked
down at her hard-working customers, paying off in seconds
that two-and-a-half-year-long death. 'Frank's Club thanks
you also for its oil fields and community concerts, its
gold-paved driveways and its scholarships, its private
senators and its public laws. Frank's Club thanks you.'
But Janet never will. The best thing she knows how to do
is pray for you. How many want to be saved?

There were hands up on all sides of Ann, signaling
luck, waving bills for change. An argument broke out at
one end of the ramp between two men over the right to a
machine. Ann settled the dispute without having to call a
key man. Her wit and ease, her success, lifted her mood
out of wry, private uncertainty into a more peaceful
assurance. If she ever got tired of being a change apron at
Frank's Club, she could certainly do well as a playground
supervisor, for men had to be handled just like children or

dogs. You had to evaluate a situation quickly, choose to interfere or to ignore it. The one mistake was to stand and watch it, for males of all ages and species have to fight in presence of a female. Ann walked back to the center of her ramp, superior as if the height it gave her were her own, benign with power. It was not until she went down to the other end of the ramp that she noticed the missing slot machine.

It was not possible! Slot machines did occasionally dissappear, but never from the second floor, never from Ann's section. She looked around quickly, over toward the door, but through that crowd six men could carry a coffin without being noticed.

'Did you see the workmen take this machine?' she asked customers nearby.

'Broken,' one said. 'They must have took it to the basement.'

No slot machine was removed without her permission. 'Wise woman. Teacher among children. Idiot!' She reached for her microphone and called her emergency code number to the board. Perhaps the theft had already been seen and stopped from above. Ann looked up to check the mirror position, but her own face reflected there turned her hope to guilt. It was her responsibility. A key man and a relief change apron were with her almost at once. And she did not know how many, among the new customers approaching the ramp, were plainclothesmen. She stepped off the ramp and saw Bill approaching.

'A put-up fight at the other end,' she said to him. 'I thought it was the real thing.'

'Why didn't you call a key man then?'

'I thought I could handle it.'

'You know that isn't your job.'

'Yes, I know.'

She did not resent his anger. It was a matter of pride as well as importance to keep anything of this sort from happening. He was no angrier with her than she was with

142

herself. She answered his questions as accurately as she could, repeated her answers, admitted discrepancies of detail. She even tolerated suggestions that she might, in fact, be involved in the theft. Bill knew her better than to consider the possibility, but it was a routine part of his job to be suspicious. The fact that he had loved her and that she had hurt him made him only a little more brutal than was necessary.

After talking with Bill, after reporting to a security officer, Ann was allowed to return to her position. She had missed her long break. The crowd was heavy, almost as heavy as on a Saturday night; and, as Ann walked back and forth, both rushed and nervously alert, her back burning, she felt an undefined hostility in the crowd. Demands for change were curt. Jokes had an edge of malice. And faces, unless she could look directly into them, were sinister and grotesque. Something in the peculiar, artificial light, in the coolness of the air conditioning, distorted the sun-tanned, summer sweating skin of perfectly ordinary people. They were perfectly ordinary people, Ann reminded herself again and again, countering this new mistrust which was sometimes close to fear. It was not even extraordinary that, in a crowd of this size, there were crooks. Some hospital attendants stole drugs. Some bank managers embezzled money. There were aldermen who helped themselves to the collection plate. Why did she try to defend the Club? It was an argument she had lost half a dozen times with Frances. 'Take an ordinary man,' Frances would say, 'better still, take a man honest enough to walk three blocks to return too much change to a clerk in a drugstore. What would he do in Frank's Club?' And Frances was right. He'd have no compunction about trying to cheat any change apron out of a few dollars. Part of the excitement for the tourist was his feeling that he had crossed the moral boundary of society as he crossed the threshold of a gambling casino. The fact that

143

the reputable casinos were operated on a code of honesty more rigid than in any bank made no difference. No public relations scheme would ever destroy the myth that a gambling casino is run by gangsters, staffed by petty criminals whose only purpose is to trick a man, to cheat him, to steal his money. 'And who's to say they aren't gangsters?' Frances would demand. 'Who's to say you aren't a petty criminal?' Frances would say Ann got what she deserved. Any man had a perfect right to trick, cheat, and steal back as much as he could get.

'That was a ten I gave you.'

Ann held up the bill folded around her middle finger. It was a five.

'They ought to put you in the floor show for sleight of hand.'

'This is the bill you gave me, sir.'

If pressed by a customer, Ann would have to offer to have her apron emptied. A cashier would count her money. If she had five dollars over the amount of her IOU, the customer was right. On a Friday or Saturday night, only luck let you balance any time in the evening. Everyone made mistakes. And even the automatic coin rollers were not absolutely accurate. A nickel could get into a roll of quarters. But the mistakes were eight per cent of the time in the customer's favor. If you held your job, you learned not to make mistakes in the Club's favor. The Club could not afford it. But the myth persisted. Gambling, condemned generally, reluctantly condoned occasionally, had to be evil.

'This goddamned machine is fixed! They're all fixed!'

'Yes sir, they are. The Club collects fifteen per cent. If you play long enough, you'll lose. The odds are for the house.'

'That guy cross the way got three jackpots. How much of it is he giving to you?'

Ann was used to these accusations, made angrily or amiably, and had a selection of replies to suit the

144

customer's mood. She was not usually worried by them. But tonight she had to guard against answering accusation with accusation. They were perfectly ordinary people, coming from all parts of the country into the evil desert, home away from home of every big time gangster in the States, legal headquarters of illegal syndicates, where honest politicans could still be dropped down old mine shafts and never found again, where alley murders were reported with the church news every Sunday. They were perfectly ordinary people, free at last to be fearful, malicious, greedy. Then home they'd go to the good, green, well-watered plains of the Lord to tell what they had seen, the coarse women, the obsessed men, the deserted children, never guessing that these picturesque inhabitants were tourists like themselves. They were perfectly ordinary people. You had to love the whole damned world to love anyone at all.

'Hear you're giving away slot machines tonight,' the relief said as she stepped up on to the ramp.

'Only to old customers or relatives,' Ann answered.

'I've got five extra minutes for you if you'll give me a share in your cut.'

'You can have everything I get out of it.'

'Sold. Take your time.'

'Thanks.'

Ann passed Silver on her way to her floor locker.

'You didn't have to do it,' Silver said in a quiet, conspiratorial tone. 'Joe and I don't even want one. It would ruin the high-class decor of my living room.'

'It's the thought that counts,' Ann answered.

'Don't worry about it, love.'

'No,' Ann agreed tiredly.

It was hard to get through the crowd. Ann moved both cautiously and impatiently, trying to protect her money and her painful back. Once free of the weight of her apron, Ann felt no more than a slight, physical relief. She wished she did not wear a uniform and could for a few

145

minutes disappear into the crowd, talk with or stand silent with, feel with these people who had suddenly become the enemy. But her white, ten-gallon hat and her frontier clothes made it impossible. She was even branded with a name. She had no hope of anonymity. At the bar, drinking tomato juice, she wondered if she was being watched. It was ridiculous! Just because a couple of sharp, professional crooks had taken advantage of her, she didn't need to get a third-rate case of paranoia over it. She must relax, think of something else. If she decided to go home tonight with Silver, she should call Evelyn. She did not have time. She had to get back.

Again on duty, Ann put her mind to the problem of the night. She had not said definitely that she would have a drink with Evelyn. She would be asleep. Or Ann could tell Silver that she had to go home and meet her tomorrow. But it was Silver's last free weekend. And Ann was not at all sure she wanted to go home to Evelyn.

'Change!'

God, they could take a whole row of slot machines and she wouldn't notice. She must concentrate, not on Evelyn, not on the negative nature of the universe, not even on this peculiar, human population, but on money, machines, and mirrors. The noise raged up at her, filling her head with a pounding, useful emptiness.

Ann checked out her apron at quarter past three, but she was not allowed to leave until she had answered more questions and signed a statement. Silver was waiting for her in the employees' lounge.

'Well, how does it feel to be a big-time gangster?'

'Lousy,' Ann said. She was too tired and discouraged to joke.

'It's not important,' Silver said, trying to comfort her. 'They just make a big thing of it. Do you remember the time that drunk unscrewed the money box on my blackjack table? They asked me how long I'd known the guy. When I told them he was my manager, they put it in

146

the statement and asked me to sign it. Jesus! It's their job to keep the slot machines and money boxes screwed in, not ours. Just screw them.'

'Yeah,' Ann said.

'Do you want to go back to your place?'

'I don't know, Sil. I don't know what I want to do.'

'You need a drink.'

Ann lay on her stomach on the carpet in Silver's living room, silent, playing with the ice in her glass. Silver was finishing a T-bone steak she had cooked for herself.

'You know, Hiram O. is going to survive the loss.'

'Sure, I know. It just made me feel funny, as if the whole crowd was . . . I don't know. Do you ever get tired of it? Do you ever wonder why you work there? Do you ever . . . think about it?'

'Not much. You think too much.'

'I remember once I found moths in my closet, holes in everything. Everywhere I went I kept thinking of those moths, eating away there in the dark. I couldn't stop thinking about them.'

'What's eating at you now?'

'I don't know. Just things in general.'

Silver got up and walked over to Ann. 'Come on. Roll over and give us a foot.' Ann rolled over on her back and offered her right boot to Silver. 'Now the other one. You know, you could live with Joe and me if you wanted to.'

'What?'

'But you don't want to, I know.'

'I've got a place to live.'

'To eat and sleep.'

'And work. That's all I want.'

'I'm going to tell you something, love,' Silver said, kneeling down beside Ann and beginning to undo her belt. 'And you're to shut up until I'm finished.'

'I'm not promising. Look out for my drink.'

'I'm looking out. You're the one who ought to be looking out. You're about to get hooked, little fish,

147

hooked and landed. I want you to make damn sure the bait you swallow is what you want.'

'Look who's talking about getting landed.'

'I'm talking because I know,' Silver said with real fierceness. 'You need somebody, whether you know it or not. I watched you play around with the idea that it might be Bill. He's a nice guy. I was sorry for a while that it didn't work out. Then Joe said to me, "He isn't smart enough for her. She'd ruin him in a year." '

'Thank Joe for me, will you?'

'Sit up,' Silver said. She had unbuttoned Ann's shirt and was about to take it off. 'Now it's this Evelyn Hall. I haven't anything against women, and I don't know her. But I know you. Lie down.' Silver took hold of Ann's trouser legs and pulled. 'How smart is she?'

'Very.'

'How good is she in bed?'

'Well . . .'

'And how disappointed were you when you found out that she really wanted to go to bed with you after all?'

'What do you mean?'

'Love, when little boys want to marry their mothers, they have a hard enough time of it, but they manage. When little girls want to marry their mothers . . .'

'I thought you said you charged for analysis. How much is this going to cost me? I want to be sure I think it's worth it.'

'Fierce,' Silver said softly, 'very fierce. If you want a woman, have a woman, but remember you're a woman. You need some man-handling. How many women do you know who can . . .'

'One,' Ann said, letting her body go with a strange reluctance, almost like grief, desire answering skill, will answering love, without really wanting to.

They slept until after noon, and Silver would not be hurried with cooking or eating. Then she had to dress herself for the occasion of shopping in Hollywood-blond

148

lavender, Cinderella slippers on her long, tan feet. Ann watched her put on her jewelery. She decorated herself as Frances decorated a Christmas tree, hanging great, bright ornaments everywhere. Finally she turned to Ann for a approval, the clattering of metal on metal like a muted nickel jackpot payoff.

'You're marvelous,' Ann said.

'Got up like a common whore,' Silver answered, mimicking an unknown, ideal, female enemy.

'I wonder if I ought to take time to change.'

'I'm certainly not going to go into Magnins with you looking like that.'

'All right, but we'd better hurry.'

'I'll put my clothes in the car. We can eat downtown and change at the Club.'

It was well after two when they arrived at Ann's house.

'Are you coming in with me?'

'I am,' Silver said, exaggerating a real determination.

But Ann, in her own preoccupation with meeting Evelyn, did not realize until she was introducing them in the upstairs hall that Silver had, of course, had a real female enemy in mind. There was a moment of tension in which Silver seemed to hesitate between the extremes of hauteur and crudity, in which Evelyn recovered from a shock her expression serenely concealed.

'I better change,' Ann said.

'Come in and have a cigarette with me, Silver, while you wait.'

'Thanks. Don't be long, Ann.'

It was something between an assertion of possessiveness and a plea. Ann understood Silver's uncertainty in the use of her name. She had not called Ann by name more than three or four times in four years they had known each other. Ann turned away at once, grateful not to have to cope, but she would certainly not take long. The sooner she got Silver away from Evelyn the better. Even in ten minutes Silver could do irreparable damage, but perhaps it was just as well. Evelyn had wanted to know what kind of world Ann lived in. Now she would find out. Ann reached into her closet for something to wear that would not be a comment on Silver's garishness. She chose an apricot cotton she had bought to please Bill. Silver had also been delighted with it. 'I like that new plunging waist line.' Then she put on earrings, which she hardly ever wore, and a bracelet and a ring.

'Got up like a common whore,' she murmured, but, as she glanced at herself in the mirror, she caught in her own eyes the same look of critical hopefulness that she had seen in Silver's. 'Have your cake and eat it, that's what you want.'

She hurried down the stairs, apprehensive about what might already have happened.

'All set,' she said, looking quickly at Evelyn.

'Evelyn's coming with us,' Silver said.

'Are you?'

'It sounded like fun.'

'She's promised to come to the wedding, too. We can pick out your dress today.'

'My dress?'

'I have to buy you a dress,' Silver said, almost reproachfully. 'I'm going to be in champagne. Evelyn and I have decided you should be in caviar.'

'Black?' Anna asked, 'or red caviar?'

'Pewter,' Evelyn said quietly. 'The color of your eyes.'

'Won't it be a little dreary?' Ann protested, fighting down the same ridiculous tenderness that had threatened her so often in the last weeks.

'Subtle,' Silver corrected. 'Are we ready?'

They went out together, stopping only for a moment to explain to Frances that they would not be back for dinner.

'Did you get the wedding invitation?' Silver asked.

'I did,' Frances answered. 'I'll be there.'

Ann and Evelyn had already started out the door.

'I'm sorry about last night. It was too late to call.'

'It's all right. Will you be home tonight?'

'I don't know,' Ann said, and before she could say anything more, Silver had joined them.

When they got to Magnins, Silver and Evelyn approached the clerk together. Silver, in her role as bride-to-be, mixed earnestness with comedy, vulgarity with parody. Evelyn, quick-eyed and quiet, defined the range of Silver's taste and confined herself to it with tact and good humor. As Ann watched them, she still felt tentatively protective of Silver, whose gaucheness made her seem suddenly very much younger and more vulnerable. In a way, though her makeup revealed rather than concealed the hard use she had put herself to, she did actually look five years younger than Evelyn. For Evelyn had let her hair begin to gray, and her aristocratic bones and candid intelligence gave her face an authority and quietness that is always associated with age. Ann studied Evelyn for any faint sign of condescension. Was it there in the way she seemed to keep Silver from any outburst of graphic appreciation when Ann tried on a dress too tight for her? Was it there in Evelyn's almost uncanny ability to reassure Silver at the very moment she was discouraging her from making a choice in outrageously bad taste? If she was condescending, Silver obviously did not feel it. Ann had rarely seen her so wholehearted in an effort to please anyone; and, in her own eyes, Silver felt she was succeeding, for she grew less assertive and more geninely good-humored every moment. When Ann had tried on all the dresses Silver and Evelyn had selected, they had found nothing that really pleased them.

'Don't you want to look for yourself?' Ann asked.

'No, not now. Let's go to that classy little shop around the corner. I've never been in it.'

'I can't bear the place,' Ann said. 'Anyway, everything's outrageously expensive.'

'You're not paying for this,' Silver said. 'I am.'

There was no one else in the shop, and the only clerk was on the phone.

'Where do they hide the clothes?' Silver asked, starting over to the closed cupboards.

The clerk half turned, alarmed, as if she expected a raid. Evelyn touched Silver's arm and nodded to a settee. The clerk turned back to her hushed conversation, reassured but still uncertain.

'This reminds me of the female trade,' Silver said suspiciously. She would not sit down with Evelyn but stood looking around. 'You know that corset shop on West Second they closed about a year ago?'

Ann laughed.

'I'm not kidding. I'm not letting you in that dressing-room alone.'

'Don't worry,' Ann said, grinning. 'I'd scream.'

'Cigarette?' Evelyn said.

'No thanks. Is this really on the level?'

'I think so,' Evelyn said, amused.

'I'm sorry to keep you waiting,' the clerk said to Evelyn, ignoring Silver and Ann. 'May I help you?'

'I hope so,' Evelyn said, her dignity suddenly cool. 'Miss Childs is looking for an afternoon dress.' She nodded to Ann as she spoke, suggesting the color and material.

'Size twelve?' the clerk asked, her eyes never seeming to have looked anywhere but at Ann's face.

'Usually,' Ann answered.

'Won't you sit down?' the clerk suggested to Silver, her tone subdued to politeness by Evelyn's manner. 'I'll bring a chair for you, madame,' she said to Ann, 'and then I'll show you what we have.'

Silver sat reluctantly, but she too, seemed subdued.

'If it isn't on the level,' Evelyn said, picking up Silver's phrase and suspicious tone, 'I'll bet they're losing money.'

Silver relaxed into a guffaw of laughter. Ann looked down at Evelyn with surprised admiration. Then their

152

attention was directed to the clerk, who had brought out three dresses.

'That's the one,' Silver said immediately.

'Exactly,' Evelyn agreed.

'Hadn't I better try it on?' Ann asked.

'I suppose so,' Silver said, arching her invented eyebrow.

Ann, in the dressing room, had an almost overpowering desire to scream. It was an hilarity that came from a need to do something with the tense energy the afternoon had created in her. She felt reckless and uncertain. The dress, paler in color than she had imagined, was like smoke or moonlight, and, though the folds of material were decorous, only softly suggestive, the effect was of something transitory that at any moment might simply be cast aside. It was a magnificent whim. To model it properly she should step out in it and then step out of it in one free, exalting gesture. Only her conventional underwear really prevented her. How sad it was that madness was so frail and easily inhibited. She walked out, wistful, to Silver and Evelyn.

'My God!' Silver said softly.

'I think it suits your daughter, don't you?' the clerk said to Evelyn.

'She's not my daughter,' Evelyn said, her eyes on Ann, her quiet voice so final that the clerk could not even apologize. 'It becomes you.'

'You're almost unbelievable, little fish. It's a good thing I'm not worried about competition,' Silver said. Then she turned to the clerk. 'How much is it?'

'A hundred and fifty dollars.'

'I'll write a check.'

'Sil . . .' Ann began, sobered by the price.

'It's worth twice that. Don't argue.'

'But its . . .'

'Hush. Go take it off carefully before it disappears all by itself.'

153

Ann stood, reluctant to let Silver win the argument. She could buy it herself if Silver wanted her to wear it to the wedding. To let Silver buy it made Ann really uncomfortable. She looked over at Evelyn, but Evelyn would not help her. She had obviously withdrawn from this moment of the afternoon because it had nothing to do with her. Ann went back into the dressing room, the secret hilarity gone, the dress nothing more to her now than an embarrassment; but, if she was going to let Silver buy it, she must be glad of it. She did not want to ruin Silver's pleasure. Ann had never been so aware of considering Silver before. The self-consciousness of it troubled her because her very concern seemed a kind of criticism of Silver which she was refusing to acknowledge. Was it Evelyn's criticism, or was it her own? Ann rejoined her two friends, determined to be pleased.

She did not, therefore, complain when Silver suggested that they should go to the top of the Mapes for an early dinner. Ann did not like the place. It irritated her to have to thread her way through gaming tables to get to the bar or the dining room. And the noise of the three or four machines being played got on her nerves. Away from the Club, she did not want to have to put up with it. Silver had thought Evelyn should see the view, but the desert and mountains were as unreal as a picture postcard from here, and the town looked cluttered and dusty and embarrassed about itself. Ann struggled to hide the impatience she felt with the world Silver wanted to show Evelyn.

'Why don't you come down to the Club with us after dinner?' Silver suggested.

'Not tonight, Sil!' Ann protested at last.

'Tonight's the best night. You haven't seen Frank's Club until you've seen it on a Saturday night.'

'I should get back,' Evelyn said. 'I've taken off enough time today. I'll come down some other night.'

'You should have been there last night,' Silver said.

Ann got up from the table and excused herself. She went into the ladies' room, washed her face with cold water and ran cold water on her wrists. She did not want to be reminded of last night. She was suddenly terribly tired, and the thought of going back to work depressed her. She did not even want to go back to the table. The gaiety had worn off, like champagne in the middle of the day. She felt stale and strained and a little unreal.

'Are you all right, Ann?'

'Yes, I'm all right,' Ann said, startled by Evelyn's appearance in the room.

'You look tired.'

'I am a little, just for the moment.'

'I'm sorry you have to work tonight.'

'Well . . .' Ann said vaguely. 'Oh, I wanted to give you the keys to my car. Would you drive it home for me?'

'Sure, but how will you . . .' Evelyn did not finish her question, obviously regretting it.

Ann wanted to say that she would come home, but the very power of her desire prevented her. She dreaded another night with Silver and was angry with that dread. She felt her silence turn Evelyn turn away. 'I'm afraid, Evelyn,' Ann wanted to say, and 'Take me. Somehow make me come home,' and 'I don't know what to do, Evelyn,' and 'I've got to go home with Silver.' But she said nothing, and they went back to the table in silence. Silver had already paid the bill and was anxious to leave. Giving Evelyn Ann's dress to take home, they parted company with her in the alley.

'It's a beautiful dress, Sil,' Ann said, as they walked up the alley together.

'I wonder why I've never bought you anything before,' Silver said. 'I used to like to dress my women as well as undress them. I guess I've lost the knack since Joe.'

They were silent.

'You don't really want to come back with me tonight, do you?'

155

'I do, sure. I'm just tired.'

'I wish I could decide which one of you to be jealous of.'

'Jealous?' Ann asked genuinely surprised, for, though she had felt on this afternoon somehow unfaithful to Silver, her infidelity had been to Silver's person, not to the relationship between them. 'You aren't really.'

Silver turned and looked down at Ann with tired impatience. 'I sometimes don't understand how a person with brains like yours can be so stupid about people.'

'But why should you be jealous? You never have been. What about Joe?'

'What about him?' Silver demanded, stopping and turning on Ann, but she broke her pose of rage almost before she had taken it up. 'Little fish,' she said quietly. 'Little fish, I've bought you a wedding dress, the only present I ever gave you. Pewter.' Her voice went wry. 'The color of your eyes.'

'Sil, don't!' Ann said, astonished.

'No, I won't.' They had reached the employees' entrance. 'I'll meet you here tonight and give you a lift to your place.'

'I don't want a lift to my place,' Ann protested angrily.

Silver smiled, recovering something of the self-assurance Ann so loved in her. 'I know you don't, love. I know you don't. But I'm giving it to you anyway. We can't argue with the game warden.'

'I don't want to go home, Sil!' Ann said, her voice an urgent, tight-throated whisper so that she would not be overheard by other employees passing by them.

'You two taken to the streets?' Joyce asked, coming up behind them. 'I didn't recognize you for a minute.'

'We'd better change,' Silver said. 'We're late.'

Ann pulled off her cotton dress and slip, kicked off her shoes, and stood in her bra and pants taking off her jewelery.

'Not bad,' Joyce said, standing by her, adjusting the

cord on her hat.

'I didn't know you were interested,' Ann answered lightly.

'I'm not,' Joyce said. 'Just curious.'

Ann turned quickly to the locker and took out her skirt.

'Ann, I'm just kidding around.'

Ann did not trust her voice to answer. She buttoned her shirt roughly and reached for her trousers.

'Then you do mind,' Joyce said.

Ann could not distinguish between concern and malice. 'Get off my back,' she said tightly. 'And stay off.'

When she turned around, Joyce had gone. Ann took her hat and apron and hurried up the stairs. She was late, and the crowd that confronted her when she pushed open the door would neither take her in nor let her through. She hesitated for a moment in the deadly cold air, in the brain-splitting noise. Then she stepped into that wall of human flesh, using her elbows and the heels of her boots to cut a way through.

At three thirty, when she walked out of the door, she had no idea how the hours had passed. Only her legs and back told her that she had stood and carried the weight for the allotted time. Silver was waiting.

'Lose anything tonight?' she asked, amiably.

'Nothing but my mind,' Ann said.

'I had a rare time,' Silver said. 'A slightly stoned man of God was preaching to the dollar machines, "Man can't live by bread alone." I should think he'll be glad to know it tomorrow morning unless he's on the American plan. And this other guy, a real philosopher type . . .'

Silver talked their way to the car, talked their way to Ann's house. When she stopped the car, she was still talking.

'Oh, shut up, Sil,' Ann said, taking hold of the lapels of Silver's shirt and offering her mouth as an interruption to the endless story.

157

'Have a good time, little fish,' Silver said gently. 'I'll see you in church.'

Ann got out of the car, and Silver pulled away quickly and noisily like a high-school kid. The light in Evelyn's bedroom went on. Ann looked up at it, resentful and glad.

'Lady of the City, Mother,' she said softly as she walked up to the house, 'Game Warden, Lover. Rich Ann, Poor Ann, Beggar Ann, Thief. "Take. Eat," said the serpent.' And then she sang, 'You're the apple of my eye.' But, as she closed the front door behind her, she knew she had hopscotched to the final square. 'The game's up,' she said in her sheriff's voice, but it really was. 'I didn't hear you, Mother, until the fourth time you called. And now I'm on the first step. And now I'm on the second step . . . Evelyn?'

Evelyn opened the door and took Ann into her arms.

'I'm so glad you're home,' she said quietly.

'I want a bath,' Ann said, 'and a drink.'

It was a long bath, in which Ann entertained herself with phrases of songs, punch lines of bad jokes, and a muted Sunday rhetoric that ranged from bits of Plato to a good imitation of Billy Graham. The rehearsal over, she was ready to entertain Evelyn. She drank two large Scotches to accompany herself and tried not to notice whether Evelyn was amused or not. Then she got up and stretched herself out on the bed next to Evelyn. She closed her eyes and heard, echoing in the painful, empty vault of her skull, her mother's voice, hard and clear, 'Don't. It's not worth the money.' What in hell did that mean? She was asleep.

When she woke, Evelyn was up and dressed, reading at her desk.

'Frances!' Ann said.

'Good morning, my darling. It's all right. I told her you'd had a couple of drinks with me and fallen asleep.' Evelyn got up and walked over to the bed. 'Which is quite true.'

'Did you sleep?'

'Very well. And so did you, except for one or two initial nightmares.'

'That must have been pleasant for you.'

'It was. You're lovely asleep.'

'But awake . . .?'

'Shy and full of conversation. Interesting conversation though.'

'You say so little.'

'You don't give me a chance. The minute you stop talking, you're asleep.'

'Talk to me now,' Ann said.

'And I'm not sure that what you say isn't often misleading.' Evelyn held Ann's face in her hands gently. 'Do you always tell such long, irrelevant stories?'

'Probably.'

'There's only one solution then. I must have you like this, and, while you're telling and telling, I can find my own ways about you. But perhaps your body can mislead me, too, take sudden turnings I only clumsily follow. . . .'

'I want you.'

'In a while, my darling. In a while. You mustn't be impatient. You're hardly awake.'

Ann turned, the longing of her body straining against the last reluctance of her mind, and she felt Evelyn's tentative, almost casual beginning gradually give way to an authority of love. Ann was held urgently, brought into being, then restrained, caught again, held, until she wanted nothing ungiven, until she wanted nothing, until she came to wonder, not asking any longer, but naming, 'Evelyn.'

'Yes, darling. You must teach me to do that.'

'Now.'

'No, not now. You must get up and have some breakfast.'

'Evelyn?'

159

'Little fish,' Evelyn said, rumpling Ann's hair, for a moment roughly. 'It's an odd name for you.' Then she got up, took a towel and left the room.

'Lady Macbeth,' Ann muttered viciously, but it did no good.

She could not manage to be quite hurt, quite angry, quite frightened, or quite guilty. All the possibilities of negative emotion were there, however, threatening the stronger, single desire, which, like the scent of Evelyn's perfume, was personal rather than sexual. She wanted to be with Evelyn. She wanted to know Evelyn. She wanted to be able to love Evelyn, whatever that meant. Half a dozen vague clichés came into Ann's mind, jumblings of prayer book and movie magazine that had to do with fidelity, procreation, and healthy sexual attitudes. And with them came the half-formed cartoons. She got up out of bed. She hadn't lost the battle against tenderness. She had changed sides. And now she faced her really formidable enemies. Line them up. Name them. Choose among those to be killed, those to be captured, those to be converted. For, if she was to love Evelyn, she would have to fight her own whole damned world, and some of it she could not live without.

Ann dressed and went down to get some breakfast. She tried to be as casual with Frances as Evelyn had been. It shouldn't be difficult because Evelyn had used Ann's own tactics. She had told the truth. But Ann had always used the truth to confound Frances, not to reassure her.

'I heard you slept with Evelyn last night,' Frances said cheerfully.

'Not exactly,' Ann wanted to say, but she checked herself. Then, as she watched Frances cracking an egg into the pan, she wondered why she had always kept herself away from Frances; for, conventional and blind as Frances tried to be, she was both intuitive and generous. For a moment Ann was actually tempted to say something, to ask a straight question, but her habit of

160

isolation was too strong. Instead she said, 'Two eggs please, Frances,' using the stupid, ancient ritual of food that Frances would understand.

In her own room, she did not take out her sketchbook. She sat staring at the empty table, staring at the implications of the decision she seemed to have made. She was going to court Evelyn, not simply her body, but her mind and her heart. 'Don't. It's not worth the money.' Wise advice, perhaps. Odd how clearly she still held her mother's voice in her unconscious, a voice she hadn't heard for nineteen years. 'And you're one of the enemies I'm going to have to kill'. Somehow linked to that broken and grotesquely mended bone of memory was the lust of Ann's body. Her proud sexuality, the range of her experience and the inventiveness of her skill must all be irrelevant now. If, in making love with Evelyn, her body yearned for obscure intimacies, they must no longer be substitutes for, a defense against, intimacies of person with person. Here was an enemy to be converted. But her real terror was for the world she lived in, that Evelyn did and would continue to find it empty and appalling. Ann could not leave the desert. In her human loneliness, the landscape had become her home. And she found it hard to imagine leaving the Club. Already she felt herself threatened with losing the visions she had there, which would mean losing the light she worked by. And her work? She did not know about that. Why must she fight this battle at all? Who was Evelyn to ask it of her? Did she ask it of her? Ann did not know. She asked it of herself. If she did not, she would lose something of herself that seemed terribly important. 'I don't even know what it is.' Ann's eyes focused for a moment on the children. Perhaps it was something she had already lost along the way of these last four years, old habits of thinking, friends. Her friends had belonged to her father's world. Most of them she had not seen since his death, except by accident. There were one or two people at the University

161

she still called on very occasionally. There was Kate Buell. She hadn't seen Kate for months.

'I want Evelyn to meet Kate Buell,' Ann said that evening at the dinner table.

'What a good idea,' Frances said. 'You'd love Kate, Evelyn.

'Who is she?' Evelyn asked.

'She'll tell you about herself much better than we can,' Walter said. 'She never stops talking.'

'She's an old lady,' Ann said. 'Her husband was a newspaper man. She's the daughter of a miner, raised in Virginia City. She's lived in Nevada all her life. Why don't I see if I can get her to come out to dinner with us on Thursday evening? She loves to be taken for a drive.'

If Ann could find enough, recover enough of a world Evelyn could understand and like, the Club she went to at night might not be important, a privacy she could keep. But, after a night's work there, Ann came home uncertain. The light in Evelyn's room did not go on. She had not asked Ann to wake her, but her door had been left slightly ajar. Ann hesitated, then stepped quietly into the darkness of the room.

'Are you awake?'

'Yes.'

'Don't turn on the light.' Ann sat down on the edge of the bed and felt Evelyn's hands reach for her shoulders, her neck, her face. Ann leaned down and kissed her. 'Really awake? Do you want a cigarette?'

'Can you find them in the dark?'

'I think so.' Ann touched objects on the bedside table until she located the package, the matches tucked neatly into cellophane. She lit a cigarette, held the match a moment, then shook it out. 'Here.'

'How are you?'

'I'm not sure,' Ann said.

'Do you want a drink?'

'No.'

162

'Come to bed then.'

'Do you want me?'

'Very much. Now.'

There was no urgency in Ann's own body at first, only the desire to know Evelyn, to discover her desire, to serve it. In a physical simplicity she had never known before, could not have believed in, Ann joined Evelyn to the very images of her blood, speaking its wild, natural, insistent poetry until the silence they lay in was sleep.

'Ann?'

It was dawn.

'You mustn't stay, darling.'

Reluctantly Ann roused herself enough to get up. When she looked down at Evelyn, she was already asleep again. Ann turned away quietly and went to her own room, knowing that one of her enemies in Evelyn had already been defeated.

On Thursday Ann felt some confidence as she set out with Evelyn to get Kate Buell at the residence hotel where she lived.

'Why don't you drive now and let me maneuver doors and things?' Ann suggested as she got out of the car.

'You'll have to tell me where we're going,' Evelyn said, sliding over into the driver's seat.

'I will. I'll be right back.'

Ann brought Kate down to the car proudly. She was a tiny woman, still light stepping and certain voiced at seventy-five. She was delighted to be going out, delighted to be meeting someone new, for she was aware that her conversation sought out fixed points in the past, that certain memories had become the refrain of her day; and old friends, though patient, could not feel the new wonder she did each time she recounted one of the richnesses of her life. A new audience always made her happy. But she was not simply absorbed in herself. She liked people. She liked ideas.

'Those new cartoons in the *Territorial Enterprise* are

simply brilliant, Ann,' she said, after they had settled in the car. 'Have you seen them, Mrs Hall?'

'No, I haven't. I haven's seen any of Ann's cartoons yet.'

'You must. It's a real gift she has, not just for drawing. Wit. Intelligence. Range. You know, I often think cartoons, the really good ones, are the most accurate record of our particular history. I don't mean to belittle other things, but I think the time will come when people recognize the significance of this kind of comment much more than they do now. Ann, I was troubled by the one in the *New Yorker* about a month ago.'

'Were you Kate?'

'Yes, I thought I could see that odd streak of inhumanity that's in so much psychological humor these days. Are you working full time now?'

'Turn right here, Evelyn,' Ann said. 'No. I'm still at the Club.'

'I wonder how much longer that's going to be necessary for you.'

'All my life, I suppose.'

'Perhaps. Fidelity to any human place, except the heart, seems to me a dubious thing. But the landscape, that's a different matter!' Kate looked ahead. 'Are we going out of town?'

'Yes, to a restaurant on the Tahoe Road.'

'How lovely. Ann tells me that literature is your field, Mrs Hall.'

'Yes,' Evelyn said.

'I have a great guilt about literature. I used to read it. Now I can't read anything but fact or theology. And I wonder why. As we get old and begin to prepare ourselves for the new life, I think we should turn more and more to literature where fact and philosophy meet; but we don't. We dwell, instead, in an actual past and indulge ourselves in mysticism, a fearful division. I still read Shakespeare, but only the comedies. Do you both see

164

the light on the Virginia Hills? Don't let an old woman's talking distract you. Do you like the desert, Mrs Hall?'

'I'm beginning to,' Evelyn answered. 'It's still a little awe-inspiring.'

'There is no gentler, more beautiful place on earth, I think. I'm quite foolish about it. I tried to move away once several years ago. All my good friends are in the City. My doctor's there. It seemed sensible to live there; but, do you know, though I loved it for a month, I couldn't stay. And it's not my own past I missed. I can take that with me. It is this desert, the smells of it, the colors of it, the silence of it.'

'Kate, have you read that newish book out on ghost towns?' Ann asked.

'Yes, I have. I bought a copy, something I don't often do nowadays. Have you read it?'

'Not yet.'

'Perhaps I should give it to you. Shall I?'

'I'd love to borrow it.'

'No, I'll give it to you. Remind me on the way home so that I don't remember after you've gone and feel embarrassed about my forgetfulness. It is lovely of you to think of me, Ann. I don't get out often enough these days. It's hard to make the effort.'

Ann directed Evelyn on to the Tahoe Road, and they did not drive very far before they came to the restaurant Ann had chosen. It was still some distance to the mountains, but the building stood on a rise of ground that allowed a long, wide view of the desert to the north.

'I think this is the place where young Ernie Trool plays the piano,' Kate said. 'Do you know him, Ann?'

'Not really. I know who he is.'

'Your father knew his father. Ann's father knew everyone in town,' Kate said to Evelyn.

'Not quite,' Ann said smiling. 'You're the one who knows everyone in town.'

165

'Not anymore. I did when I ran the newspaper. Then I certainly did.'

'You ran a newspaper, Mrs Buell?' Evelyn asked.

'I certainly did and very badly, too,' Kate said, patting Evelyn's arm.

It was Evelyn's arm, she took, going up the stairs, Evelyn she asked to advise her about cocktails, Evelyn she addressed herself to more and more.

'Come on,' Ann said, when the waiter arrived with the cocktails. 'Let's go out on the terrace. Will you be warm enough, Kate?'

'With a martini, I'll keep both of you warm as well.'

It was not a large terrace. There were just three tables, and they were the only people to come out of doors. Kate stopped in the middle of a story about the newspaper.

'Now listen,' she said, and surrounding the human stillness she commanded was the total stillness of the desert. 'If I lost my sight, if I lost my sense of smell, I would still know where I was.'

Ann watched Evelyn look out over the near sage into the far space of the evening, the desert already in the shadow of the great mountains, and she hoped she could read in Evelyn's face some new awareness of the freedom and the peace of this still, unpeopled earth.

'I must call you Evelyn', Kate said suddenly. 'It's such a lovely name. Would it embarrass you to call me Kate? I know I'm an old woman, but everyone I love calls me Kate.'

'Kate,' Evelyn said, smiling down at the old lady. 'Of course, I'll call you Kate.'

'There are virtues in being old. Loving, for instance, is a very simple matter. One is no longer afraid of the instincts of the heart. You have one of the loveliest faces I've seen, Evelyn. It's like your name, something one wants to say.'

Ann smiled at Kate's direct delight, at Evelyn's unembarrassed pleasure. She heard Evelyn turn Kate's attention then to the ballads her life had become. Ann

166

had listened to these stories from the time she was a small child. She loved the familiarity of them, and sometimes, under her breath, she spoke with Kate the phrases that had not been altered in fifteen years. Her attention never really shifted, but sometimes Kate's voice became the evening stillness, as light as the sound of some night bird. Ann rested.

They left the terrace when their dinner was served and went in to Ernie Trool's piano playing. Kate had to go over and speak to him at once. Evelyn and Ann went to the table.

'Isn't she wonderful?' Ann said.

'Yes,' Evelyn answered. 'Your world is full of wonders.'

'Your lovely face, like your name,' Ann said quietly, 'something one wants to say.'

Ann drove back along the night road toward the brilliant fragments of light that were Reno. Then she went up with Kate to get the book Kate wanted to give her.

'Will you bring Evelyn to see me again before she goes?' Kate asked.

'Yes, Kate, soon.'

As Ann turned away, she felt in Kate's phrase, 'before she goes,' a sudden urgency. She hurried back to the car, as if a simple moment or two could make a difference. She had so little time. She had already wasted so much of it.

'Are you going to show me some of your work?' Evelyn asked as they were driving home.

'Yes,' Ann said.

'Tonight?'

'If you like.'

Ann offered Evelyn first the collection of cartoons she had done for local papers. Most of them were occasional pieces, making use of Nevada history or current events. There were a few protest cartoons, directed at the Nevada testing grounds. Evelyn stopped to study one rather careful sketch of an atomic explosion, captioned: 'And

167

the desert shall rejoice, and blossom as the rose.'

'They're all fairly standard stuff,' Ann said.

'Are you a pacifist?'

'I don't suppose so,' Ann said. 'I have reactions, moments when I think about changing the nature of the world, but I suppose the only thing you can change is your view of it. Shut one eye, cross them, close them both.'

'Yet you produce protest cartoons.'

'They sell. Oh, I don't mean I don't feel something about them, but cartoons aren't very serious. They're moments in time. They don't last.'

'Then you don't agree with Kate?'

'I like ideas. Here, this is a collection of stuff I've sold in the big world.'

Evelyn turned page after page without comment.

'Like Kate, you find that streak of inhumanity that's in so much psychological humor these days,' Ann said.

'The sketching is brilliant. No, it's not that they're inhuman. They're reluctant, somehow. Do you know what I mean? A kind of self-conscious satire. Not self-conscious. Oversimplified? It's hard to say. I like individual ones. I don't really know very much about cartoons.'

'A little cowardly is what they are,' Ann said. 'Just a little dishonest.'

She reached for a final book, reluctant as her cartoons were, to expose the real vision she had. She had not ever shown *Eve's Apple* to anyone, but she had to show it to Evelyn. She knew quite simply that the sketches in *Eve's Apple* were the only real work she had ever done.

'And where have you sold these?' Evelyn asked, taking the book from her.

'I haven't. I haven't sent them out.'

Ann watched over Evelyn's shoulder as she turned the pages in silence. The awareness of an audience gave Ann the first distance from these sketches that she had ever

168

had. She saw her own style, only hinted at in her published work. The drawings had size and weight. The lines were not threatened by tentative satire. They were boldly ironic.

'Ann Childs,' Evelyn said finally. 'You're a moralist!'

'No,' Ann said. 'I have a knowledge of good and evil. That's all.'

– 7 –

Evelyn often spent evenings in Ann's room, exploring her library, which was a random richness of unsettled taste. At first Evelyn had looked for books which she wanted to use; but, as she discovered underlined passages and comments in margins, she began to piece together the scattered commonplace book of Ann's private study. She would sit at Ann's table, surrounded by books, copying quotations.

From Goethe:	'Man is not born to solve the problem of the universe but to find out where it is.'
From Conrad:	'All claim to special righteousness awakens in me that scorn and anger from which a philosophical mind should be free.'
From Langer:	'Paradox is a symptom of misconception; and coherent, systematic conception, i.e., the process of making sense out of experience, is philosophy.'
Langer again:	'. . . peculiar Christian conception that identifies the devil with the flesh, and sin with lust. Such a conception brings the spirit of life and the father of all evil, which are usually poles apart, very close together.'
From Cooper:	'Men feel far more than they reason, and a little feeling is very apt to upset a great deal of philosophy.'
From Toller:	'I have respect for nothing but my work. The work commands me; that is all I serve.'
From Sappho:	'. . . . . . . But I say Whatever one loves, is.'

Ann had not underlined a verse which caught Evelyn's attention:

> Now I know why Eros,
> of all the progeny of
> Earth and Heaven, has
> been most dearly loved.

She did not write it down. She was not, at the moment, so much interested in finding her own reflection as she was in finding Ann's. These books were like old photograph albums, through which she searched to find the candid or posed moments of Ann's mind. In some of the quotations she could hardly recognize Ann, a blur among dozens of youngsters who identified with the large, euphoric generalities of western intellectual heroes, but perhaps Ann was being ironic. Where she did not comment, Evelyn could not be sure. Occasionally, and always in the most cryptic and particular statements, Evelyn recognized at once that idiosyncratic imagination which was Ann; however, though Evelyn could always recognize it, she could not always understand it. She looked down at another marked verse in Sappho:

> People do gossip
>
> And they say about
> Leda, that she
>
> once found an egg
> hidden under
>
> wild hyacinths.

For the arrogant, the world is a vicious but essentially harmless place? Evelyn's was a willing, but uncertain suspension of disbelief. The pieces of Ann did not quite fit together, the several separate worlds she seemed to live in, her amoral behavior and her moral judgment, her sympathy and her rage, her brashness and her delicacy. Who was she?

Evelyn set the book aside and stood up. It was only two o'clock. She had, perhaps, two hours to wait. 'And now I know why Eros . . .' she said quietly, as she stretched and yawned, a suggestion of desire informing all her nerves. Extraordinary . . . not that she should feel desire but that she should not have felt it, consciously for years. And with the awakening of her body had also come passions of other sorts which were not really new because she dimly recognized them as belonging to a person she had almost grown into before her life had taken the long detour of marriage. She had never been, except in her mind, a real adventurer, but she had not been afraid; or, if she had, fear had been no more than a seasoning that had increased her appetite, particularly for people. Before her marriage to George, and even during the first few years after the war, they had both had a lot of friends; but, as they grew apart from each other, they had isolated themselves. George was the first to refuse people, but Evelyn had also withdrawn, not wanting the simplest kind of intimacy for fear that it might expose her failure. Now she was exposed, and the very vulnerability that had terrified her – had she expected to be stripped and whipped in the public square? – gave her a reckless courage. For someone who had had nothing but stock responses, and most of them negative, for almost ten years, the anarchy of desire and curiosity seemed a mind of salvation. Evelyn gave herself to it with the zeal of a convert.

No, she gave herself to Ann. It was only through Ann that Evelyn reached out to this world. She felt she could be interested in and care about anyone and anything that mattered to Ann: Silver, the desert, Kate, cartoons. That

173

was Evelyn's nature. When she had learned to play the piano, she did not want to be a concert pianist; she wanted to be an accompanist. When she had begun to draw, her ambition was to be a portrait painter. And her love of language had not turned her to writing but to criticism. She took the value of her own identity from the person or idea she served. Was that true? Was she weak then, not, after all, crushingly strong as she had seemed to be? Was she dependent? 'Sure,' George would say, 'the way a puppeteer is dependent on a puppet. And you have an appetite for people, all right. You eat them.' 'Not the tough ones,' she answered and heard in her own voice, for the first time, the ancient, unspoken scorn for her husband's weakness. 'I'm ashamed of him. I was humiliated by him.' And she had felt some kind of monster, incapable of sympathy, incapable of love. She had been a kind of monster. He had created her so, asking of her a subservience to his ailing will, which demanded both that she support him in the public world and depend upon him in their private living, be his manhood and his wife. And she had tried, an error she could hardly blame him for entirely. She chose to try to hide her own sense of inadequacy. As she scorned him, she scorned herself. Neither of them should be ashamed of anything in themselves but their willing participation in the obsolete pattern their marriage had become. What difference did womanhood make?

It was curious that, at the very time she was giving up all the external images of womanhood, Evelyn should become increasingly aware of her own femininity, and it was not a synthetic maternity as she had expected it to be. Oh, at moments Ann sleeping was a child, her child. And sometimes, when she saw the thin, vicious scars on Ann's wrists, she had to fight down an animal rage which was protective. But these emotions were occasional. Now,

174

waiting, she had a wonderful, physical impatience to have Ann home, and her memory of the nights before made her anticipation confident. She had grown almost vain about her body, and she had begun to discover, underneath the strict discipline she had imposed upon her mind, an inventiveness. She could talk whimsically, sometimes even wittily to call up in Ann not admiration so much as delight. Evelyn wanted to be charming, provocative, desirable, attributes she had never aspired to before out of pride, perhaps, or fear of failure. Now they seemed almost instinctive. She was finding, in the miracle of her particular fall, that she was, by nature, a woman. And what a lovely thing it was to be, a woman.

'I'd like to go back to Pyramid Lake,' she said to Ann when she came home.

'Would you really?'

'Yes, and I also want to go to the Club. I almost went down tonight, and then I was a little afraid to without asking you first. When Silver suggested it on Saturday, you were so firm.'

'I didn't think you wanted to go.'

'You make love with Silver, don't you?' Evelyn asked suddenly, surprised at her own directness.

'I have.'

'Do you make love with a lot of people?'

'Not a lot. Some. Do you mind?'

'I don't know,' Evelyn said, but she remembered the fierce physical jealousy she had felt when Silver had bought the dress for Ann. She did not want to lie. 'Yes. I suppose that's terribly backward . . . reactionary of me, is it?'

'No.' Ann smiled. 'Fidelity is one of those green, sane words that grow like weeds in everyone's garden.'

'You don't approve of it?'

'I don't know. I think I'm allergic to it, that's all.'

175

'Must I be promiscuous to avoid giving you a rash?'

'No,' Ann said sharply.

'Oh? It's only your own fidelity you're allergic to.'

'Don't make it sound so final. I have a transient personality. I outgrow things or move away from them. Tomorrow I might decorate a whole house with fidelity and find I can live with it without so much as an itch.'

'For a while.'

'For a while,' Ann agreed. 'I don't really understand how people take the marriage vows. How did you? It's one thing to forsake the past, but how can you forsake the future?'

'I suppose it never occurred to me that I had one.'

'Is that why you married George?' Ann asked roughly. 'I'm sorry.'

'It's all right. One direct question deserves another. It's just that I don't seem to be able to answer yours as easily as you answer mine. I think I married him because I thought I loved him. And I wanted to be married. But it can't be as simple as that, can it?'

'I don't think that's very simple. Why did you want to be married?'

'I wanted children. I wanted to live in a house. I wanted to be a woman.'

'Is that being a woman?'

'I thought so,' Evelyn said, 'but I was a very conventional young woman, darling.'

'Why are you divorcing him?'

'I have to,' Evelyn said.

'Talk to me, Evelyn,' Ann demanded. 'Talk. I have to hear. I have to know.'

Evelyn looked steadily at Ann. If she told her, really told her, of the grotesque inhumanity she had helped to create and maintain over these last years, what hope would there be of surviving it? Would Ann find anything left of her that was delighting, perceptive, loving? The dangerous euphoria of the last days snapped like a nerve in the back of her neck. Pride and anger rose to cover fear. Evelyn had been out of her mind to enter into this relationship. Yes, out of her mind. Ann was an attempted moral suicide from which Evelyn had just come to.

'Evelyn,' Ann said from a great distance. 'Evelyn, listen to me.'

'No,' Evelyn said.

'I have to know, Evelyn. I love you. You have to tell me.'

Evelyn turned toward the door.

'Evelyn?'

'Do you have any idea what you're doing?' Evelyn asked. 'I don't suppose so. I suppose in a way you're quite innocent, but I'm not.'

'No,' Ann said wryly, 'you've been thrown out of the garden.'

Her answering anger touched Evelyn as no gentleness or pleading could have done. She reached out and took hold of Ann's shoulders. 'Not for eating apples, though. I eat people.'

'A mixed mythology,' Ann said. 'Why are you afraid?'

'I'm not afraid.'

'You are.'

'I'm afraid for you then.'

'I don't believe that. You may be afraid of me, and perhaps you ought to be. I don't know. I suppose, in a way, you're quite right: I don't know what I'm doing, except risking a dubious but essential world on a whim called Evelyn Hall. *You* may be someone I want to eat. Who knows? I think I won't eat you, though. I don't think you'll let me. And you can rest assured in me, too. I shall be nobody's meal.'

'You don't know. You don't know.'

'What are you afraid of?'

'Myself,' Evelyn said. 'I can't imagine that you could, knowing me, love me. And I can't imagine, if you did, that it would be a good thing.'

'Why?'

'Ann, my husband is in and out of a mental hospital, and his doctors have told me the only thing I can do for him is to divorce him. I'm some kind of poisonous alter ego for him, an ideal, a judge. I told the doctors I couldn't divorce him. I had married him. They sent me to my minister who very gently and tactfully explained the moral loopholes, how one can escape through the infinite insight and generosity of God. Apparently, in the eyes of God, if you've done a fairly thorough job of destroying someone, you don't have to go on being faithful to him. You can quit. Not only can you, you're required to break the letter of the law to observe the spirit. That assumes, of course, that something of the spirit has survived. I have to divorce George. I have no other choice.'

'You don't want to divorce him?' Ann asked.

'Shall I tell you the truth? No, I don't. I'd rather he'd die.'

'Why are you horrified? Do you think it's an unusual feeling? It's as normal as imagining how sorry the world will be when you're dead. He probably wishes you were dead, too, or wishes he were dead. It's about the same thing.'

'But I *have* destroyed him.'

'You have not. That's an arrogance you damned well better get over.'

'Arrogance?'

'I don't know the man,' Ann said quietly, 'but I assume he's had some experiences that have had nothing to do with you. Did you give birth to him? Did you raise him? Did you go off to war with him? You may not have helped him any, Evelyn. You may even have clarified his nightmares, been the subject of several of them. But destroy him? No. He's still alive, after all. The doctors tell you you can help him by divorcing him. What's so appalling about that? Have you ever thought you could

178

have an operation for him? Have you ever thought you could have his dreams for him? Have you ever thought you could die for him? There are things people have to do alone. Going mad is one of them. Apparently he has to go mad, and you can't go with him. He has to be free.'

'But not to go mad,' Evelyn said. 'In order to keep from going mad.'

'What have you done to him?'

As Evelyn began to speak her monologue of petrified guilt, she realized that she had at last come to the trial she had expected, but not in the public courts of law to be judged and sentenced by official strangers. They conspired with her to set her free. Nor was her confession to be offered to God, Who had, by casually forgiving, apparently already condemned her. Her judge was to be this young image of herself, whose arrogance and morality and innocence she curiously believed in. As Evelyn watched Ann's face, she found she could speak not only of guilt but of anger and of need. And finally she could ask: 'And what on earth does my love for you mean? Isn't it some final perversion of inadequacy and need?'

'You've been talking about the sin of putting moral names to immoral behavior. Perhaps you can make the same mistake in reverse, call love perversion.'

'But how do you know it isn't a rationalization?'

'I don't,' Ann said. 'Loving you scared hell out of me.'

'*Do* I look like your mother?'

'No, not at all.'

'Do you really remember her?'

'Very well,' Ann said. 'The last time I saw her I was six. I was playing in the sand. We lived in Carmel. I saw her walk away down the beach. She never came back.'

'Where did she go?'

'To one of her lovers, I suppose. Dad said she suffered from nymphomania. He blamed himself for being intolerant, which is only to say he was in love with her and didn't get over it.'

179

'What about Frances?'

'He was fond of her. But I think, to the day he died, he hoped he'd find Mother again. He had me, too, of course. We both used to look for her. It was a game we played. Even after Frances and Walter moved in, Dad would always say, "Who's Daddy's sweetheart?" The answer was "Mommy is." Then he'd say, "Who's Daddy's other sweetheart?" I was. Frances wasn't really even in the hierarchy. He was good to her. He cared about her, but he kept right on looking for Mother.'

'How did you feel about her?'

'I thought I adored her. I suppose I really hated her, jealous of her hold on my father, hurt by her leaving of me, but I didn't know it until he died. I've been busy murdering his image of her ever since.'

'And doesn't that have something to do with me?' Evelyn asked.

'Yes,' Ann said, 'I think so. I've always made love with women to prove to myself that they aren't, after all, the mother I'm supposed to be looking for, to prove that she doesn't exist. So you could probably say my loving of you is a perversion and a destructive one.'

'Does it feel that way to you?'

'No, not at all,' Ann said, 'but my feelings can be very willful.'

'I'm not really afraid of *your* feelings.'

'No. You see yourself as a classic case history. And, if you're doomed to sexual inadequacy and sterility, you anyway have enough morality left not to take out your frustrations on people you really care about. If forced to a choice, you'll keep dogs.'

'I think so,' Evelyn said, refusing to flinch at Ann's brutal accuracy.

'Evelyn. Evelyn. You're not as simple as that. You're not in a textbook. You're a human being.'

'And you?'

'I'm less certain about me,' Ann said, grinning. 'But I'm

willing to behave as if I were human. I'm willing to gamble on the possibility. And so are you. Why have you loved me at all?'

'Lack of social orientation. Latent homosexuality. Moral amnesia. Masochism. Revenge. But I'm willfully ignorant in these matters. My terms are probably very inaccurate.'

'And so, though you hate to hurt me, you know you've made a terrible mistake. You hope I'll forgive you. You hope we can go on being friends.' Ann's tone was uncertainly comic, an occasional syllable tipping into satiric anger. 'Why have you loved me at all?'

'Because I couldn't help loving you,' Evelyn said, feeling the tight control leave her voice. 'Because I can't help loving you, your wild, inaccurate emotions, your bizarre innocence, your angry sense of responsibility, your wrong-headed wit, your cockeyed joy, your cowboy boots, your absolutely magnificent body, your incredible eyes. I can't help it. I don't know how anyone could.'

'There've been thousands, I should think,' Ann said, the warmth returning to her voice. 'But I'm glad you're not one of them. I don't intend to let you go, Evelyn.'

But what do you intend to do, Evelyn wondered, and what do I intend to do? She could recover from this particular, personal fear and moral panic in Ann's arms, more certain of Ann than she had been, more certain of herself. But each moment they spent together involved them in a relationship they must somehow take responsibility for. It was easy enough to forsake the past, but could you forsake the future? Perhaps. Nothing before her mattered so much as being with Ann now.

Being with Ann, Evelyn found it hard to remember what it was in the desert that had so terrified and appalled her. She drove the easy, straight road to Pyramid Lake as comfortably as she might have driven the road to Santa Cruz, but she was glad that they would not arrive at the boardwalk and crowded beach. There were few places left in the Bay Area where anyone could go and expect even an uncertain privacy. Privacy was what she wanted. They were both already growing restless with the caution they had to use when they were together in the house, reticent in other people's company, always aware of the thinness of walls, the vulnerability of doors when they were alone. And dawn, which came so soon after Ann got home, was becoming a symbol of the world's intrusion. They could not ever sleep a night through together.

'Shall we go to the same place?' Evelyn asked.

'Yes, I think so.'

'Does anyone else go there?'

'I've never seen anyone else, and it's a weekday anyway. There won't be anyone else on the lake at all until supper-time.'

'Good,' Evelyn said. 'We can swim without suits.'

'You are getting reckless.'

'I feel reckless all the time. This afternoon I want to be reckless.'

Evelyn drove toward each rise of ground, expecting the water; but, when they came upon it, it was as if she had never seen it before, a great reach of sky that had fallen suddenly and quietly upon the land. She did not pull over to the side of the road; she let the car drop over the crest and down to the lake shore.

'I like the way you drive,' Ann said.

'Do you? How do I drive?'

'I'd have to show you. It's the next turn off.'

The sun was hot, the sand fiery under foot, but a cool, dry wind came off the lake that gave a freshness to the air. Evelyn stopped for a moment before she walked down to the beach. The long, clean line of the horizon was broken only occasionally by an outcropping of rock, clearly defined against the heat-washed sky, and the massive shadow reflections of the land trembled on the wind surface of the water.

'See the islands out there? They gave the lake its name,' Ann said. 'I've never been out to them, but the story is that they're a treasure hoard of Indian arrowheads . . . also alive with rattlesnakes. I wonder if it's true.'

The mention of rattlesnakes made Evelyn look around her quickly. She had before been so absorbed in the psychic dangers of the desert that it had not occurred to her to consider its simple, natural dangers.

'Don't worry,' Ann said. 'You don't often see them this close to the water.'

'But, if they're on islands. . . .' Evelyn said and then hesitated. 'I don't really care. I'm not afraid of them.'

She walked down to the water, to the waves of white shells along the shore. She stooped down for a handful of them, curious to discover them again. Their tiny perfection, infinitely repeated, seemed the more miraculous because of the huge, simple size of the landscape. It was no wonder that a Christian God had not been at home here. It would take the many anamistic gods of men less confident of their own dominant spirit to describe the powers of this world. Evelyn thought of the Catholic Church in Virginia City. Faiths transplanted changed their nature or died in climates alien to them. Like the redwoods of California. She had heard that in Australia they had grown with dangerous speed for sixty years and then had died. She felt no terror in the idea, only a shifting of focus. Perhaps people also changed. Evelyn looked up into Ann's watching eyes.

'What are you thinking?'

'I was wondering if people changed when they moved from place to place.'

'The word is "adjust," I think. People change, standing in one place.'

'Or don't adjust and don't change.'

'Why do you still wear your wedding ring?'

'I can't take it off,' Evelyn said. 'I've tried.'

Ann knelt down beside her and took her left hand.

Slowly, but without hesitation, she eased it off Evelyn's finger, held the empty gold ring in her hand for a moment, and then gave it to Evelyn.

'How did you do it?' Evelyn asked, bewildered.

'I worked one summer at a jeweler's.'

Evelyn looked down at the ring and at the white band of skin that remained around her ring finger. 'I wonder what I'll do with it.'

'It's a tradition in Reno for people to throw them into the Truckee. Then old men fish for them and sell them cheap to the kids who come from California to get married.'

'So that's why they were shouting at me.'

'Who?'

'The old men below the bridge. They were panning for gold.'

'That's right.'

'I don't think I want to do that,' Evelyn said. 'I wonder if there's anything you can do with a wedding ring that isn't embarrassingly symbolic.'

Ann made no suggestion.

'Well,' Evelyn said, 'thanks,' and she dropped the ring into her jacket pocket, its weight immediately reminding her that this was only a temporary and not at all satisfactory solution.

'I'm good at buttons, too,' Ann said, a gentleness in her teasing. 'And zippers . . . and hooks.'

'Ever work in a corset shop for the summer?'

'No,' Ann said. 'I'm an honest amateur.'

'Are we really safe?'

'I don't know about me,' Ann said. 'You're certainly not.'

'Oh, neither are you, my love.'

She reached for Ann, but Ann turned out of her arms quickly and waded into the water. A dozen yards away, but still in the shallows, she turned back to Evelyn. For a moment Evelyn did not move. The candor of Ann's absolute nakedness, not caught in unselfconsciousness like a young nude in a romantic painting, but fully aware of her erotic power, roused in Evelyn an arrogance of body, a lust that burned through her nerves like the fire of the sun they both stood in. This was the freedom she wanted, an animal freedom exposed to the emptiness of the sky and land and water. As she stepped forward, Ann flipped into the water and was gone. 'I know why you're called Little Fish,' she said softly, and the power of her body, as she swam, was an aggressive power. She was a stronger swimmer than Ann, confident in the chase. Not thirty yards from shore, Evelyn reached out with her left arm and caught Ann's thigh. Ann rolled over on her back, and they came together, turning, weightless in the water.

'In the sun, too,' Ann said. 'On land.'

And it was Ann, then, who dominated and controlled their bodies. Her free, inventive wildness, the physical intimacies she demanded, aroused every vague, animal desire in Evelyn that had been left unnamed, her body growing as demanding as Ann's until Ann's ecstatic cry broke the world silence like the cry of some mythical water bird. They lay still then, exhausted and peaceful.

'Is that what it's like with Silver?' Evelyn asked.

'No,' Ann said. 'Not like that.'

'With anyone else?'

'No.'

'My God, I feel possessive of you. It frightens me a little. If I think of anyone else making love with you, I want to go at them with a meat ax.'

'That *is* a little excessive,' Ann said. She was idly tracing Evelyn's backbone with her lips. 'I hate to cover you, but I'm afraid you'll get burned.'

She got up and walked over to where they had left their clothes. Evelyn watched her, still unaccustomed to her independent nakedness.

'You'd better put these on,' Ann said. 'Do you want to wash off first? I'm going to. We're just a bit sandy.'

'I haven't the energy,' Evelyn said, grinning. 'I'll just brush off and take a swim later.'

She sat up and dusted her shoulders and breasts with her shirt before she put it on. Then she stood up reluctantly to pull on her underwear and trousers, watching Ann, who had swum out about a hundred yards from shore. Just as she was about to sit down again, Evelyn became aware of the sound of a distant motor. She listened. It was not a car. It must be a speed boat. She looked down the lake, but the curve of cliff blocked her view.

'Ann?'

Ann waved.

'Can you see a boat?' Evelyn shouted, but the sound of the motor was now so loud that she knew Ann could not have heard her.

She squinted at the stretch of water where she expected the boat to appear. There must be at least two of them. She wished Ann were out of the water and dressed. Damn the boats! Then suddenly, not around the cliff but over it, came a helicopter, no more than a hundred feet off the ground. Evelyn could see the two men in it quite clearly. They were in uniform. It was an army plane. The men saw her, grinned and waved. She did not wave back. The plane dropped fifty feet and hovered right over her head. Then it shied off, leaving her in a storm of sand, and went out over the water. They had seen Ann. Through an open window, they were shouting and waving, the plane not twenty-five feet above the water, hanging there like an obscene, giant insect.

'Get away!' Evelyn shouted. 'Get away from her!'

Her ridiculous, ineffectual fury was lost in the racket of the motor. What were they doing here? What right had they here? The plane dipped away from Anne and came back over the beach. The settling sand rose up again.

'Damn you!' Evelyn shouted. 'Get out of here!'

She saw their good-natured faces again as they waved.

The plane rose up and moved off along the eastern shore.

'How did you like that?' Ann called as she came in to the beach, staying under water until she could reach the towel Evelyn waded out to give her.

'I didn't. What on earth are they doing here?'

'I don't know. I suppose every now and then they do a routine inspection. Lucky, weren't we?'

'You don't really mind, do you?' Evelyn asked.

'No. I thought it was funny, didn't you?'

'I should have,' Evelyn said, 'but I didn't. I was furious.'

'Why?'

'I want you to myself, I suppose.'

'Ah, darling,' Ann said, laughing. 'I'm not a fish. They'd have to get closer than that to do any real damage.'

'I'm sure they were flying lower than they're supposed to.'

'No doubt about that. Evelyn?'

Evelyn grinned reluctantly. 'There's sand all over the picnic basket.'

'Never mind,' Ann said. 'I'll take you into town and buy you a steak, how's that?'

'That's fine.' Evelyn heard the plane engine getting louder again. 'But let's get out of here quickly.'

Ann pulled on a shirt and trousers, and they grabbed their belongings and started up the cliff. They needn't have hurried so, however. The helicopter stayed a sedate distance up and out from the shore, the men nodding and saluting with exaggerated politeness. It was not until they had driven some way that Evelyn thought of her ring. She reached into her jacket pocket, knowing that it was gone. She said nothing about it to Ann. Losing it was probably the best thing she could do with it. She looked down at her hand. It would take longer to lose the mark it had left.

Though Ann did not actually refuse to take Evelyn to

the Club, she was vague about setting a time; and, since Evelyn had asked to go, Ann was monosyllabic about her evenings at the Club. Perhaps the stories she had told and the explanations she had given created a Frank's Club that existed only in her own mind, an image which she did not want destroyed by Evelyn's independent view; but the Club was too important to Ann for Evelyn to be able to ignore it. When a specific invitation was not forthcoming, Evelyn decided on a time of her own. Silver had said that Saturday night was the night to see the Club, but Ann had protested. A Friday night seemed to Evelyn the right compromise. She wondered when, during the evening, she should go. Her own nervousness about the town made her consider going before dark; but, because she was determined to explore all of Ann's world without fear, she chose instead the early hours of the morning. After all, Ann moved about the public streets unescorted at three and four o'clock every morning. There was no reason to be afraid.

There was a problem about getting down to the Club. Evelyn could not ask for Ann's car, and she did not want to ask for Walter's. He would offer to go with her, and, because his company would be a great comfort to her, she did not want it. A cab at that hour of the night, ordered for Frank's Club, was an impropriety Evelyn was reluctant to commit. She smiled at herself. She could come to Reno for a divorce. She could lie naked in the public day making love to another woman, but she could not call a cab at midnight to go to a gambling casino. She chose, instead, to walk.

The quiet, residential streets, dark with carefully planted trees opening occasionally to the clarity of desert sky, were not at all unpleasant, and Evelyn felt an exhilaration to be on her way at a time when the hours usually dragged with her waiting for Ann. She met no one until she turned north on University Avenue, walking past the darkened Public Library and the Post Office to the

188

bridge that crossed the Truckee. There were not many people, but there was no furtiveness even in the single loiterers who stood along the bridge, quite unself-consciously enjoying the coolness of the night. Evelyn had only one moment of uncertainty as she passed the courthouse on the north shore. There were half a dozen old men sitting on its shadowed steps, perhaps the same old men who spent their days on the banks of the river, waiting for the unwanted gold people tossed to them like stale bread to the ducks. Evelyn was glad she wore no ring and glad in the dark that no one could see how recently she had taken it off. When she turned to walk toward Virginia Street, she saw ahead of her a bright neon day and crowds of people. It was exactly the same scene she had encountered at nine o'clock that first morning, but at this time of night it seemed more natural, like a carnival or country fair. The crowds were friendly. People shouted to each other from across the street, sang, shook hands with exasperated motorists stalled in the pedestrian traffic, joined together, handed each other money, set out for another casino sure of winning again or winning back what they had just lost. There were drunks, but they were not isolated. People jollied them along, helped them when they stumbled, leaned them up against walls or offered to buy them another drink. And the rhythm of the machines gave a rhythm to the noise until it seemed to Evelyn that they were all part of a huge, exuberant jazz symphony. There were even couples dancing to it here and there along the sidewalk.

At the open doors of Frank's Club, Evelyn did not even hesitate. She moved in with a crowd and was not aware of the change of atmosphere until she was well into the building. Then the cold air and the suddenly magnified noise struck her into a more defensive alertness. She was enclosed in the crowd. There was still gaiety in the eddies of movement between slot machine clusters and gaming tables, but the dominant tone had shifted to a stagnant

189

sea of people intent upon maintaining the positions they had achieved. Evelyn let herself be carried uncertainly from the edge of one group to another until she was caught in a cul-de-sac behind the escalators. To her left an exaggerated Judy Garland, dressed in clothes like Ann's, barked the comic results of the game she dealt to a roaring, delighted crowd. Evelyn was held there by her peformance, unable to understand the game or to hear most of what she said, but aware of the skill she used in her certain entertainment. She was marvelous. Then Evelyn saw a change girl to her right, who seemed raised several feet above the ground on the waving hands of the crowd. She, too, had a kind of command of the chaos she was there to serve. Evelyn looked all around over the crowd to the change stations, but she could not see Ann anywhere. She could not imagine that she would ever really find her. She worked her way toward a cashier's cage and stood in what seemed to be a line. If she could get to a cashier, she could ask for change for the opportunity of asking where Ann might be. The line did not move. Evelyn saw people feeding in from the sides of the cage and so worked her way again to a position which would inevitably carry her past the cage.

'Nickels please,' she shouted. The cashier did not even look up. 'Excuse me. Could you tell me where I could find Ann Childs?'

'Who?'

'Ann Childs. She works here. A change girl.'

'Sorry,' the cashier said, shaking her head.

'Or Silver?'

'Silver? What kind do you want?'

'No a person named Silver. I'm looking for a person named Silver.'

'Oh. Silver Kay?'

'Yes, that's it.'

'I think she's up in the Corral.'

'Where's that?'

'Second floor. Off the escalator, turn left.'

'Thanks.'

'My pleasure, love.'

It was not easy to get on the escalator and terrifying to get off, but, having achieved both successfully, Evelyn felt a relieved confidence. If she could find Silver, Silver would know where she could find Ann. And even in this crowd, Silver might be noticeable. Evelyn turned left, as she had been directed, and found herself in a room the size of a ballroom, crowded with slot machines and people, who moved about apparently quite unconcerned about the huge stage coaches that were suspended from the ceiling.

'Well, Our Lady of the Lake,' someone said behind her, 'You've kept your promise after all.'

'Silver,' Evelyn said, more pleased than she could have imagined to see Ann's friend. 'I never thought I'd find you in this crowd.'

'Having a good time?'

'Well, not yet. I'm still trying to find my way around. Where does Ann work?'

'Right over there where I can keep an eye on her.'

'There she is!' Evelyn said, in her voice an unguarded surprise and delight.

'Doesn't she know you're here?'

'Not yet.'

'You'd better go over and let her know. I think she's just about ready for her long break. She can show you around.'

'May I come back and see you later?'

'I'll be right here, love, unless they pack me to the basement for overhauling.'

Evelyn did not go right to Ann's ramp; she stood a little distance away, where Ann would not be apt to see her, and watched Ann work. She was incredibly quick and graceful; and, though Evelyn could not hear what was said to her or what she answered, she could read in the swiftly changing expressions of Ann's face the fragments

191

of concern, amusement, doubt, and authority that her job required. On the ramp, a little above and apart from the crowd, she was perfectly at home. Evelyn saw her reach for a microphone that hung just above her head, and then she heard Ann's voice, magnified, call off the numbers of a jackpot from across the room. If Evelyn had once thought Ann's job somehow degrading to her, she thought it no longer. She had a quite childish desire to say to the people standing near her, 'Do you see that girl? I know her,' for everyone in the insignificant crowd must be a little in awe of the people who actually worked here, who understood and controlled the multicolored magic of the machines. Evelyn found her way into the crowds and finally took a place by a nickel slot machine at the end of Ann's ramp. She opened the roll of nickels she had brought from the cashier and put one in. She pulled the arm and watched the wheels spin. Nothing happened. She put in another, then another. On the fourth nickel, she thought she heard a bell ring, and a great number of nickels spilled into the cup.

'A jackpot, girl!' said an affable man standing next to her. 'Good for you!'

'What do I do?'

'Get the change girl. Here, like this. Just wave and whistle until she comes.'

Ann turned around at his sharp whistle and saw Evelyn. Evelyn grinned guiltily.

'The lady's got a jackpot.'

'Don't play it off, ma'am, until the key man comes.' Ann said, a warm amusement not quite hidden in her professional tone. She leaned over to see the machine number and said more quietly, 'What the devil are you doing here?'

'I missed you,' Evelyn said softly and saw in the quick direct look Ann gave her nothing of disapproval. 'It's fun.'

'I'll be off in five minutes,' Ann said.

Ann's relief arrived with the key man to pay off the waiting jackpots. Evelyn walked with Ann to her floor locker.

'Can I buy you a drink?' she asked, holding up the dollars she had been given.

'No, but you can buy me something to eat. When did you come? How did you get down here?'

'I walked.'

Evelyn watched Ann take off her apron, fold it carefully and put it in her locker. Then she brushed both hands together briskly and obviously before she turned the key and pinned it back on to her shirt.

'Why do you do that?'

'To show I have nothing in my hands. If you forget, you can be fired.'

They went together to the restaurant and ordered sandwiches and coffee.

'I think I'll come down here every night,' Evelyn said. 'It's much nicer than waiting for you at home, and think of all the money I could win.'

'You can lose what you've won tonight,' Ann said firmly. 'But you're not to spend a penny more. It would be just like you to get gambling fever.'

'Do you think I'm the type?'

'I do, my darling, for fevers of all sorts.'

'I'm pretty safe. I don't know how to play anything but the slot machines.'

'You'd learn. Anyway, you can lose enough to scare you without ever graduating to the dime machines. And I can't keep an eye on you because you mustn't play in my section. It's against the rules for relatives, and I wouldn't be able to convince anyone that we're not related.'

'Of course not. We are.'

'Are you going to stay a while?'

'Until you're ready to go home if you'll let me.'

'Do you really want to?'

'Of course,' Evelyn said. 'The noise was a little

appalling at first, but you get used to that, don't you?'

'In a way,' Ann said.

'And everybody's having such a good time, almost everybody anyway. I love watching you work.'

'Well, you mustn't do too much of that. I'll start giving away all the House's money.'

Evelyn did not go back to the Corral with Ann, feeling Ann a little uneasy at having her there. She was amused by Ann's quite serious warning to her. Perhaps Evelyn felt safer in the Club than Ann did. She stayed on the second floor and began to watch roulette. It was not really a difficult game. She got a couple of dollars' worth of chips and lost them almost at once. It was quite an easy game to lose. The crap table was much more complicated. Evelyn did not understand the betting at all; and, because people took turns with the dice, she felt nervous about standing too close to the game. Also there was a kind of intensity in the players and dealers that she did not feel elsewhere. The slot machines really were simpler and more fun. But, even near the slot machines, though the crowd had thinned a little, there seemed a growing tension. Fewer people seemed to be playing casually. There were not as many conversations as there had been an hour ago.

'I said cap these two machines,' an old woman shouted at a change girl.

'I'm sorry. There's still too big a crowd to save machines.'

'Call the floor boss. I play here every night. I want these machines capped.'

'I'll cap one, all right?'

Evelyn turned away from this argument only to find herself witnessing an even more unpleasant scene, a young husband tyring to persuade his obsessed wife to stop playing two dollar machines.

'Honey, I don't have any more money. It's all gone.'

'Let me see your wallet. Come on.'

'I've got to have enough to get us out of here.'

'You were lying to me!'

'Listen, you've lost over two hundred. You've got to quit.'

'You're a rotten spoilsport, tight-fisted, mean, stingy . . .'

'Honey, please . . .'

'All you ever think about is money!'

'All right, take it!' he said in disgust. 'You make me sick.'

Evelyn turned away again. She wanted to go back to Ann's section where everyone seemed to be having such a good time, but she could not. It was against the regulations. Perhaps she could find Silver, but Silver was gone. Where she had been, there was some kind of minor commotion. An old man in a clerical collar was shouting. As Evelyn drew nearer, she could hear something of what he was saying.

'There can be no divine faith without the divine revelation of the will of God! Therefore, whatever is thrust into the worship of God that is not agreeable to divine revelation, cannot be done but by human faith, which faith is not profitable to eternal life!'

'Get that crackpot out of here!' someone shouted.

Two uniformed men stepped up to him and began to move him through the crowd. Evelyn stepped back to let them through.

'There can be no divine faith without the divine revelation of God!' he shouted again. 'This is Vanity Fair. Who judges me but Hate-good? Who are you, all of you, but Malice, Live-loose, Love-lust, Hate-light . . .'

Vanity Fair. Of course, she had heard of it all before. He was quoting Faithful's final speech in *Pilgrim's Progress*. Faithful was tried at Vanity Fair and died there. Crackpot the old man might be, but he knew his Bunyan, and he knew Vanity Fair when he saw it? 'When they were got out of the wilderness, they presently saw a town

195

before them . . .' Evelyn heard him shout just before the elevator doors closed behind him: 'I buy the truth!'

The money in her hand was suddenly distasteful to her, but she resisted being moved by an old man's fanatic moralizing. She could get rid of the money by feeding it back into the machines it had come from, a solution that would free her from both the little guilt and the morality that threatened her. She started to put a nickel into the machine she stood by only to discover that it took dollars. Well, she had a silver dollar. It would be quicker. Evelyn put the dollar in the slot and pulled the handle. The wheels spun and jarred to a stop one by one. A light went on. A bell rang.

'No!' Evelyn said, appalled. 'I don't want it. Stop!'

But the silver dollars crashed into the cup and onto the floor, and a smiling change girl called the jackpot into the board. A key man counted out a hundred and twenty dollars into Evelyn's reluctant hands.

'Will you play it off, please?'

Evelyn put a dollar into the machine, pulled the handle and turned away, but the machine spilled out eighteen dollars.

'I don't have to play that off, do I?' Evelyn asked, frantic.

'Not if you don't want to.'

She turned away, desperately wanting to get out. She would find Ann. She would tell her that she had to go home; but, when she arrived at Ann's ramp, she was not there. Evelyn looked at her watch. It was after three.

'You're late,' Ann said, standing right behind her in the crowd.

'Oh darling, I've done the most awful thing'

'What is it?'

'I've won all this money!' Evelyn said, offering it up to Ann.

Ann looked down at the money, then at Evelyn, and began to laugh. Evelyn's horror broke. It was funny. Of

196

course, it was funny.

'It frightened me so for a minute,' Evelyn said, and then she, too, began to laugh.

– 8 –

Ann had not expected the Club itself to accomplish Evelyn's conversion. She had hoped to keep Evelyn away from the Club entirely and to win her approval by means of a short course in the history of Nevada and a careful abstraction of the Club, revealing it as an ideal symbol of man's industry in which Ann felt obligated to participate. Trained in the intricacies of defensive logic by her elaborately intellectual father but disciplined in emotion by the shrewd and cryptic wit of the practical world she lived in, Ann had organized an argument to be presented in impressive fragments, offered to Evelyn casually as entertainments, a sort of subliminal advertising for Ann's own point of view until Evelyn would one day put all the pieces together with the love of coherence she had and speak Ann's view as if Evelyn had discovered it. The plan had been working very well before Evelyn's visit to the Club.

From the book Kate had given her, Ann collected stories of the hundreds of failures to settle the desert, the mining towns turned to ghost towns because the ore ran out or the railroad did not come through. Unionville was typical in its decline. First the church went, moved and converted into a saloon, the bell sold to call ranch hands in to supper. Then the railroad passed on the other side of the mountain, and the courthouse was lost to Winnemucca. Finally even the newspaper folded, and the largest mine closed, its owner claiming that he had spent

199

three million dollars trying to live in Unionville. It was finished. And over and over again the same thing happened, the rush, the boom, the decline, the death. Nevada's incredible wealth of gold and silver built not one city that could survive the desert and the mountains. Not one. It wasn't really fair to count San Francisco, was it? Its wealth did not come from the actual produce of the mines but from stock speculation, and, when the last mines closed, San Francisco could feed on the fertile valleys and vast forests of California, on the sea. In Nevada, there were no great valleys, and even the sage, for miles around the mining cities, had been burned for fuel. There was no water. Elsewhere in the world the God of the Jews had brought forth in the desert spring water from the jawbone of an ass. In this desert, there boiled up nothing but the poisonous sulphur of hot springs. There was nothing to support civilization but the man-made railroad and highway, built not to reach the desert but to cross it.

It was here Evelyn had interrupted the secondhand raw material Ann offered her to discover the present Nevada for herself. Ann wanted her to see not the fact but the meaning of Frank's Club, Ann's meaning. For Frank's Club was man's answer to the poverty of the land. Reno had grown up along the railroad, along the highway, without a mine to its name. It invented its own. The casinos were Reno's gold mines, but synthetic and perpetual, correcting the flaw of nature. They could accommodate any number of prospectors. They could support not only the town but the scattered population of the state. When Reno built a church, Frank's Club supplied both the money to be spent and the souls to be saved. The town could maintain a courthouse and perpetuate laws that restored gold even to the river. It was a sound economy which exported nothing but advertising and imported human beings at their own cost to feed the inhabitants. A perfect kingdom, based on

200

nothing but the flaws in human nature. It thrived.

And this was the economy, obscured only by a confusion of other minor enterprises, of thriving civilization everywhere in the world. But elsewhere you could be deluded by just that confusion. It was extraordinary how other industries could create the illusion of value, the hallucination of salvation through products as meaningless as automobiles and cosmetics, text books and cameras. It was true that casino owners spoke more loudly than any of the other kings of industry to defend their contribution to society. They could speak more loudly because theirs was the purest activity of civilized man. They had transcended the need for a product. They could maintain and advance life with machines that made nothing but money. And the only requirement, after all, was life, all needs subsidized (food products, housing, education, law religion) by the lucrative desires of mankind. This desert town was man's own miracle of pure purposelessness.

Ann had prepared herself to defend this vision against any other, but she had chosen Evelyn's own world of the university as the enemy she would have to equal or defeat. The pursuit of learning was, after all, as pure of purpose as gambling, only archaic enough to need subsidizing. She had heard from the secular pulpits of the classroom that learning had value in itself, but there was nothing of more intrinsic value in learning than there was in gambling. For eighty per cent of the people in Frank's Club gambling was no more than an entertainment. For eighty per cent of the students in the classroom it would be generous to say that learning had even entertainment value. Only a small minority in any group developed a passion for anything. For every obsessive gambler there was undoubtedly a young Faust in the atomic laboratories. And, if there were a few who loved learning for learning's sake, surely there were many more who loved gambling for gambling's sake. Human nature was the same in the casino and in the ivory tower. But in the casino the vision was unclouded. You loved the world for its own sake or not at all.

It was a beautiful argument, but Ann had no opportunity to use it. Evelyn had asked for and taken the facts instead. Reluctantly, Ann let Evelyn drive her down to the Club every evening and pick her up sometimes an hour, sometimes two hours early. After the first night she did not gamble. Apparently winning all that money had had a more sobering effect than losing would have done. Evelyn had no interest in playing either the machines or the games. She came, she said, to be near Ann, but often at the end of shift Ann had to go in search of her, finding her engrossed in observing a particular dealer or change apron or gambler. On the way home, Evelyn was often silent, but sometimes she would ask technical questions about the operating of the Club that gave no room for theoretical answers, and sometimes she would comment briefly on an incident, usually insignificant in itself but given a not quite explicit importance by Evelyn's view of it. If Ann countered with a view of her own, Evelyn offered no more than a disinterested silence. She was never critical. She did not seem disturbed by anything she saw. Ann very much wanted to ask her what she was really thinking and feeling, but both their bodies were so demanding that, when they were at last alone, always aware of the threatening dawn, their conversation was fragmentary, crude with desire or elaborately incoherent with the last brilliance before sleep.

During the day, when they might have talked about the Club, Evelyn shared her work with Ann; and, since it apparently did not occur to Evelyn to defend her interest in teaching and learning, Ann could find no opportunity to attack it. Instead, she settled to a study of poetry, learning the discipiline of its higher grammar, tracing the folklore of its imagery. Once she challenged Yeats's view of salvation in *Sailing to Byzantium* only to be shown

202

that he challenged it himself in *Among School Children*, and his criticism of education seemed so reasonable and undisturbing to Evelyn that Ann could only accept her clarifications of the text in silence. The poetry was, in fact, so interesting that Ann often forgot to be pre-occupied with her own world. In Evelyn she had fond a companion for her mind whose knowledge and perception far outreached her own, and she was eager to learn.

But her contentment was threatened again each night when she looked up and saw Evelyn standing alone in the crowd, at once detached and absorbed. What was she seeing? What judgment was she making? In her concern, Ann worked inaccurately, and several nights running she was either over or under her ten-dollar limit when she checked out. The third time Bill had to sign for her, he spoke with impatience.

'If you can't keep your mind on your work, you'd better keep your girl friend out of the Club.'

'Follow that logic far, and you'll have to fire yourself,' Ann answered angrily.

'Meaning?'

'How often have you signed for Joyce this week?'

'You forget she hasn't been working long. She's doing damned well for a beginner.'

Ann censored a nasty retort and turned away. She was angry because Bill was right. She was also angry because Evelyn's presence in the Club had obviously become a subject of general knowledge and speculation. She did not really care what people thought, but they could keep their ideas to themselves. It was her own fault. She should not let Evelyn come down to the Club.

'You don't have to be in such a hell of a hurry,' Silver said, catching up with Ann as she went downstairs to put away her hat and apron. 'She's waiting for you.'

'Sorry, Sil. I didn't see you.'

'You don't see anybody these days, love.'

'Don't *you* start in on me.'

203

'Then don't let her come down every night.'

'Why shouldn't she?'

'She doesn't belong here, love. She makes people nervous, you for instance.'

'Maybe I don't belong here either!' Ann snapped.

'Maybe not.'

'Don't get at me, Sil.'

'I can't leave you completely alone until after the wedding, love. There's a rehearsal Wednesday afternoon. Joe didn't see why we couldn't have it Thursday afternoon. I had to explain to him about not seeing the bride on the day of the wedding.'

'How are you going to manage that?'

'He's spending the night at the Mapes.'

'Do you want me . . .?'

'No, love,' Silver said smiling. 'There are no instructions to the maid of honor to sleep with the bride the night before the wedding. It doesn't say *not* to, of course, but I think they have in mind a last night of chastity, a last night in Daddy's old pajamas, a last night of solitary weeping for one's girlhood. I can't remember mine very well. Perhaps I'll weep for yours.'

'Sil . . .'

'Go along now. Don't keep her waiting.'

Ann had to go back into the Club to find Evelyn. Her own nerves were raw by this time of night, and she hated going back into the noise and crowds she had just escaped. As she pushed open the back door, she ran into Walter.

'What are you doing here?'

'Having a drink on Bill,' he said, anger raising the pitch of his voice. 'Really on him. I threw most of it on him. Where's Evelyn?'

'In here somewhere. What's the matter?'

'Nothing,' he said. 'Forget it.'

'Walt?'

'Listen, Ann, some guys, when they get hurt, don't have

204

the sense to keep their mouths shut. Bill knows a lot of people. Things get around. I just came down to see if I could knock a little sense back into him.'

'What things?'

'It doesn't matter. Are you going to get Evelyn or shall I?'

'I'll get her, but I want to talk to you, Walt. I want to know what's going on.'

'She shouldn't come down here. It's no place for a decent woman.'

'Has Bill been talking about Evelyn?'

'And you. It's partly your fault. I know you don't care what people think. You can afford to be indifferent. But Evelyn isn't a change apron. She's a university professor. It makes a difference.'

'What difference?' Ann demanded.

'Sometimes I don't understand you,' Walter said, tiredly, tightly. 'But I'm a simple, heterosexual male with an unexceptional I.Q. I haven't even got an Oedipus complex. My only problem is that I'm a reactionary about women. I still think that's what they are.'

'You're a nice guy,' Ann said gently.

'Exactly. I'm going home.'

'Have a drink with us?'

'Thanks anyway. I'm tired.'

'I'm sorry, Walt.'

'*I'll* never mention it again,' he said, but his attempt at the old joke was not really successful.

Ann watched him out of the door and then turned to find Evelyn. She was watching a blackjack game where the betting was heavy, her eyes were passive, and the stillness of her body made her seem in a kind of trance.

'I could leave you here all night and you'd never know the difference.'

'Sorry, darling,' Evelyn said, smiling. 'I wait here not to be in the way.'

Ann regretted her sharpness at once. How was Evelyn

to know that it was just her unobtrusiveness that made her conspicuous? How could Ann explain it to her? She did not understand it very well herself. Bill's viciousness, even under the circumstances, was uncharacteristic of him. And Silver's controlled jealousy made no sense at all. As for Walter, though his knight-in-shining-armor complex had sometimes made him clank a little, she had never heard him talk about decency before. Understandable or not, there was a conspiracy developing that Ann could not be indifferernt to. In that much, Walter was right. She ought to protect Evelyn. But Ann did not know how to tell her not to come down to the Club again without offering an explanation. Damn Bill! Damn them all! Why couldn't she and Evelyn be left alone? There was so little time. Evelyn would go to court a week from today, from yesterday by now. Only one week. Why should Ann say anything? Mightn't it be better just to be silent, to take the time they had, live in terms of it, and then let the whole thing go? Perhaps that was what Evelyn was doing. She accepted the present because it bore no relationship to the future. And wasn't that the attitude Ann herself advocated? Before she had known Evelyn, yes, but now the temptation to take what there was was not as urgent in Ann as the temptation to risk the present for the future. She did not want Evelyn now as much as she wanted a world in which Evelyn was possible. But she did not know what world that was, and in her ignorance and in her need she was silent.

Evelyn did not go down to the Club early on Tuesday night. She had been busy with her own work. On Wednesday, Ann explained that she would have dinner with Silver, Joe, and Bill after the rehearsal and probably have a drink with Silver after work.

'Might you be out all night?'

'I don't think so, but don't wait for me.'

Bill was waiting for her on the sidewalk outside the new Episcopal church. Dressed in a business suit, he always looked both younger and sterner than he did in frontier clothes, a choirboy who had outgrown his innocence but not his moral malice. Ann checked her anger. She must somehow also check his for today and tomorrow. It could wait.

'They're already inside,' he said irritably. 'You're late.'

'I'm sorry,' Ann said, her upper lip curling over her teeth. 'I couldn't find my plate.'

It hurt him to have to smile at their old joke, but the habit was stronger than his will. And his reluctant amusement gave Ann a brief, unkind pleasure. Her cheerfulness grew more resolute. She inquired about the emotional state of the bride.

'She's having an argument with the minister. She's determined to walk down the aisle. He says, without anyone to give her away, she should come in from the vestry. She says she's giving herself away, and that ought to do.'

'Is Joe being any help?' Ann asked, a straight question possible now that she felt herself in tentative control of his mood.

'None at all. When the minister said there wasn't any point in her coming down the aisle by herself, Joe suggested that she could take up a collection as she came. I decided to wait for you out here at that point.'

'I wonder if the wedding's still going to be here,' Ann said, as they walked up the steps together.

'Apparently Silver is an Episcopalian,' Bill said. 'And the minsiter has, thank God, a sense of humor.'

'It's all so unlikely,' Ann said.

'That's what Joe and Silver like about it.'

Bill held open one of the great doors. Ann hesitated, caught for a moment by the direct, bitter regret in Bill's eyes. There was no way around it.

'Let's be as civil and unsymbolic as we can, shall we?'

'I'm making an effort,' Bill answered coldly, nodding her through the door.

She walked by him into the church, empty but for the three quarreling figures at the other end of the center aisle.

'Look, I'm a J-J-J-Jew, at nose and heart anyway,' Joe was saying as he sat down on one of the altar steps. 'It doesn't matter to me what we do.' Then he saw Ann and Bill and leapt up again. 'Here are two more Christians for you, F-F-Father. Be consoled. The b-b-balance of power has shifted.'

'What's the problem now?' Bill called as they walked down the aisle.

'Silver wants me to go one step f-f-further into the sanctum-s-s-sanctorum than I'm supposed to so that, when we kneel, I can have a s-s-substitute for my Adler Elevators. Help me reason with her, Ann. She's not bigger than both of us.'

A compromise was finally achieved. Silver would walk down the aisle, but Joe would kneel beside her on the proper step. The rehearsal could now proceed. Ann and Bill stood quietly in their places, listening to the vows and watching the ritual movements. A nervous seriousness had come over Joe. His stammer was more pronounced than usual, and he sweated a little. Ann wondered how he really felt about marrying Silver. That he loved her there was no question, but taking Silver to wife was no ordinary gesture. Joe was only two or three years older than Ann, a tiny, highly geared man, passionately indifferent to his job on the local newspaper, devoted to his ambition to be a highly successful writer of pornography. With his ghetto intelligence, his amoral sentimentality, and aggressive, delicate body, he had chosen in Silver as unlikely and right a mate as he could find. But Ann could not see why he would want to marry her. What relevance God's holy ordinance had to their union she could not understand. The minister handed a prayer book to each of them, and the rehearsal was over.

It was still early. They had time for several drinks

208

before they went into the Mapes dining room for dinner. There was an embarrassment among them when they sat down together. Bill and Joe had had an argument about who was to be the host. Silver and Joe had had an argument about what it meant to 'plight thee my troth.' Bill and Ann were no more than unnaturally polite to each other. Ann's attempts at humor, unsupported, did nothing but increase the tension. She reached for an inconsequential question to break the silence that had fallen.

'Is it two weeks you're taking off, Sil?'

'I've quit, love.'

'Quit?' Ann repeated, unbelieving.

Silver looked at Joe. He picked up a prayer book and paraphrased as he read.

'Almighty G-G-God, Creator of mankind, who only art the wellspring of life, has already bestowed upon these His s-s-servants the gift and heritage of ch-ch-children.' He put the book down and smiled tenderly at Silver.

'He means I'm pregnant,' Silver said, and she blushed willfully.

'Didn't you know?' Bill asked, a mild malice in his tone.

'I haven't had a chance to tell her,' Silver said, in the quickness of her answer a regret for any malice of her own in telling Ann this way.

Ann sat very still, fighting down the angry panic that had come over her, for she had realized suddenly that it was not Bill's reluctance to be pleasant that was creating tension. It was her own presence, and Silver wanted her to know it.

'Well, what do you think of that, love?'

It could not have been an accident, not with Silver and Joe; and, if it had been, Silver was not without recourse. They wanted a child. Naturally. They wanted a child.

'When she couldn't adopt you,' Joe said, 'she wanted a little f-f-fish all of her own, one the g-g-game warden couldn't take away.'

Ann turned to Joe, feeling that she would smash his face in, but in his expression there was nothing but nervous concern. And he was a little drunk. Perhaps they all were. What difference did it make? Any of it.

'Order champagne, Bill,' Ann said. 'We must drink to the new little fish.'

Then she laughed with a free loneliness that broke the tension and gave them all, except Bill, a moment of pure relief. He ordered the champagne and offered an earnest toast to procreation. When they left the hotel, Joe and Silver parting for the last time before the wedding, they were all recognizably drunk.

'That's what I should have done to you,' Bill said, as they wandered down the street toward the Club. 'Not man enough, that's what, but I have to tell you something. I've solved my problem. I've got a girl who's already got a baby and I'm going to marry her.'

'Are you?' Ann asked.

'Yep, aren't I, Sil?'

'You say so,' Silver answered.

'Well, but I asked her last night.' He turned to Ann. 'Right after that little bastard, Walt, pitched a drink at me. And she accepted.'

'Joyce?'

'That's the one,' Bill said. 'So listen, honey, I'm sorry about all that I said about your girl friend. Each to his own taste, eh? Shall we shake on it? No hard feelings?'

Ann took his hand and looked up at him. He was beginning to cry.

'It's just that I'm moved,' he said, grinning, 'by my own bigness of heart. I didn't really mean to apologize. I've just had you fired.'

'Jesus Christ, Bill, can't you lay off? Don't you think she's had enough for a while?'

'It was your idea, wasn't it? You said I ought to fire her, like we fired Janet, for her own good. It's for your

210

own good, honey. After tonight, you're free.'

Ann turned away from them both and walked down the street. If she had any serious doubt about her own sobriety, it left her when she met Joyce at their locker. Her smile was the last, clean, sharp pain Ann needed to clear her head. She was so sober that she could keep herself from saying, 'Thanks,' with all the gratefulness she felt. She was a good loser. As she offered careful good wishes, she was also offering a world that she had lived in a long time. It was odd that she should be saying goodbye not to Janet, not to Silver, not to Bill, but to Joyce, the kid she had expected to be fired within a month.

Perhaps the champagne had not quite worn off, after all, for Ann walked through the crowd to the jazz beat of the machines with a lightness of spirit she could not explain. And, when she mounted the ramp and looked out over the familiar human landscape among whose guns and stage coaches and mirrors she had spent the last four years of her life, fiercely defending it, fiercely loving it, she had no sense of regret. 'Fidelity to any human place, except the heart, seems to me a dubious thing.' Ann turned to the sharp whistle of a key man and went down to witness a payoff.

At four o'clock in the morning, alone in her room, Ann began a series of sketches, shaping in lines what she could not shape in words, that curious variety of experiences for and against which man is required to bear witness. But the fragments did not satisfy her. And so at last she turned her pencil against herself, bearing witness against the witness she was, and let herself become one of her own cartoons.

It was Evelyn who woke her early in the afternoon.

'There's a telegram for you, darling.'

Ann reached for it, not awake enough at first to know what it was, but, as she unfolded it, she remembered. She read the brief, impersonal message which relieved her of her duties at the Club. She could pick up her pay check, turn in her hat and apron within the next forty-eight hours.

'Anything wrong?' Evelyn asked.

'No. Just a bit of Bill's weak wit.'

'What time are you due at Silver's?'

'A little after seven. Are you going with Walt and Frances?'

'I thought I would.'

'It won't be much,' Ann said.

'Weddings never are, according to Frances.'

'She'll have a good cry just the same. Maybe that's why.'

'You don't much want to go, do you?'

'Well, I'm less reluctant than I would be if it were my own.'

'It was a long night.'

'Very,' Ann said, but she kissed Evelyn only absent-mindedly as she got out of bed. 'Have you decided what you're going to wear?'

'I haven't much choice really. I didn't think, when I packed, that I'd be going to a wedding.'

'I suppose not,' Ann said, grinning.

'I have a blue dress that ought to do.'

'Blue? Yes, I like you in blue.'

And Silver in champagne. Ann had not seen her dress, and, when Silver opened the door to let her in, Ann was surprised into approval. Silver could never have been simply respectable, nor could she be subtly elegant. She had the preposterous figure of a Petty Girl, a gorgeous vulgarity of breast and thigh, and she displayed her body to the public with a professional flair, but often with a mockery of decorations. This dress had a pure boldness that was beyond indecency, and the only jewelry Silver wore was a real diamond and sapphire bracelet.

'It's gorgeous, Sil.'

'I'm gorgeous, love. Joe picked it out. He says clothes don't make the woman; men do, and they want to see

212

what they're in for. Drink?'

'Thanks.'

The Scotch had been set out on the bar. Silver reached for ice and did not measure as she poured.

'I wondered if you'd turn up at all,' she said.

'Did you? It never occurred to me,' Ann said, taking the drink. 'I should have called.'

'Did the telegram come?'

'Yes.'

'I'm sorry,' Silver said. 'I'm so damned sorry.'

'It doesn't matter. I would have quit anyway. I just hadn't realized it yet. I didn't know you were going to, of course.'

'What are you going to do?'

'I don't know,' Ann said. 'I don't have to do anything.'

'About Evelyn, I mean.'

'I don't know. I don't have to do anything about her either.'

'Don't you?'

'Don't sound so moral,' Ann said, smiling. 'Joe can make an honest woman of you. I'm not in the same position with Evelyn.'

'You're going to let her go?'

'I don't even know that I have a choice. If I have one . . . no, I won't let her go.'

Silver went over to the bar to pour herself another gin.

'Do we have time?' Ann asked.

'No,' Silver said. 'I'm just taking it. Both the bride and the groom have the privilege of at least fifteen minutes in which to contemplate what a sick, sick, fucking, Christ-awful thing getting married is. That's what the book says – or words to that effect.'

'Come on,' Ann said, taking the drink from Silver's hand. 'Swear to God and save the dirty words for Joe. We're *not* going to be late.'

'And what do I say to you, little fish?'

'Nothing,' Ann said. 'Be speechless. Come on.'

Ann stood at the end of the long center aisle and looked at the backs of the hundreds of people who filled the church. On Silver's side, the front pews were filled with her ex-employees, backed by a small army of ex-customers. Toward the back was a colorful representation from Frank's Club out on their long break, the key men holding their hats, the change girls and dealers wearing theirs. Among them, looking as out of place as they would have in a Charles Addams cartoon, were Walter, Frances and Evelyn. Joe's side was drabber, but as crowded, and here and there flash cameras sat on laps like small children peering over the pews. A door to the right opened, and Joe stepped out, as tiny and stiff as the groom on a wedding cake. Bill was right behind him. Ann turned back to Silver and smiled.

'He looks like a prize in a shooting gallery,' Silver whispered.

'Well, let's go get him. I'll help you carry him home.'

The organ stopped playing. The crowd shifted and then stood as the wedding march began. Ann set out slowly and cheerfully down the aisle, past the bright shirts and white hats, past the sudden, quiet blue of Evelyn's dress, past the cameras and business suits, past the pastels of prostitutes to the two men who stood waiting. Only once did she look directly at Bill, but neither he nor Joe was looking at her. Their attention was tensely focused behind her. Only when she turned to take her place did she realize that Silver was not following her. Ann looked back and saw Silver still standing where she had been. She must have been waiting to have the aisle entirely to herself, but a long moment passed, and she did not move. The organ went on playing. The minister nodded at Silver encouragingly. Still she did not move. Apparently, after all, she could not give herself away. Then Joe, as easily as if it had been planned, walked up the aisle to her and offered her his arm. They walked down the aisle together, and the women in the congregation began to weep their easy tears of vicarious relief and triumph. One more among them was about to be saved. Even Ann's throat tightened as that ridiculous pair arrived before the minister to take their vows they neither believed nor clearly understood for reasons their unborn child only partially explained, for reasons neither they, nor those who witnessed this marriage, would ever quite believe or understand.

'Wilt thou, Joseph . . .' forgotten man, cuckolded by the angel of life before he ever got to the alter '. . . take this woman, Silvia . . .' Silvia? Who in hell was she?

'I w-w-w-will.'

'Wilt thou, Silvia . . . forsaking all others . . . ?' A vow only your enemies would help you keep.

'I will.'

From this day forward, Joe stammered his promise to love and to cherish. And Silver promised back, giving her troth, for what it was worth, defined in her mind not as fidelity but as some hidden part of herself which Joe would have the ingenuity to discover.

'Bless, O Lord, this Ring . . . perform and keep the vow and covenant betwixt them made (whereof this Ring given and received is a token and pledge) . . . Those whom God hath joined together let no man put asunder.' Unless you've worked in a jewelers' store and know how without the slightest awkwardness or pain. . . .

They had knelt and stood, kissed and turned to the mounting joy of organ music, in whose hilarious upper registers Ann could almost imagine bells and falling coins. She turned and took the arm Bill offered her to follow them out of church. On the way up the aisle, she saw Joyce, near the back on the groom's side. She looked away to find Evelyn, in whose expression she could read nothing but simple acknowledgment. 'You're going to let her go?' If I have a choice, no, I don't intend to let her go.

'What do you intend to do then?' Evelyn asked. She was

215

standing at Ann's drawing table, looking at the sketches Ann had done the night before.

'Anything that will keep you here,' Ann said.

'I have a job, darling,' Evelyn said. She walked over to the bed and sat down beside Ann. 'I have to be back in California at the end of next week.'

'Give it up.'

'You can't give up a job just like that. Anyway, what would I do? I've given George the house and the car. I have my books and my clothes and about two hundred dollars in the bank. That's all.'

'I have plenty of money. I'll buy you a house and a car. If you wanted another job sometime, you could get one here.'

'When you got tired of supporting me? When a young man as handsome as Bill, as dear as Joe, and a good deal brighter than both of them came along?'

'I'm not going to marry anyone.'

'You can forsake the past, but how can you forsake the future?'

'But that's one thing I know.'

'How can you know, darling? Perhaps women live better together for a while, but men and women seem to be such an unbreakable habit in the scheme of things that, why, even Silver and Joe finally marry.'

'For a while then,' Ann said.

'Give up my job, perhaps not be able to get another? And, if I did teach here, what kind of a life would we have, I at the University all day, you at the Club all night?'

'That's no problem,' Ann said. 'I've been fired.'

'Fired?' Evelyn repeated. 'Why?'

'Oh, these things happen. It doesn't matter. I would have quit anyway.'

'What will you do?'

'Darling, my father left me money invested in things, and I make pretty good money on cartoons. I don't

216

really need to work.'

'Then why don't you come to California with me?'

'I don't think I could, Evelyn. I don't think I could leave.'

'Why not?'

'I don't know.'

'Afraid of being saved?'

'Perhaps,' Ann said, smiling. 'Or of being turned into a pillar of salt somewhere along the way.'

– 9 –

When Evelyn went down to breakfast Friday morning, she found Frances and Walter sitting with their coffee. They were both self-consciously silent for a moment. Then Frances got up and hurried off to the kitchen to fix Evelyn something to eat.

'I'm afraid I'm going to have to dash,' Walter said. 'I'm already late.'

Evelyn sat down alone to eat the grapefruit that had been set out for her. She had probably interrupted nothing more than the rare moment of privacy Frances and Walter had, but she felt uneasy. When Frances came back into the room with a plate of bacon and eggs, her cheerfulness seemed strained. She spilled Evelyn's coffee when she tried to pour her a second cup and made a complicated task of cleaning it up. Evelyn wanted to ask her what was wrong, but Frances was not shy. If she wanted to talk, she would; if she did not, the kindest thing Evelyn could do was to ignore her nervousness.

'What time's your appointment with the lawyer?' Frances asked.

'Not until ten thirty. I have lots of time.'

'Evelyn, I don't want you to think I'm meddling in your private affairs. That's the last thing I want to do.' Frances hesitated, as if she were waiting to be encouraged or cut off, but, when Evelyn offered no comment at all, she went on. 'Walter's told me something very unpleasant this morning. He should have told me days ago but he didn't.

I can understand why he didn't, but he should have, just the same. I don't know whether it's really important or not, but, if anything happened and I hadn't let you know about it, I'd never forgive myself.'

'What is it?'

'It has to do with Bill. He's been in love with Ann, you know. Up until several months ago, all of us thought she was probably going to marry him. Then, just like that, it was over . . . for Ann anyway. It wasn't for Bill. Of course, he was hurt, but I never would have thought, even so, that he could behave the way he's been behaving.'

'How has he been behaving?'

'He's been doing a lot of talking, Evelyn. About Ann, mostly, but for some reason I don't quite understand, except that he must think it's a way of hurting Ann, he's been talking about you.'

'About me?'

'I wouldn't say anything about this at all if Bill hadn't told Walter he was thinking of going to your husband's lawyer. Walter told him he was out of his mind.'

'To my husband's lawyer? To say what? To do what? Why?'

'To make trouble in the divorce proceedings. Evelyn, I haven't any idea what arrangements you've made. I don't know anything about your divorce. It's none of my business, but, if there were any possibility that your husband would like to make trouble . . . sometimes men do, at the last minute, because of money or . . .'

'But what could Bill say? What was he thinking of saying?'

'He was thinking of offering evidence to prove that you and Ann . . .' Frances hesitated in embarrassment '. . . are lovers. He even asked Walter if he'd testify, and he said he could get the names of a couple of army pilots who were in a helicopter. It sounded just crazy to me, and Walter said he was pretty sure Bill wouldn't go through with it, but he wasn't positive. If you went into court without knowing and something came of it . . .'

Evelyn sat, staring at Frances.

'It may be nothing at all Evelyn. It probably isn't. Do forgive me. I just didn't feel I had any right not to say something. You know Walter and I would do anything we could. He was terribly upset. He didn't even want to tell me.'

'Dear God,' Evelyn said softly.

'Has he any evidence? Is there any real danger?'

Evelyn did not answer.

'What is all this about a helicopter?'

'One afternoon when we were swimming at Pyramid Lake, one flew over, that's all.'

'How did Bill find out about it?'

'I don't know. Ann thought it was funny. She probably told it to him or to Silver, just as a funny story. Has Walter talked to Ann about this?'

'Not really, not about Bill's going to the lawyer anyway. I think he did tell her that Bill was being unpleasant.'

'So he fired her because of me.'

'Fired her?'

'Yes,' Evelyn said. 'She was fired yesterday.'

'Well, that, anyway, is no cause for anything but celebration. Bill may not know it, but that's the biggest favor anyone ever did for Ann.'

'Do you think so?' Evelyn asked wryly. 'If she'd chosen to leave, that would be one thing.'

'Choose or not, she's out of there. That's what matters. Oh, Evelyn, if you'd only take her with you, get her right out of here . . .'

'I may not get out of here myself,' Evelyn said. 'Ann's lost her job. She may be dragged through court as well. If she is, I won't have a job either."

'Would your husband make trouble if he could?'

'I wouldn't have thought so, but I wouldn't have thought a perfectly strange young man would take it

221

upon himself to go to a lawyer either. There are a great many things I wouldn't have thought. I'll simply have to find out.'

'If there's anything I can do . . .'

'Do?' Evelyn repeated. 'It's been done, Frances. Excuse me.'

Frances had already excused her. She wanted love for Ann and did not much care how she got it. Had she no capacity for moral indignation or at least moral doubt? Did it never occur to her, because of the sentimental trash that filled her head, that love might be a devastating obscenity? Frances cherished convention. How could she then so willingly trade her dream of Ann's white wedding for what might turn into a vicious absurdity in the public courts of law? Her own white wedding had, of course, turned into a vicious absurdity in the public courts of law. And so had Evelyn's. Or so it was about to. Three people. Ann's father, Ann's mother, and Frances had all been willing to let Ann suffer the ruined exposure of their own lives.

'I will not,' Evelyn said aloud in the empty quietness of her room.

But how could she stop it? If Bill had spoken to the lawyer, if the lawyer had written to George, would George be tempted to do anything about it? He did not want the divorce, had only agreed to it under pressure, finally persuaded by being offered all of their joint property; but he could accomplish nothing by a counter-charge. Evelyn would have let him get the divorce in the first place if he had wanted to. But would he be tempted, because he felt her his judge, to expose her, to ruin her academic career? She would be no better than he then.

'I am no better,' she said. 'And I never have been.'

But she had confessed this truth to herself before. She had already seen that her own needs had been as destructive as his. It was George who had not known it.

222

Would he choose, given the revelation and opportunity, to prove it? There was no real evidence. What could those two army pilots say? Neither Walter nor Frances would testify. Silver? The whole thing was a vicious absurdity!

'Vicious absurdity or not, it's true.'

And could she, under oath, deny it?

'I could not.'

Evelyn picked up her purse and gloves, went back downstairs, and left the house. She did not turn toward town. She chose instead the street she had walked her first evening in Reno, past the morning lawns of playing children, past the neighborhood store, to the short hill, that little rise of ground that could obscure the fact of empty miles of desert. Evelyn did not hesitate. She walked on up the hill and along the three short blocks that brought her to the desert's edge, cut off from the town by nothing but a broken bit of barbed wire fencing. She ducked through it and stepped out onto the desert itself. The heels of her shoes sank a little in the sandy soil, but she went on walking out into the sun that this morning seemed robbed of its intensity by a cool wind coming off the mountains. The scent of the sage was still hot and clear as spice, but it was not as strong as it had been. And the bolder colors, which she had once had to look for, revealed themselves even in the greater distances. This vast, empty, silent place promised autumn. Evelyn could feel it. 'If I lost my sense of smell, if I lost my sight, I would still know where I was.' 'There was never water here, not fresh water.' The earth requires the insignificant vulnerability of living cells to build its silence of dust and fossil, consuming life, transforming death into monumental mountains and grains of sand. No man's investment of sons will ever claim this land, nor will his genius for destruction change it. The scattered seed and the shattered atom fall indistinguishably together upon the silence like fertile rain, the land reclaiming man.

Evelyn had walked half a mile into her own vision of

223

the desert before she turned and looked back at the curiously regular edge of town she had left; 'When they were got out of the wilderness, they presently saw a town . . .' And Faithful was tried there and died there, but for defending his convictions, not for giving them up. If he'd surrendered divine faith to human faith, he would not have been killed; nor would he have escaped, however. He would have stayed.

Evelyn began to walk slowly back the way she had come, neither Faithful nor Christian. There is no allegory any longer, not even the allegory of love. I do not believe. Even seeing and feeling, in fact, what I do not believe, I do not believe. It's a blind faith, human faith, hybrid faith of jackass and mare. That's the only faith I have. I cannot die of that. I can only live with it, damned or not.

'If nothing happens, if Ann isn't dragged into this, I'll let her go. I'll never touch her again.'

And if she is?

'I won't go to court. I won't get the divorce. I'll go back to George. If only she isn't dragged into this, I swear I'll . . .'

Swear to whom?

'To chance, to fate, to the little gods of the desert and the lake, to the one large god whose ordinance I may not, after all, break, to everything I don't believe in, to everything I know, to my own blind, human faith. I'll never touch her again.'

It seemed a long way back to the broken barbed wire. It seemed a long way back past the house, where Ann must still be asleep, to the center of town and Arthur Williams' office. As Evelyn rode up in the elevator, she made herself think, not of the universal images among which she could not quite find her place, but of the petty, unpleasant facts which were her own to deal with.

'Here for the dress rehearsal?' the secretary quipped cheerfully.

Evelyn nervously considered her dress, which was not

224

what she had planned to wear in court, before she recognized the irrelevant humor that was intended. Her belated smile was a wry apology, a social straw the secretary floundered for through three measures of unmusical laughter. In the embarrassed silence that followed, Arthur Williams' office door opened, and a grim-boned, awkward woman struggled out through the elaborate, ritual farewell Arthur Williams imposed on all his clients. Evelyn, as apprehensive as she would have been if she were about to be asked to dance, braced herself for his greeting, but she was better prepared than she had been before and managed to maintain some dignity of her own in spite of him.

'I've been able to arrange a hearing for ten o'clock Monday morning,' he said quietly once he was settled at his desk. 'I assume you'd like it private.'

'Please,' Evelyn said. 'Is it possible?'

'And customary. There shouldn't be any reason for the judge to refuse. Has Mrs Packer agreed to be a witness?'

'Yes.'

'Good. Now, you'll have to answer a few questions about your place of residence because only permanent residents of Nevada can be granted divorces. When I ask you for your address, you must give Mrs Packer's address. I will also ask you if you have any other home or place of legal residence. The answer is "no." Then I will ask you if it has been your intention, and still is your intention, to make Reno your home and residence for an indefinite period of time. The answer is "yes." '

'But I plan to leave Reno almost at once.'

'An indefinite period of time is variously defined, Mrs Hall.'

Because the plane might be late, she could swear that she intended to make her home in Reno for an indefinite period of time? Evelyn wondered if the divorcees who stayed on in Reno were those who, having broken their marriage vows, could, nevertheless, not bring themselves to commit perjury. It was a last ditch morality she knew she could not take seriously. Perhaps, being able to answer two of the three questions honestly was an unusual privilege. She was learning to treat laws as most people treat poems, making them mean whatever she wanted them to without reference to the author's intention or achievement. Her aptitude tests had always indicated that she would be a clever lawyer.

Arthur Williams went on to outline a number of factual questions: the date of their marriage, the date of their separation. He explained why the written agreement of settlement should be entered as evidence but not merged in the decree the court might award.

'Then I will ask you to describe to the court the defendant's acts of cruelty upon which you rely as a cause for divorce. You need only mention his refusal to work, his extravagant spending, his extreme rudeness to your friends, his indifference to you.'

'And those facts are enough to establish cruelty?'

'Anything that has caused you extreme suffering is cruelty in the eyes of the law, Mrs Hall. People have been granted divorces whose complaints seem extremely petty. It is not the act itself that's important. It is the effect of that act upon the plaintiff.'

'I see,' Evelyn said. Plaintiff was an unpleasant word. It whined into sound and then cut itself off with martyred abruptness. One consolation was that she could be called the defendant. It was a title that seemed more accurate.

'It sometimes helps to remember that you are not on trial. Your husband is, in absentia of course; so it needn't be unpleasant for either of you.'

'I wish I found that comforting,' Evelyn said. 'Mr Williams, is there any possibility that the divorce might be contested?'

'I had assumed not. Are you expecting your husband to cause any trouble?'

'Not expecting, no, I . . .' Evelyn hesitated. She could

226

not bring herself to ask the questions she must ask because, with them, she would be forced into explanations she could not offer. 'No.'

'It's natural for you to feel a little nervous, Mrs Hall, but there isn't any reason for you to worry. Everything is in order. It's a perfectly straightforward case.' He smiled reassuringly. 'Now, are there any other questions you'd like to ask?'

She must ask him to phone George's lawyer, to find out, but all she could force herself to say was, 'Do I just go to the courthouse?'

'I'll meet you and Mrs Packer right by the main door at quarter to ten. If there are no delays in the court, it shouldn't take much longer than twenty minutes.'

He got up, and Evelyn felt in the tension of his body his intention to end the interview. She could not allow herself to be danced out of the room until she had somehow managed to tell him of Bill's threat.

'Do you happen to know Ann Childs, Mr Williams?'

'Ann?' Her question had obviously thrown him more violently off pace than she could have anticipated, for he echoed the name as if to ward it off, and his body froze in an incompleted gesture. He had to struggle into movement and speech. 'Her father was my partner.'

'I didn't realize that. Of course, you know her then. Do you know any of the people who work with her at Frank's Club?'

'Know them? Yes, I know them,' Arthur Williams answered, and he seemed to take this question as a kind of lifeline, for he pulled himself up to it with a rhetorical vigor that was almost desperation. 'The husband of that wretched woman you just saw leaving this office, for instance. He was a dealer until his gambling habits were too much even for the management. He was always paid in cash, of course, and given a free dollar chip with each week's pay, but he was allowed to lose only all that he earned, no more. Most of my local clients are employees

227

or customers or married to employees or customers. I had a man in here the other day who makes twenty thousand dollars a year, and his children don't have shoes because his wife can't stay out of the casinos. He's begun to use company funds to pay her debts. She'll send him to prison eventually. Yes, I know them. I know them all because their stories are all the same. And I could tell you stories, such stories of suffering that you wouldn't believe. You've been in the casinos, I suppose?' He had begun to pace his office, but he stopped to pose his question.

'Yes,' Evelyn answered tentatively. His growing excitement was alarming to her in the same way his elaborate manners had been. She wished he would sit down again behind the desk which seemed to inhibit and discipline his responses, but he remained standing.

'And what did you think of them? And what do you think of those of us who live here, tolerating places like that ... even working in them? It's true: most of the people who live in Reno are numb to them. We're just like the Germans who turned a blind eye to the exterminating of the Jews because we stand by and do nothing about these Buchenwalds of our own. Why? I'll tell you why. The gambling interests in this state are getting so strong that they control the laws of the state. People are afraid, and they have reason to be afraid. When I spent money trying to back an honest politician, my wife was threatened and so were my children. And people don't even realize what's happening. The political power building up in this state will control the whole country soon, and then it will be too late.' He paused, standing under the picture of his father in judge's robes. 'It's already too late for most of us. When I came to Reno twenty years ago, Frank's Club was nothing. These places began as penny roulette wheels in the backs of stores. Look at them now. And who speaks out? The University? No. The churches? No. Pay Caesar what's due to Caesar, they say. But Caesar's paying them. There's no state tax.

And there isn't a department at the University or a church in town that doesn't have a hand in someone's pocket. The ministers drive Lincolns and go to the Islands for their vacations. Even the Catholic Church is silent. My wife's a Catholic. She begs me not to argue with the priests. She's afraid something terrible will happen to me if I speak my mind to anyone. I ask myself, if all the people who know in their hearts that gambling is a sin, one of the blackest sins there is, would speak out, would it do any good? Maybe not. Maybe not now. We have to protect our children.'

'Why on earth do you stay here, feeling like that?' Evelyn asked.

Arthur Williams paused, the rhythm of his protest broken. 'My wife has sinus trouble,' he said, the force gone from his voice. 'The climate's good for her.'

'Surely there must be other places. . . .'

'Yes,' he said. 'Maybe if we'd moved ten years ago. . . . We used to talk about it. I'm not as young as I was then.'

He turned away from Evelyn and stared out of the window. Once she would have found such an outburst of morality ending in so pathetic a confession at least pitiable, at worst contemptible. Now, as she looked at the back of the small gray man in the gray suit, who was perhaps contemplating the destroying price of his own Lincoln, she saw only how like George he was and how like herself. She felt neither pity nor contempt. Everyone must vacillate between a vision of himself as plaintiff and as defendant, as Able and Cain. And the world must always seem to be either the Garden of Eden, from which he is about to be expelled, or a circle in hell, into which he has wandered like Dante or Orpheus only to find that he can't get out. How guilty the innocent always feel, how innocent the guilty. And, if paradox is a symptom of misconception, then the world itself is probably misconceived, a profound error in the very nature of things.

'Excuse me,' Arthur Williams said at last, turning to

229

Evelyn. 'You were asking about Ann Childs.'

'It doesn't matter,' Evelyn said.

'She was a gifted child. I tried to help her. I couldn't.'

He did not want the interview to continue, but he seemed unable to end it. Evelyn herself had to make the move that would free him. He did not even go to the office door with her. On the way out of the building, Evelyn remembered one of the drawings in *Eve's Apple* and now recognized in it Arthur Williams' particular stance in the universal dilemma. This was not the discovery she had gone to make, however. She knew no more about Bill's activities than she had this morning after breakfast. Evelyn realized that, if she was going to find out what he had or had not done without exposing herself or Ann, she had only one choice. She must see Bill himself.

She had not been to the Club before in the early evening, but her sense of time deserted her almost immediately after she had let herself be pulled through the doors by the urgent and inevitable crowd. The noise she was prepared for still sent its violent and continual prophecies like currents of fear along her nerves. She was afraid, not in decorous timidity as she had once been, not in anticipation of personal encounter. It was pure claustrophobia which embraced her like the intimacy of her own skin but with a pressure so appalling that, for the moment she suffered it, it was a physical agony she did not imagine she could endure. Then it was over, and she was moving quite naturally through the crowds, carefully stepping onto the escalator, even more carefully stepping off, just as if she were going to find Ann at her accustomed station by the guns. But the Coral, for all its gross familiarity, was a different place without Silver's garish presence and uncertain greeting, without Ann's preoccupied and unnatural height in the far corner. Both their positions were filled by young women Evelyn had never seen before, but they were not new; they worked

230

with an efficiency and personal assurance of employees who had been there for some time. Evelyn checked her resentment of them both, for, though she missed Silver and was angry about Ann's dismissal, she certainly should be as happy as Frances to know that Ann was free.

Evelyn herself should be free now to see the Club as she would have seen it if Ann had not been working there. Would she have taken an attitude similar to Arthur Williams'? He saw it as a place of the most corrupt usury and human suffering, a Buchenwald, the third ring of the seventh circle of hell. If it was not moral, it was visual melodrama. Nothing here recalled the terrible, skeletal despair of the Jews, nor were there the contorted expressions of greed and rage that were accredited to the money breeders. If the crowd reminded her of anything at all, it was a cluttered drawing of Hogarth, and even that was in exaggeration. Where was the suffering, innocent or guilty? She could see it here and there in the desperate and in the resigned; but most of these people were tourists. There were no tourists in Buchenwald and only a few distinguished tourists in hell. Surely no one enjoyed himself.

But Evelyn was not here to define the moral climate of Frank's Club. It should not really matter anymore. That it did was only an indication of Evelyn's private uncertainty. She studied the general to avoid the particular. She was studying the crowd to avoid Bill, not to find him. Evelyn forced herself to look for Bill, but she could not see him. She went to the cashier to inquire.

'He's on his break, love, but he ought to be back to check in with us in about ten minutes.'

'Thanks.'

As she found a place to stand and wait, claustrophobia threatened her again. She focused her eyes on a sign: FRANK'S CLUB FOR FUN AND GAMES. And she focused her mind again on the crowd with determined and cheerful detachment. People were having fun. If the

231

Club was making money which made the Dicks family rich and powerful, it was also creating a rather marvelous, mock welfare state, based on the redistribution of wealth by means of acts of pure charity, support of education and religion, road building . . . and law buying, but Ann would argue that all industry buys laws. PLAY ONLY WHAT YOU CAN AFFORD. The Club encouraged moderation. Had there ever been such a sign at a department store sale? If the employees were given free dollar chips with their pay, surely the practice was no different from the ten per cent discount and generous credit (carrying compound interest) granted to any clerk. Frank's Club felt a particular moral responsibility to its employees, teaching and reteaching the Golden Rule. Ann had brought home the latest paraphrase: ALL YOU HAVE TO DO IS PUT YOURSELF IN THE OTHER GUY'S PLACE AND DO HIM LIKE YOU'D LIKE TO BE DONE. THIS IS IT IN ESSENCE. There was a failure in aesthetic values, one had to admit; but in the culture of North America Frank's Club could not really be singled out for its bad taste. Its writers and interior decorators had at least some dim sense of historical tradition. She was begging the question, of course. Frank's Club was corrupt in its purpose, and no matter how amusingly, honestly, and generously that purpose was carried out, it should not be overlooked or excused. Hiram O. Dicks made money out of men's weakness for gambling. Was gambling evil in itself then? A good many churches did not think so. Bingo had become an important source of income. Then the evil must be in fact of private enterprise. Hiram O. Dicks made money. Even the dimmest witted congressman could recognize this morality as subversive.

Her mind was playing games much more dangerous than any Frank's Club could offer. If she could accept this place as a microcosm, no better and no worse than any other, simply representative, she could as easily rationalize the last vestige of her private morality into meaning-lessness. And she wanted to. Her fear was that she could not accept this world, that she could let Ann go.

'You wanted to speak to me?'

'Yes, Bill, I do.'

'Can I buy you a drink?' he asked, cordial but uneasy.

'Thank you, no,' Evelyn said. No sociability could alter the directness of the question she had come to ask, and neither delay nor privacy would alter the threat of his actual aggressive presence. 'I've heard this morning that you were thinking of going to see my husband's lawyer.' Bill's face tightened, and his cheek was shadowed by a flickering nerve. 'Have you seen him?'

'No,' Bill said. 'I was angry. Anyway, there was nothing he could have done.'

'I had to be sure,' Evelyn said.

'I loved her.' He spoke with energetic, defensive anger. 'I wanted to marry her.'

'I understand that.'

'Do you? Do you really know what it's like for a man to watch the woman he loves . . . doing what she's doing? It made me mad.' He stopped, forcing himself to be quiet. 'It doesn't matter now. It isn't any of my business. I suppose I should apologize.'

'No,' Evelyn said.

'Is she going away with you?'

'I think not,' Evelyn said.

They stood, looking at each other. Then Evelyn turned away and walked through the crowd to the down escalator. If anyone should apologize, she should or Ann should. But Ann, at least, had the sense to know that she could not marry Bill. If he was suffering now, he'd get over it. He did not have to live for sixteen years with a woman who could not be his wife and yet could not bring herself to admit it. Evelyn wondered if he'd ever know how lucky he had been.

Ann was free then, of the Club, of Bill, and, because

233

there was no threat of countersuit, of Evelyn. Evelyn could let her go, and now she must. Why? Because, even spared this particular exposure, the world would not let them alone for long. There would be other Bills, a great many more of them in Berkeley than in Reno, who, loving Ann or not, would be self-appointed judges. And few of them would be as reticent about taking action as Bill had been. They would live among an army of special assistants to the Dean who felt morally obliged to uphold that old dictum: marriage is the best life for a woman. Clichés were only a sin in literature. In life, if they happened to be true, there was no intellectual campaign that would defeat them. Did she believe that marriage was the best life for a woman? Of course. She believed it just as she believed that this huge, arcade was not, as Ann would have it, only another of the many mansions of God. As Ann would have it. Ann could not argue for the Club. And she would not argue against marriage. She would say, 'for the while then.' And, if she ever wanted to marry, Evelyn would let her go. But she must let Ann go now. If she would not let Ann go under these circumstances, she never would.

'No, I never would. I love her.'

There was no one downstairs when Evelyn got back to the house. Walter had gone out with his new girl. Ann was probably in her room working. Evelyn found Frances upstairs in Virginia's old room, making up the bed.

'Are you expecting someone new?'

'Sunday or Monday,' Frances said, 'and another the middle of the week.'

'I saw Bill. He hasn't gone to the lawyer.'

'Well, that's good! I did think he had more sense than that, but you never can be sure of people. I should have gone down there myself. That's what I should have done. I wouldn't have had to bother you at all.'

'I'm glad you told me,' Evelyn said. 'It's something I ought to know. Is Ann in her room?'

234

'Yes.'

'I'll go on up.'

Ann was sitting in her armchair surrounded by newspapers. She got up quickly as Evelyn came into the room.

'Where did you go?' she asked.

'Just out on errand, darling. Don't look so worried.'

'I didn't know where you were. I went down to your room, and you weren't there. You weren't anywhere in the house.'

'Well, I'm back now,' Evelyn said, smiling. 'What have you been doing?'

'I've been reading the ads. There's a house for sale on the bluff overlooking the river. Most of them are too big, but this one isn't. Look.' She picked up the paper. 'Three bedrooms and a den. I wanted to go look at it this evening. I wonder if it's too late.'

'Ann darling . . .'

'I know you have to go back. I know you can't just quit, but I was thinking that maybe you could find out about a job here before you go, maybe for January, maybe even for next fall. I could buy a house, and we could come back.'

'We've got to talk,' Evelyn said. 'No, don't sit over here. Sit over there in the chair.'

Ann sat down obediently, her eyes concerned but trusting. Evelyn realized that this final suggestion of compromise was only preliminary to total surrender. Ann would go to California and stay. Evelyn had only to ask. For a moment, she wavered in her resolution, but Ann's very vulnerability forced Evelyn to be hard. She must not take advantage of Ann's need.

'I've just been down to the Club. Did you know that Bill was thinking of going to George's lawyer to tell him about you and me? He didn't, but he might have. You might have been involved in the court proceedings, very nastily involved.'

235

'He never would have done it. Anyway, I wouldn't have cared.'

'Maybe not, but I would have cared. It frightened me, and it still does frighten me to think what might have happened. You're young, and you're independent. Scandal isn't anything that troubles you.... It does trouble me. Practically, I could be badly hurt by it. I could lose my job, and I care very much about my job.'

'Yes,' Ann said quietly, 'it's different for you. I understand that.'

'Lots of things are different for me, Ann. I care what people think. I care about morality. I like to do the right thing.'

'How do you know what that is?'

'Sometimes I don't. I haven't been at all sure that divorcing George is the right thing. I agreed to it only because anything else I thought of doing seemed even less right. So many little dishonesties are involved; so many rationalizations are necessary. It's a demoralizing business. It makes you begin to question the meaning of everything you believe. But that's rationalizing, too. Failure to live up to what you believe is right doesn't destroy the value of it. And one failure doesn't justify giving up entirely. Or suggesting that someone else give up.'

'Give up what?' Ann asked.

'I can't really argue about it,' Evelyn said in sudden desperation. 'I know I talk in clichés. I can't help it. I feel we're wrong. Ann. It isn't right. It isn't natural. I can't go on with it. I don't want to.'

Ann looked down at the newspaper in her hands. She was crying.

'Ann,' Evelyn said softly, 'forgive me.'

'Nothing to forgive,' Ann said, looking up. 'I had a lovely time.' She got up. 'I think I'll go out for a drive. Maybe I'll take a look at that house, just for the hell of it. I'll see you.'

Evelyn was left, sitting alone in Ann's room. She got up quietly and walked to the door, but she did not go right out. She turned to look back at the room, at the chair where Ann had been sitting.

'Why didn't you argue, even a little? There isn't any argument for a lie. And it is a lie, my darling. Nothing else I've ever known has been as right and as natural as loving you. And there isn't anything I wouldn't risk . . . except you.'

Evelyn went back downstairs. Frances had finished preparing the room across the hall. There would be someone new Sunday or the next day. Evelyn went to her own room and sat down at her desk, but she could not work. It had been weeks since she had felt the absolute weight of time, for, as trapped in any evening as she might have been, Ann had always been at the end of it to set her free. Now there was nothing to anticipate but Monday morning when, with her suitcases already packed, she would go to court to offer up, with guilt and goodness, the little perjuries that would free her of nothing important any more.

The expected guest did not arrive on Sunday. Monday morning not only Frances and Walter were up for breakfast but Ann. Evelyn had hoped that somehow they would not have to meet again today after the tense hide-and-seek they had been playing all weekend. There was nothing left to say. Yet, when she saw Ann sitting at the breakfast table, she could not help being glad.

'Evelyn,' Frances said, 'I'm awfully sorry. I'm expecting a guest about ten thirty, and I think I must be here to greet her, but Ann could go to court with you. She's as good a witness as I would be, and she's got the car.'

'Couldn't Ann meet her?' Evelyn asked. 'It's just that I think Mr Williams is expecting you, Frances.'

'It's happened before,' Frances said. 'It won't matter to him. Ann knows what to do just as well as I do.'

'I'm sure she does. I just hate to . . . I wish I didn't have

237

to ask either of you.'

'I won't stay in the courtroom,' Ann said. 'I'm called first. Then I can leave.'

'It isn't that . . .' She looked down at Ann who was obviously no more eager to witness than Evelyn was to have her; but, as it happened again and again, she seemed to be the only one who was available. Apparently no vow Evelyn could make would keep Ann out of court.

'If you'd waited until next year, I could have done it,' Walter said, getting up from the table. 'I guess you'll be gone tonight by the time I get home. We're going to miss you around here, but I guess you're glad it's over.'

'Will you come see me if you're ever in the Bay Area?'

'You bet I will.'

'Goodbye, Walt.'

'Goodbye.' He took the hand she offered and then quickly and shyly kissed her on the cheek. 'Take care.'

'I'm afraid Walter really is going to miss you,' Frances said.

'I'd better go up and get dressed,' Ann said. 'What time does your plane leave, Evelyn?'

'Three o'clock.'

'Are you packed?'

'Just about.'

'Anyway,' Frances said, 'you'll both be home for lunch.'

'Yes,' Evelyn said, 'Mr Williams says it doesn't take more than twenty minutes.'

Frances smiled. 'I'll miss you myself.'

As they drove together to the courthouse, Ann offered no amusing stories or interesting bits of information to disguise the real silence between them, nor did she sulk. She was simply quiet, her attention given to stop signs and pedestrians. Evelyn watched her and wanted to speak, but there was nothing honest that she could say aloud. She was silent, therefore, until they walked up the courthouse steps together and met Arthur Williams in the lobby.

'Mrs Packer couldn't come,' Evelyn said.

'How are you, Ann?'

'Fine, Arthur.'

'Ann's practically a professional witness,' Arthur Williams said to Evelyn. 'When she was ten, she already knew court procedure better than her father and I did. How are Frances and Walter?'

'Just fine,' Ann said.

'We can go right on up. If you'll show Mrs Hall where the waiting room is, Ann, I'll come and get you when it's time to go into court.'

They rode together in the elevator to the second floor. Then Ann and Evelyn went together to the waiting room where several other people had already settled in the uncomfortable wooden chairs. A young man got up to give them a place to sit together. Evelyn nodded and smiled, but she did not speak her thanks. She could not bring herself to break the apathetic silence of the room. It was neither shabby nor dirty, but it was small and bare, and the people in it only exaggerated its lack of personal definition.

It was a room Evelyn had become familiar with on the stages of a dozen little theaters and coffeehouses, the set located by the dialogue as a prison cell, a bus depot, a room in hell. The young man coughed discreetly into his hand. A woman reached into her purse and then furtively slipped a tranquilizer into her mouth, swallowing it without water. Someone's stomach growled. Everyone shifted guiltily. Evelyn felt the beginning pressure, the dizziness and slight nausea that she had become almost accustomed to since she had arrived in Reno. Her hands were cold, and her mouth was dry. She prayed that it would not be long. She must try to relax. She looked over at Ann and saw in the stillness of her body and the quietness of her face an unselfconscious patience, a serenity that Evelyn had seen before often, at the bar in

Virginia City, on the beach at Pyramid Lake, on the terrace with Kate, and, yes, sometimes even at the Club when she moved among the crowds of people, 'almost a professional witness,' bearing witness to the world, at home in it. Ann became conscious of Evelyn and turned to smile, in her eyes nothing of her own need, only gentleness and reassurance.

'It won't be long,' she said, and her voice did not seem to threaten the frail dignity of silence that the others kept.

Then Arthur Williams was at the door, signaling to them. They got up and followed him down the corridor to the courtroom, which was empty except for the clerk, the judge, and a young woman who was talking with the judge. Ann and Evelyn walked down to the front of the room and sat down in one of the pews. Evelyn had to check her instinct to kneel.

'Would you like me to wait outside after I'm through?' Ann asked quietly.

'Not unless you'd rather,' Evelyn said, and then she added, though she knew she should not. 'I'd really like you to stay. I wonder when George's laywer will arrive.'

'She's here.'

'She? That young woman?' Evelyn asked, surprised.

'Yes. She's the one Arthur almost always uses.'

The young woman had taken a seat to the left and in front of them. Arthur Williams spoke to the judge for a moment and then stepped back.

'Hall against Hall.'

'Your honor, may we have a private hearing?'

'That will be the order of the court.'

Ann was called at once as a witness and sworn in. Then Arthur Williams asked her to state her name and address.

'Do you know this lady?' Arthur Williams turned and indicated Evelyn.

Ann looked down at Evelyn, her eyes unguarded. 'I do.'

'She is Mrs Evelyn Hall, the plaintiff?'

'Yes.'

'When did you meet Mrs Hall?'

'In my home on July twenty-seventh.'

'And she has lived at your home since that time?'

'She has.'

'From July twenty-seventh, up to and including the present time you have either seen Mrs Hall in Reno, Nevada, each and every day or you know that she was here all of that time?'

'I do,' Ann said again.

The young woman, representing George, stepped forward.

'Are you in any way related to the plaintiff?'

Ann hesitated. 'We are not related.'

'No further questions.'

Ann returned to her seat, and Evelyn was directed to take the stand.

'Do you swear to tell the truth, the whole truth, and nothing but the truth, so help you, God?'

'I do.'

'Will you state your name, please?' Arthur Williams asked.

'Evelyn Hall.'

'Are you the plaintiff in the case in which George Hall is the defendant?'

'I am.'

'And is the defendant your husband?'

'He is.'

'Where do you reside, Mrs Hall?'

She gave the address.

'When did you come to Reno, Nevada, to reside?'

She gave the date.

'Do you have any other home or place of legal residence other than your home here?'

'No.'

'When you came, did you come with the intention of making Reno, Wahsoe County, Nevada, your home and residence for an indefinite period of time?'

241

'Yes.'

'And has that been your intention since?'

'Yes.'

'And is it still?'

Beyond Arthur Williams, Evelyn saw Ann. It had not been her intention at first. It had not been her intention ever. And it was not her intention now, but it was her desire to be here or anywhere with Ann, a desire which all her intentions denied.

'And is it still, Mrs Hall?'

'Yes, it is,' Evelyn said, in her voice an uncertain resonance.

The questions were factual then. Evelyn answered them with easier control. The written agreement of settlement was submitted as evidence and accepted as Exhibit 'A,' a term Evelyn could almost smile at.

'Mrs Hall, you have alleged as cause for divorce that the defendant has treated you with extreme cruelty during the marriage and that the cruelty was mental in nature. Is that true?'

'Yes.' Her mouth was dry again.

'Would you please tell the court just what the defendant's acts of cruelty were upon which you rely as a cause for divorce?'

'He refused to work,' Evelyn recited. 'He ran up debts . . .'

'Please speak to the judge, Mrs Hall.'

'He refused to work. He ran up debts.' Evelyn could think of nothing else to say. She turned back to Arthur Williams. 'I supported him.'

'Is it true that he was extremely rude to your friends?'

'Yes, yes, he was.' Evelyn turned back to the judge. 'He was extremely rude to my friends.'

'He did not want them in the house?' Arthur Williams prompted.

'No.' She spoke to Arthur and then turned to the judge. 'No.'

'But he did not welcome your company either and yet would not let you go out?'

She must stop playing this child's game of telephone. She must speak for herself. Somehow, for a sentence or two, she must leave some kind of truth, no matter how partial, on the record.

'He's bitter and despairing and frightened,' she said. 'He's afraid to care about anyone. He's afraid of the responsibility. Afraid of being destroyed, or afraid of destroying. He can't care about anyone. It's too much of a risk.'

'This inability to make friends and indifference to you,' Arthur Williams said, cutting in on her, 'caused you unhappiness and tension?'

'Yes,' Evelyn said, alarmed at his abruptness.

'It has, in fact, had a serious effect on your own emotional and mental health?'

'Yes.'

'What in your opinion would be the effect on your emotional and mental health if you had to resume life with the defendant and he treated you as he has in the past?'

'I would become as frightened and despairing as he.'

'Therefore, because you do not love him anymore, there is no possibility of reconciliation?'

'Not love him?' Evelyn repeated. Not love him anymore? Suddenly the bewildering and shaming charade was transformed into reality. Before her were the two lawyers, man and woman, like witnesses at a marriage. Beside and above her the judge waited to hear her answer, the one simple, truthful answer that would speak her failure and set her free. 'No, I don't love him anymore. There is no possibility of reconciliation.'

'Plaintiff granted a decree of divorce. The agreement now in evidence marked Plaintiff's Exhibit "A" is approved, is adopted as part of this decree by reference. The agreement is not merged in the decree and shall

243

continue to exist as a separate and independant document.'

Arthur Williams offered Evelyn his hand and helped her down from the witness stand.

'You and Ann wait for me in the downstairs lobby. I'll be a few minutes with the papers.'

Ann and Evelyn walked out of the courtroom together and rode down in the elevator to the lobby.

'Well, that's that,' Ann said and they were alone together. 'All you need now is your diploma.'

'How long will that take?'

'Five or ten minutes. Time for a cigarette if you want one.'

'Let's go out onto the steps, shall we?'

They stood together in the warm, morning sun, looking down at the bridge and the river. A couple of old men sitting below them, turned to stare and then turned away again. Evelyn looked up at the clear, immense, and empty sky. Then she turned to Ann and saw in her eyes the darker color of the day.

'It's a terrible risk, Ann.'

'And the world's full of mirrors. You can get caught in your own reflection.'

'And destroyed?'

'Or saved.'

'And I'm afraid of the one, and you're afraid of the other. We're a cryptic cartoon, my darling. It should be one of your best.'

'I'll only draw it if I can live it.'

'In a house by the river with me and your five photographs of children?'

'Anywhere.'

'For the while then,' Evelyn said. 'For an indefinite period of time.'

And they turned and walked back up the steps toward their own image, reflected in the great, glass doors.

244

Pandora Press is a feminist press, an imprint of Routledge & Kegan Paul. Our list is varied – we publish new fiction, reprint fiction, history, biography and autobiography, social issues, humour – written by women and celebrating the lives and achievements of women the world over. For further information about Pandora Press books, please write to the Mailing List Dept at Pandora Press, 11 New Fetter Lane, London EC4P 4EE or in the USA at 35 West 35th Street, New York, NY 10001–2291.
Some Pandora titles you will enjoy:

ORANGES ARE NOT THE ONLY FRUIT
Jeanette Winterson

'Like most people I lived for a long time with my mother and father. My father liked to watch the wrestling, my mother liked to wrestle. . .'

'The achievement of this novel is to make us squirm with laughter, then make us acknowledge how utterly sad it is when the needs of self-preservation turn what has been sacred into a joke.'
Roz Kaveney, *Times Literary Supplement*

'*Oranges* is a brilliant first novel – at once witty, gripping, imaginative and touching.'
Time Out

Paper £4.50   Fiction   086358 042 4
Winner of the 1985 Publishing for People Prize for First Novel

THIS PLACE
Andrea Freud Loewenstein

'An energetic and passionate novel which grips the reader's attention with unholy force. It is an extraordinary evocation of a closed world – female bodies and female minds struggling against an imprisonment equally dire whether enforced or self-imposed, and written with charity and understanding.'

Fay Waldon

'Loewenstein vividly creates, through a naturalistic fidelity to voice and description, a stifling inferno.'

Michele Roberts

Cloth £9.95   Fiction 086358 039 4
Paper £4.95   086358 040 8

CHARLEYHORSE
Cecil Dawkins

This is an explosive gallop through the family fortunes of mother and daughter on their huge ranch in Kansas.

Mother is a megalomaniac, daughter as stubborn as the bulls she manages; Cecil Dawkins's novel reworks traditional Western themes and is guaranteed to make you laugh, cry and see red.

Cecil Dawkins lives in New Mexico.

Cloth £9.95   Fiction 086358 096 3
Pandora edition not available in USA or Canada

NATURAL SELECTION
Margaret Mulvihill

Maureen works as a slave in a London publishing house and lives on the borders of literary London. Life is a series of groggy mornings, tedious days working on other people's manuscripts and planning illicit meetings with Martin. Until a certain manuscript falls mysteriously into her hands. . .

This witty novel describes a publishing world filled with sex, adultery, plagiarism, opportunism . . . as well as books.

To be read in the bath while eating expensive chocolates.

Cloth £9.95   Fiction 086358 064 5
Paper £3.95   086358 058 0

A WOMAN CALLED EN
Tomie Ohara

Written by a major modern Japanese novelist, this book won two major literary awards on its publication in Japan.

Based on fact, the novel is set in 17th century Japan and centres round En who at four years old is confined with her family to a single house, isolated from society and human contact, when her father falls from political favour. There she remains for 40 years but she prevails, strong and refusing to be defeated.

Written in the formal classical style of the 17th century, this novel is nevertheless a modern novel, movingly written and painfully felt.

Cloth £9.95   Fiction   086358 079 3
Paper £3.95   086358 082 3

LITTLE TOURS OF HELL
Tall Tales of Food and Holidays
Josephine Saxton

Painting holidays, pregnant holidays, ghastly weekends and reckless rendezvous . . . these are just a few Saxton scenarios to help you get away from it all, with these cautionary tales about campers, hampers and oily foreign muck for gastronomiques and holiday makers everywhere.

These stories are specifically concerned with the more macabre or stultifying aspects of eating and holidaying. Josephine Saxton is able to unravel the disturbing implications behind the most innocent and everyday activities with an acute and very witty eye for detail in sharp and brilliant prose.

Cloth £9.95   Fiction   086358 094 7   176pp
Paper £3.95   086358 095 5

STEPPING OUT
Edited by Ann Oosthuizen

This imaginative collection of short stories celebrates friendship between women and explores the new lives that women are leading today. The stories range from love stories to friendships and betrayals, to the relationship between sisters and women in conflict

with contributions from
Anna Livia   Honora Bartlett   Barbara Burford
Michelene Wandor   Ann Oosthuizen   Marsha Rowe   Jackie Kay
Moy McCrory   Andrea Loewenstein   Jo Jones   Sara Maitland

Paper £4.95   Fiction 086358 488 3   176pp

PASSION FRUIT
Romantic Fiction with a Twist
Edited by Jeanette Winterson

A collection of short romances which adds a new and startling
dimension to the traditional scenario of love, lust and marriage
with stories from:
Rebecca Brown   Angela Carter   Laurie Colwin
Fiona Cooper   Sara Maitland   Bobby Ann Mason
Marge Piercy   Josephine Saxton   Aileen La Tourette
Lorna Tracey   Michelene Wandor   Fay Weldon

Paper £3.95   Fiction 086358 070 X   200pp

AUTOBIOGRAPHY OF A CHINESE GIRL
Hsieh Ping-Ying
With an introduction by Elisabeth Croll

This is the story of Hsieh Ping-Ying, a Chinese girl born at the
beginning of this century who rejected the traditions of the old
order and eventually became one of China's leading women writers.

At school, she unwrapped the binding on her feet so that she could
run freely with the other children. As a young woman she went into
the army in order to escape an arranged marriage. As an adult she
was charged with being a communist and imprisoned.

Hsieh Ping-Ying's story takes us back to the heart of pre-
revolutionary China. She describes her relationship with her family:
with her mother and with her grandmother and the difficulties she
faced rejecting traditional constraints in order to live as an
independent woman.

Paper £4.95   Autobiography 086358 052 1   224pp

DARING TO DREAM
Utopian stories by United States women: 1836–1919
Carol Farley Kessler

Carol Farley Kessler has unearthed an extraordinary assortment of visionary writing, writings which encapsulate all the yearnings of a vanished generation for a future which has still to be made. Some women write with irony, describing journeys through time and space to parallel but inverted worlds where sober-suited women run commerce and affairs of state while men either prink and preen in beribboned breeches, or are weakened by the burden of unending housework. Other writers lay out complicated blueprints for a non-sexist society. One woman dreams, touchingly, of a fantastic future where men get up in the night to comfort crying children. The stories demonstrate that even in the early nineteenth century women were arguing that male and female 'character traits' were the product of their roles, not of their biology; and they make apparent the hidden roots of the discontent, longing and anger which was later to erupt in the great movements of women for change.

Fiction/Social History 086358 013 0   256pp
198 × 127 mm paperback

OLD MAIDS
Susan Koppelman

At 25 they were 'on the shelf'. But were they embittered spinsters or independent women?

The grim image of the 'old maid' as a ridiculous, pathetic, unlovable, unlovely and unloving creature has traditionally shadowed young women. Many have married unhappily, or submitted to constricting domestic roles, rather than face its terrors.

Susan Koppelman has discovered and collected this treasury of 'old maid' stories, written – often by 'old maids' themselves – between 1835 and 1891 in the USA. With her substantial introduction as a guide, the reader is taken on an illuminating excursion into the parlours of the nineteenth century, as the voices of single women mark out the gradual shift between spinsterhood suffered and independence welcomed.

£4.95   086358 014 9

MOTHERS OF THE NOVEL

The History of Miss Betsy Thoughtless by Eliza Haywood (1751)
Introduced by Dale Spender

The Female Quixote by Charlotte Lennox (1752)
Introduced by Sandra Shulman

Belinda by Maria Edgeworth (1801)
Introduced by Eva Figes

Adeline Mowbray by Amelia Opie (1804)
Introduced by Jeanette Winterson

The Wild Irish Girl by Lady Morgan (1806)
Introduced by Brigid Brophy

Self-Control by Mary Brunton (1810/11)
Introduced by Sara Maitland

Patronage by Maria Edgeworth (1814)
Introduced by Eva Figes

The selection for Spring 1987 includes:

Memoirs of Miss Sidney Bidulph by Frances Sheridan (1761)
Introduced by Sue Townsend

A Simple Story by Elizabeth Inchbald (1791)
Introduced by Jeanette Winterson

The Memoirs of Emma Courtney by Mary Hays (1796)
Introduced by Sally Cline

Discipline by Mary Brunton (1814)
Introduced by Fay Weldon

Helen by Maria Edgeworth (1834)
Introduced by Maggie Gee

Forthcoming in Autumn 1987:

Munster Village by Lady Mary Hamilton (1778)
Introduced by Emma Tennant
and
The Old Manor House by Charlotte Smith (1794)
Introduced by Janet Todd

The companion of this exciting series is:

MOTHERS OF THE NOVEL
100 Good Women Writers before Jane Austen
by Dale Spender

In this wonderfully readable survey, Dale Spender reclaims the many
women writers who made a significant contribution to the literary
tradition. She describes the interconnections among the writers, their
approach and the public response to their work.